A
SUSPENSE
NOVEL

THE MURDER BLOG

Sandra Gardner

Black Rose Writing | Texas

ISBN: 978-1-68513-345-0
PUBLISHED BY BLACK ROSE WRITING
www.blackrosewriting.com

Printed in the United States of America
Suggested Retail Price (SRP) $23.95

The Murder Blog is printed in Garamond Premier Pro

*As a planet-friendly publisher, Black Rose Writing does its best to eliminate unnecessary waste to reduce paper usage and energy costs, while never compromising the reading experience. As a result, the final word count vs. page count may not meet common expectations.

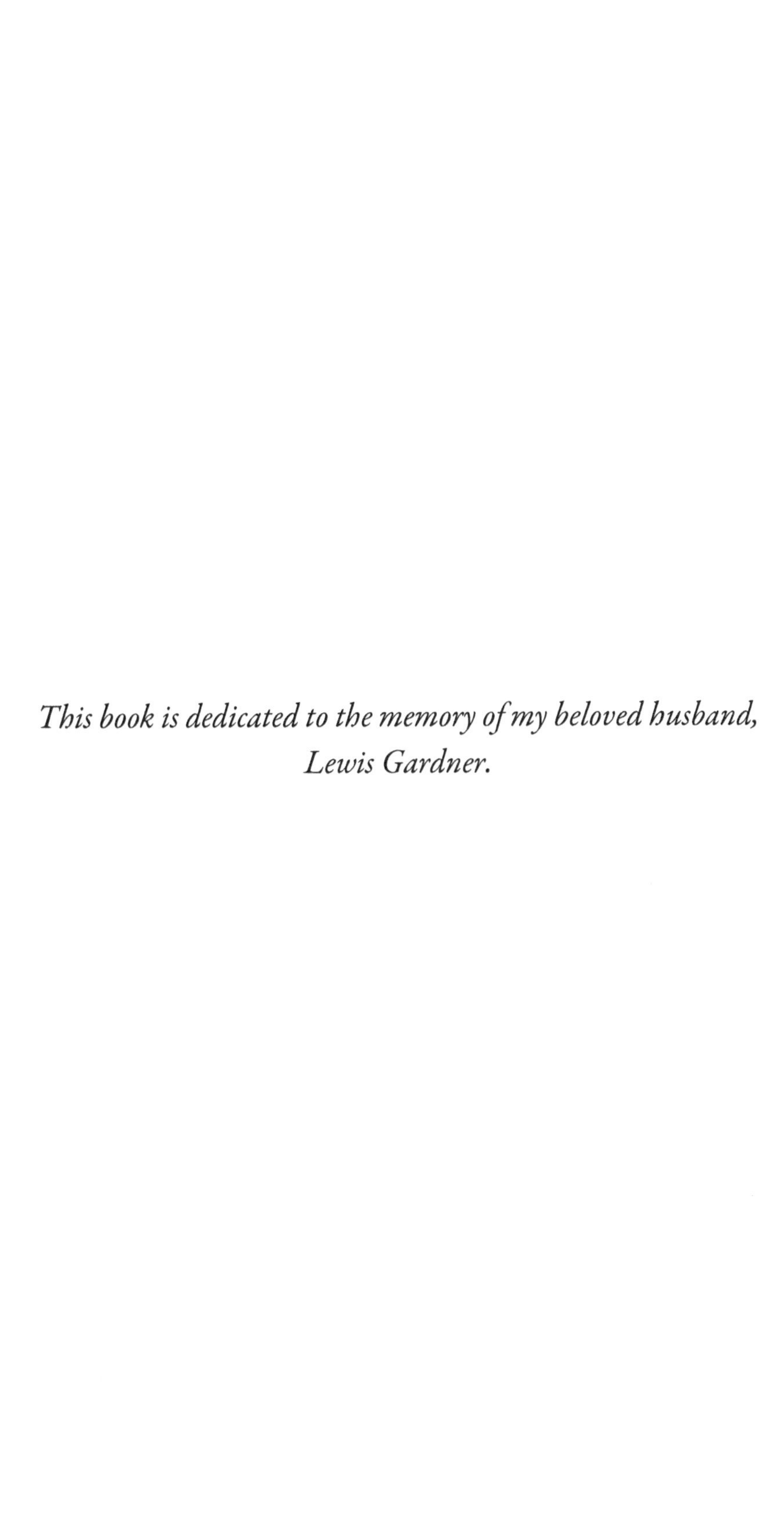

This book is dedicated to the memory of my beloved husband, Lewis Gardner.

Sandra Gardner's latest murder mystery launches readers on a roller coaster of tension from the first page! Investigative reporter Philomena Wolff must navigate dangerous relationships, family secrets, and her own fears to track down a killer before she's next. Compelling characters and a twisting plot make *The Murder Blog* a high-octane read!

–Cam Torrens, award-winning author of *Stable* and *False Summit*

The Murder Blog by Sandra Gardner is a pulsating journey in pursuit of murderers and men. Risk-taker Philomena Wolff works as an independent investigative reporter. Her success has brought with it a number of enemies determined to add her to that list of murders. One would think she would be satisfied to leave well enough alone, but the words "leave it alone" are not in her vocabulary. She decides to author a blog, *Who Killed Who*, a (surprise) blog about murders, designed to expose the perpetrators.

The blog is brilliantly interspersed with a provocative story, a masterclass in smart, intriguing writing. I particularly loved the deeply psychological backstories that lent sympathy (or revulsion in the case of the murderers), and motivation to the complex characters. I was captivated by the gutsy Philomena, who, along with her psychic sidekick Lily, leads us through a labyrinth of clues, evil schemes, and tempting, if risky, paramours. It's a turbulent ride, all the way to the thrilling conclusion.

Fans of Apple TV's *Truth be Told,* will absolutely love this book. Not that the rest of us won't share that same opinion!

–Bill Schweitzer, author of *Doves in a Tempest-The Valley of Horror*

THE
MURDER
BLOG

PROLOGUE

If I had only known what could happen, would I still have done it? Would that have made any difference?

Since I have a talent for getting mixed up in dangerous situations, probably not. It started when I got hooked on the Nancy Drew mysteries when I could barely read. The stories fed my burgeoning curiosity about what people are up to and why. This led to my snooping on the neighbors and other kids and anybody I thought looked suspicious. Most of the time, they all turned out to be perfectly innocent, of course. That was, until a series of murders of young women happened in upstate New York. The murders were never solved.

When I got older, my penchant for mysteries took a more serious turn. It made me want to solve real-life crimes, and I started a career as an investigative reporter. Exposing bad guys of all sorts in magazine articles gave me a sense of satisfaction, of doing something worthwhile. All felt well in my world – the usually peaceful Hudson Valley – where I have lived most of my life.

Then, young women in our area began going missing and turning up dead. This brought me back to the murders of many years ago. That made me sad and angry and remember a time I never wanted to think about again.

I decided to put myself out there as a crime-solver on a blog. I already had plenty of experience with bad guys as a freelance investigative reporter, a job that I was very good at. The job resulted in warnings to do me bodily harm, or worse. I was able to bluff my way through and pretend I was tough, instead of the wuss I really was, because I could talk and act a big game. I waited till I got home, shaken, worrying when my ruse would catch up with me.

I exposed scammers, con men, abusive partners, child molesters, and occasionally, even murderers in my articles. Doing it on a blog should be a piece of cake, right? After all, even with the crazy threats, nobody has killed me yet.

That was how The Murder Blog got started.

CHAPTER 1

Who Killed Who?

The blog for those with an inquisitive nose ... for murder and mayhem

ALBANY, NY: Cassie Knowles, aged 18, of Albany, disappeared on her way home from her managerial job at Jones' drugstore two days ago. Cassie is white, with blue eyes, and curly blonde hair. She was last seen wearing a dark blue pantsuit. Her friend, Maryanne Lindsey, who was with her, said Cassie ran off down a dark street after something and never came back.

If any of you have any information about Cassie, please call the toll-free number: 1-800-555-1212.

Philomena Wolff

UPDATE: Albany police reported that Cassie Knowles' body was found last night in a wooded area near her home.

COMMENTS:

From HelenO: This is so terrible. I feel for her parents.

From JazzBuff: Must be a crazy person.

From TomZ: Lock the SOB up and throw away the key.

LazyMan: Lock your doors and windows.

TammyY: I'm driving my daughter to and from work from now on. Hell or high water.

SaraH: Me, too. And if she takes a fit, too damn bad.

JimmyP: Bring the death penalty back to NY.

TomA: That's the only cure.

From Philomena Wolff: Good luck with that.

From the real Philomena Wolff: An imposter has appropriated my name. Please ignore the comments from this person. You all know that I would not post insulting comments like that.

CHAPTER 2

What I got paid for – to make a living (more or less) – was my magazine exposé articles. I tried to work on stories that could hopefully make a difference. Sometimes, I was lucky, and they did; at other times, frustration. I was proud of what I did, trying to help people's lives, the way Aunt Oly did. (More about Aunt Oly later.)

My latest assignment was on an Internet scam: a group of young men posing as investment counselors and fleecing elderly widows out of their savings. I wondered how they could face their own grandmothers. Well, they probably robbed them, too. So far, they'd been able to evade the authorities, but not for long, I hoped. Not if I could do something about it.

The best thing about my freelance writing life was that I was mostly able to work and live in the quiet of the country. After my mother died, I sold the house where I grew up and found my own place. My small, rented clapboard house on the edge of Woodstock, the artsy town in the Catskill Mountains, was, as my college friend, Robin Kramer, called it, paradise.

That it was, except for all the death threats via phone, email, and snail mail, because of my exposés. This made the local cops all too familiar with me, much to their aggravation. They made it very clear that I should not be doing what I did (which was trying to make a living) and putting myself in a perpetual state of danger. That was the name of my game, always trying to prove that I was the toughest, bravest, damn the consequences.

Back in the day, I interviewed youth street gangs in Brooklyn and the Bronx for a non-fiction book about gangs. The police drove me to where various gangs hung out, where their "club" was. The club was what the kids called their headquarters. The cops were from the NYPD Anti-Gang unit and knew these kids well. The gang members talked to them and even confided in them as sympathetic adults, likely because their home life was usually pretty sad, with single or both parents often working more than one job. Not only that, but many times, where the family lived was dangerous.

"With these youth gangs, we're not talking the old West Side Story here, with sticks and bottles. We're talking guns, lots of guns," one of the cops told me. After they let me out of the car, I took my tape recorder and notebook over to where a big, tattooed blonde girl and company were standing. It was late October, chilly, and as someone who always felt the cold, I stupidly wore only a trench coat over my clothes. I started shivering.

The big blonde sneered and said, "You scared?"

I stuck my chin out. "No, I'm cold."

After the interview, I got back in the police car. One cop turned to me, saying, "You know how many bullets these guys have? We only have six."

"Now you tell me," I said, with a shaky laugh.

For another book, a few years later, I met up with a couple of South-Central L.A. gangs, not-so-kindly introduced to me by the Sheriff's Office Gang Unit. The saddest moment was when one of the gangbangers (the cops' name for the kids), a nice-looking, polite boy of 16 told me he did not expect to live to 21. I thought of the boys and girls I knew back in Onteora High School, living safe, good lives, compared with the everyday violence facing these gang kids.

My only disaster on the L.A. adventure was due to my horrible sense of direction, getting totally lost at night in a very bad neighborhood. There was absolutely nothing around except dark streets and boarded-up buildings. I still do not know how I ever found my way back to the motel.

As an investigative reporter, I worked on some grisly stories. There was the funeral home that was leaving corpses to rot in their yard; the space heaters used in apartments without proper heating that resulted in horrible fires; the lead paint in old buildings that caused permanent learning disabilities in toddlers who ingested chips of flaking paint. The toddlers' plight got me, every time.

Dealing with all the sorrows and sleaze had led me naturally into doing the murder blog, *Who Killed Who?* Murder was the worst of the worst, and sometimes, sexual assault preceded a murder. When I thought about this, it brought back a memory I tried to push away for years, unsuccessfully.

CHAPTER 3

When I opened my laptop, there was a new message on the blog.

My dear Philomena Wolff

Since you are vigilantly following my work, I thought it fitting that I share it with you. And, appropriately enough, on your pestilential blog.

I always do it the same way. My hands around her tender shoot of neck. Gently, at first. Gazing into her wide eyes, murmuring, "I'm your savior, washing away your dirty sins, with your blood."

Of course, I'd get frustrated. Why didn't she understand this was for her own good? Why must these young women always fight me, their rescuer from eternal damnation?

I'd whisper in her ear, "Be joyful. You'll be pure forever."

She'd been perfect. Lying there, on top of the bed, so peaceful. The shot I'd given her did the trick, as usual. Before then, she'd been twisting and moaning. Even though I'd told her I was there to save her, that I'd be as gentle as I could. Well, no one could hear. We were deep underground. I'd constructed the chamber with soundproof, leaden walls.

Blonde curls, pink cheeks, big blue eyes, heart-shaped lips just begging to be kissed. Black bikini panties. (Why must they dress like whores?) And underneath ... moist and pink.

My blood was still pulsing, rushing. I needed to calm down, to finish purifying her. To enable her to lie in a state of grace forever.

I paused. There was no hurry. I poured myself a glass of wine. Ruby red. The color of blood.

Well, dear Philomena Wolff, that's all for now. I feel that we have a special relationship, you and I. Don't you?

I froze, not wanting to believe what I was reading. Then I let out a scream.

CHAPTER 4

Enough of this, I thought. Time to call in a lifeline, in the person of Lily MacCraw, my friend, blog partner, and professional psychic. Much of the time, she saw things – missing people and bodies – that other people did not. She had received the gift of what they called second sight from her ancestors.

Still shaky but a little calmer, I picked up my cell and called her.

"Oh my God!" Lily shrieked in my ear. "That filthy, disgusting message! How dare he!" Then she said, "Come right over, but drive carefully. It's pouring out."

"Great, thanks!" Not only was it raining hard, but the wind was howling. Timid driver that I was, I tried not to hyperventilate. Grabbing my keys, I managed to make it to Lily's cottage, driving very slowly, hoping my small car did not get blown across the road or get stuck in a flood. Lily lived about 20 minutes away in Phoenicia, a small town a little way west of Woodstock.

Lily inherited her grandmother Lillian's bright, comfortable cottage in the woods. Along with the cottage, she acquired Lillian's magical way with herbs and spices. More important, to my mind, was the family's gift of second sight, handed down for centuries.

When she opened the door, she took one look at me and wrapped me up in a huge bath towel. "You're totally soaked! Let's get those wet things off you." She handed me a sweat suit, sox and slippers. "Change into these and go into the kitchen and you'll feel better, I guarantee," she said, with a grin. On the kitchen table was a pot of mint tea, blue-and-white china teacups, and fresh-baked cinnamon bread on a matching blue-and-white plate.

Lily was a study in contradictions. This tough, strong woman had a kitchen that was a domestic goddess's dream: gleaming appliances, polished wood cupboard along a side wall, oak floor. Copper pots and pans hanging from beams in the ceiling. All of this came from her grandmother, who had raised her.

"I love acting like a housewife. It's my secret vice." She broke into a wide smile that showed perfect teeth, which she said was genetic, as were her strong bones and general good health. We settled in at the kitchen table, which was painted blue. (Her grandmother thought the color blue had magical qualities.) When Lily took off her frilly blue-and-white apron, her white tee-shirt showed a picture of a woman raising a fist at a man staring at her breasts, with the statement: *Don't Even Think About It.*

I sipped my tea and bit into the slice of cinnamon bread, which was, as usual, delicious. I silently thanked the universe for Lily's wonderful culinary talents, mine were nonexistent. "I remember the first time I was here, and you made that same delicious bread," I said. "I was working on the investigation of my first case, the headless torso of a young woman. You ..."

"That poor thing, cut up and thrown into the garbage." She shuddered. "And if the sanitation workers hadn't seen her, she would've ended up in a landfill and nobody would've ever found her."

"Or had no clue as to who she was or why she was killed," I said, "and still wouldn't be, if it weren't for you." I smiled at my friend.

Lily shrugged. She was the most modest, unassuming person I ever met. "I didn't do anything special. It just came to me, you know, like always."

While the police were checking missing persons' lists, Lily went to the station house and told them about her vision of the murder scene, a basement in a building belonging to the dead young woman's boyfriend's family.

"The cops wouldn't take you seriously." I made a face.

Lily said, "Well, it's hard for people to believe in psychic visions, so I can't really blame them. But eventually, they came around."

"Sure, because they had no choice. They didn't have any other leads."

When the police checked it out, they found Lily had been right. There were bloodstains in the basement. The killer turned out to be the boyfriend's father. He tried to get her into bed, and she fought him. He stabbed her to death and cut off her head, figuring that would make him safe from discovery.

"Well, I'm glad her family could finally lay that poor young woman to rest," Lily said, "and that I got to meet you then, too."

Since then, we worked on a number of cases together. Now I needed her thoughts on this horrible killer. "Do you think he sent me that disgusting post to try to scare me off my game?"

Lily snorted. "He really doesn't know who he's dealing with, does he?"

CHAPTER 5

Lily MacCraw worked with the dead for a living. She was the only woman employed at the Woodstock town cemetery, recently promoted to head gravedigger.

She liked her job, and she was good at it – very good, in fact. Digging graves gave her a chance to flex her muscles, which were great, thanks to gymnastics, martial arts, and other physically demanding activities her grandmother Lillian sent her to when she was growing up.

If not for Lillian, she always thought, God only knows what would have happened to her and Teddy after their mother died. We were loved and nurtured as well as anyone. Lillian raised us to be as strong and independent as she was. Well, it worked with me, she thought, but not with Teddy. Lily wiped tears away with her sleeve. She missed her little brother, her sister, her mother, and her grandmother. At least Lillian's strength of will allowed her to live a long, productive life, unlike poor Teddy and her mother. She tried to remember if there were other boys in the MacCraw family and what happened to them when they grew up, but none came to mind.

Lily was an attractive, green-eyed redhead, with broad-shoulders and biceps that rivaled the men she worked with. None of them dared to interfere with her, and when she gave an order, they snapped to.

That was her paid job. It supported her mission as a psychic, which was unpaid. As she explained to her friend Philomena, a real psychic had only one purpose: helping people, whether it was the police or private citizens.

Lily had been "seeing things," as her family used to say, after the "bad thing" happened. She came from a long line of Scottish women with second sight. Men were scared of them, but loved them anyway, they could not help themselves. All would usually go well until their beloved found them doing something they should not. That darned old second sight could cause no end of problems to those who engaged in nefarious doings. You did not want to be around when one of the MacCraw women found out about it.

Though nobody in town knew for sure, rumors swirled around the Mac-Craw women for generations. There were rumors about what happened to the men who fell under their spell. They seemed to vanish, never to be seen again: Were they dead? Buried in the MacCraws' basement? There was even speculation that they had turned the disappeared men into frogs or lizards. The MacCraw women were not exactly witches, however, in the true sense of the word.

Changing a human into a reptile was much too much work for the Mac-Craw women. They were far too sensible and too busy growing herbs, magical and otherwise. Changing people into reptiles, even people who deserved it, was not nice work, either – very sweaty and dirty. It could also bring about some nasty repercussions, since their neighbors already thought the women were odd and probably dangerous. Why in the world would they want to increase the populations of frogs or lizards in the neighborhood? In the MacCraws' opinion, there were far too many of the ugly things, anyway.

Believing in getting married or even living with a man was not for the women in Lily's family. They were much too independent to accommodate themselves to a man. If the neighbors whispered, the MacCraw women paid them no mind. To tell the truth, their neighbors were more than a little frightened of them. The MacCraw women emitted some kind of aura, sense, feeling, that seemed to act as a protective covering, an invisible armor. They permitted men to make love to them, to father a child, but not to stick around.

Like her mother and grandmother, Lily had never lived with a male, except for her little brother. She often thought and wondered about her father. Was he a nice man, loving and kind? Did he wonder about her? She tried asking her mother, but her mother shushed her, saying, "It's not important who he is. You have us, and that should be enough."

When nobody was at the cemetery, Lily would often lower herself into a freshly dug empty grave and meditate for a while. Someone might think this was terribly morbid and creepy, but being close to and thinking about the newly dead gave her a way into their lives. Why did they die? What were their lives like? Who loved them, who hated them? Like her ancestors, she was destined to help those who needed help – and bring harm to those who needed to be harmed.

Meditating in a grave helped her mission as a psychic: entering into that netherworld, a living person among the dead, trying to feel what they felt.

CHAPTER 6

When I was 17, one of my classmates went missing. She was discovered half-buried in the park next to the high school. Other young women were abducted and found dead. I heard people whispering the word "raped." People were scared, worrying about their teenagers. They held candlelight vigils for the missing young women in the area. The police went into the schools, talking to students about safety.

My best friend, Melanie, ended up as one of the missing. It was one day after school. We were walking home together, the way we always did. It was raining hard, and a fog was coming in. We huddled under my red-and white striped umbrella.

"Phil, I heard a kitten meowing around the corner. I bet it's lost," Melanie said, already pulling away.

My pretty, blonde friend was very tender-hearted, especially about animals. "I didn't hear anything," I said. "Besides, we're supposed to come home right after school, remember? Everybody's scared to death of the rapist-murderer." I shuddered. "I'm scared, too. It's not safe out there anymore."

She ignored me and started walking toward the corner. It was darker there, as if the sun were afraid to go there. I was, too.

"Melanie, come back!" I yelled after her. "You don't know what's down there!"

I walked to the corner and waited a long time for Melanie to come back. While I stood there watching, out of the corner of my eye, I saw a man dart from a building. I could not see too much in the rain and fog, but he was tall and skinny. He looked up for a moment. I froze and ran home as fast as I could.

I told my mother what happened and what I saw. She did not believe me, of course – she never did.

"Stop making things up, you silly girl," she said, turning back to her magazine. "You're just like your father, no sense of reality." She berated my father for not planning ahead, for not having savings, not providing a sense of security. My father never made enough money to satisfy my mother, even with long days traveling all over the state, selling insurance, which meant that he was hardly ever around.

After Melanie's mother told the police that Melanie and I always walked home from school together, two police officers came to our house. My mother put on a pretend-nice smile and pulled me onto the sofa next to her, putting her arm around me – as if she ever did that when we were alone.

The officers asked me to tell them what happened on the way home. Did I see anything or anybody? I just looked down at the floor.

My mother gave my arm a squeeze that felt more like a pinch. "Now, you need to tell the officers what you saw, sweetie." This was not a name she ever called me, or any other nice name. I almost wanted to say out loud, "Who are you talking to?"

I started shaking and could not stop. She pretended to hug me and whispered in my ear, "You better quit that, or you'll be sorry." She smiled her pretend-smile at me.

I made myself calm down and told them what I saw. "But I couldn't see his face in all the rain and fog," I said. "Now he'll come and find me because I told you." I was still trembling, even with my mother's eyes boring into me.

The officers were very nice and told me I had nothing to worry about. "There's no way he'll know anything about you," one of them said. "You'll be safe, don't worry."

After they left, my mother lost the smile and let out her anger at me for "embarrassing her by putting on such a show for the police, acting so scared." She locked me in my room and let me out just before my father came home.

That was the first time I had the nightmare: I was running in the woods and a bad man was chasing after me, trying to kill me. I was terrified that I could not run fast enough. When I finally reached my house, my mother smiled at me and locked the door to stop me from getting inside.

I woke up shaking.

CHAPTER 7

The police and members of the community organized search parties. After days of combing the area between the high school and Melanie's home, they found her body covered with leaves at the edge of the woods.

I huddled on the living room sofa, sobbing about my friend and terrified of the man in the fog. "What if he thinks I saw him? He'll come back to get me, too!"

"Who'd want you? At least your friend was a nice young woman. And pretty, too." My mother sneered, walking into her bedroom, and shutting the door.

That was my mother. She never wanted me and as much as told me I was a mistake. She probably wished I was the one in the woods.

They never found him. The attacks in our area eventually stopped. Maybe he moved, been arrested, or died.

Maybe not, because young women were going missing here again.

CHAPTER 8

Who Killed Who?

The blog for those with an inquisitive nose ... for murder and mayhem

KATONAH, NY: Andrea Tillman, 18, of Katonah, was last seen two days ago on her way home from gymnastics practice with her friend, Marla James. Andrea is white, with short, blonde hair and blue eyes. She was wearing a red sweater and blue jeans.

If you have any information about this missing young woman, please call the toll-free number: 1-800-555-7777.

Philomena Wolff

UPDATE: Andrea Tillman's body was discovered today in a field near her home in Katonah.

COMMENTS:

From PhyllisG: Maybe these parents should pay more attention to their kids.

From BenO: How can you blame the parents? Are they supposed to follow teenagers to and from school?

From ImaTechie: I agree with FredaG. I think the parents are at fault.

From RobertN: No way. You can't hover over your kids once they're teens.

From CurtS: Right, RobertN. But you have to make sure you teach them about danger, talking to strangers, etc. Stranger-danger.

From CharlieE: And it's a good idea to give them self-defense lessons. The Teen Fit gym is a great place for martial arts lessons. It's a chain, so there's a number of them.

From Philomena Wolff: Martial arts? I can have lots of fun with that, my dear.

From the real Philomena Wolff: Pay no attention to this. It's the imposter again.

CHAPTER 9

Woodstock, NY, where I grew up, is a friendly, you might say, eccentric place. It was known as the most famous small town in the world, because of the music festival of 1969 that did not happen in Woodstock. A lot of the musicians spent time in Woodstock, but the town would not allow such a large gathering. Woodstock '69, the festival of peace, love, and music, happened an hour and a half away at a farm in Bethel, Sullivan County. Tourists still stop residents on the street in Woodstock, asking to be shown where the festival was.

I learned to love the quiet, the clean air, the pitch-dark at night, the astounding view of Overlook Mountain that surprised me even after all these years.

People were laid-back, nice to each other and even to strangers, and there was always lots of music and art and theater. We even had a new theater in town, the Woodstock Playhouse, which burned down, was rebuilt, and now enclosed for year-round events. Everybody knew everybody, some were related, and some were exes who still lived together in a bunch with other exes. My childhood best friend, Melanie, was one of those kids who lived with both sets of parents and their new partners. Melanie was someone to share secrets with until …

The bad part of my childhood was my relationship with my mother. I had scenes burned into my brain that choked off any good feelings I had about myself growing up.

"I just heard our neighbor say you were the ugliest teenager she ever saw," my mother told me when I got home from school one day. "I was never so embarrassed in my life."

She was embarrassed. I went to the bathroom to throw up.

When I got all "Bs" on a report card, she curled her lip. "What have *I* got to be proud of with *you*?"

The next term I got Cs. Why even try since all I ever got was criticism?

She sent me to tap dancing class. I practiced in the back hall, so not to make too much noise in the house. I liked the class, especially the clicking sound the taps on my shoes made. For the dance recital, we wore little Dutch girl outfits, which I loved. After the performance, when I ran up to my mother, she made a face. "You are the most awkward child I've ever seen."

I acted like it did not matter, did not hurt me, whatever she said, but of course, it did. Later on, I adopted a veneer of strength, of why-do-I-care-nothing-can-hurt-me. I stuffed the overwhelming sense of shame and sadness deep inside my bones. I never knew, or maybe did not want to know, till much later, that it hobbled me, crippled my actions and relationships.

The bright spot in my life then was my father. I always knew he loved me. He tried so hard to help me with my mother whenever he could, but it was useless. I remember the conversation I overheard when I was 13 and really miserable, with a face full of acne and metal braces in my mouth. When I looked in the mirror, I ended up crying.

My father tried to get my mother to comfort me. "Phil could probably really use a hug right now. She's pretty upset about her appearance," he said.

My mother's response: "Ugh, 'Phil' is an even worse name than 'Philomena.' Please don't call her that. And as for her looks, it's her own fault."

"Her fault? How?" He was puzzled.

"Eating candy and greasy chips with her crummy friends. I never had that problem when I was a teenager."

My father just sighed. He was a high-spirited, emotionally generous man who exuded warmth wherever he went. It was a family trait.

CHAPTER 10

My father named me after his mother, Petra. His family were excitable, loving people. Our ancestors left Germany around 1870 for Greece and, just before World War Two, somehow managed to flee to America.

His close-knit family of Greek Jews (Jewish Greeks?) had emigrated together: sisters, brothers, cousins. They first came to New York City and later, all moved to the Catskills to start apple orchards. They kept an apartment building in the city that they rented out, except for one large apartment where the men who worked in the city stayed during the week.

My father was not around all that much because he always had two jobs. Though he worked hard, he was never able to make much money. When he was home on a weekend, he took me out for breakfast or to the beach on a warm day. I especially loved when we went to visit his family. My aunts, uncles, and older cousins made a fuss over me, especially my father's sister, Aunt Olympia. She was a union organizer when she was younger, living and working in New York City. Harassed by the bosses and even beaten up on a picket line by police, she was a strong woman, but very warm and kind.

"My beautiful Philomena," Aunt Olympia would coo, hugging me hard against her considerable bosom. "You look just like me when I was your age."

She went to a drawer in her dresser and dug out an old family album covered in shabby red velvet. We sat on the soft maroon living room sofa. I liked sitting there, snuggled up to her ample body, picking chocolate kisses out of the cut-glass bowl on the coffee table. As she turned the yellowing pages, I saw that she was right. It was like looking in an old mirror.

I looked at her face. "Aunt Oly (When I was little, I had trouble pronouncing her name, and the nickname stuck.), since you're still sorta pretty, that's okay with me that I look like you."

She let out a big laugh and pulled me close. Being with her made me feel good. Later, when I got older and more mature, I realized that what I loved about all of them was not so much their fussing over me, but the fact that they made me feel I belonged. I was the youngest member of a big family who had her rightful place with them.

That was not the case with my mother, who always made me feel alien, someone who did not fit. I was small for my age, olive-skinned, dark-eyed, with dark hair. That was another strike against me in my mother's eyes. She was a fair beauty: blonde, green-eyed, on the tall side for a woman.

Her family had been living in the Hudson Valley for generations. The Abbotts were among the original settlers. They even had a road named for them in Hurley, near Woodstock, where their sprawling farm had been.

My mother was more than proud of this. She showed me old maps, where the family farm had been, acres and acres. There was a pond, where the local kids would swim (called Abbott's Pond, of course). The farm was long gone, and the pond was all dried up. She took me there to see where she used to play. The family eventually turned to the more lucrative real estate business years ago and sold the farm. She still maintained that air of her birthright, of superiority: old blood, old settlers, old family, and considered my father's family pushy intruders. She made no bones about her feelings about them, my father, and me.

"What a shame you didn't take after my side, instead of those big-nosed, stunted little foreigners," she would say. I knew my mother thought I was ugly. A big Greek-Jewish nose looked fine on my father: a sign of character, I thought. "If we had more money, I'd get you a nose job," she told me.

To me, my nose was just fine. It was like my father and all his family. It was a good, solid nose. It made a statement, I thought.

Why did they marry? Aunt Oly told me that when my mother was a young woman, she was beautiful, and all the men were after her. "Evidently, she found them boring. When she met your father, a salesman, with a salesman's charm, she must have thought he was exciting." My aunt frowned. "Well, he was definitely different from what she was used to. Too bad she didn't realize that she should've stuck to her own kind." She added, "He should've, too, my poor brother!"

My mother was miserably unhappy with her lot in life. (I could almost feel sorry for her – almost.) Her family disowned her after she eloped with my father. He was not only an immigrant, but a Jewish immigrant. They were probably as snotty and uptight as my mother, not to mention anti-Semitic, hating that she married a Jew.

I became quite a rebel early on. I ditched classes, hid out in the woods, ruined my clothes, climbing and exploring. I did not discriminate in friends, either, the way my mother wanted. Looking back, I think I must have deliberately picked out the worst kids in school to be friends with, just to spite her, basically the class delinquents. That probably contributed to my fascination with crime and bad guys. I went along with them, covering school buildings with obscene graffiti, joyriding in other people's cars. Lucky for me, I was a lightning-fast runner and did not get caught. I was even on the girls' track team before rumors of my activities got me kicked off.

My mother would carry on about my behavior. "I can't hold my head up in town with you running around with those awful kids. I can just hear people whispering behind my back about it, 'She's the mother of one of those kids in that bad crowd.' Can't you find some better people to be friends with? There are plenty of kids your age from good old families."

Translation: no Jews, immigrants, or God forbid, blacks. I had no interest in getting to know people from "good old families." I was my father's daughter, through and through.

CHAPTER 11

My father's family always described the Greek islands as gorgeous and romantic. "But you couldn't make a decent living there, even with so many olive and almond trees we planted," my Aunt Oly would say. "So here we are and here we stay."

To my mind, where we lived, in the Catskills, in upstate New York, was plenty beautiful. I loved the smells of the pine trees and the sights of deer and small woodland creatures. It made me feel alive. Even after I moved away for college, it eventually drew me back in.

My studio apartment in New York City made me feel alive in a different way: the energy of people moving quickly, talking fast, Broadway, Carnegie Hall, the museums, the aromas of ethnic foods, the sounds of all sorts of foreign accents. It was always exciting.

The two lives I was living could sometimes make me crazy. I would forget which place I left something and occasionally, I woke up disoriented, not knowing where I was.

I tried to keep a reasonable schedule: the city during the week, the country on weekends. These days, though, I found myself spending more and more time upstate. I had a 10-year-old Nissan that had been through the wars of my impaired parking ability. My poor car was not only badly dented, but sported a "surgical scar," stitches alongside the part of the hood where it (I) smashed into a telephone pole. However, it was safe and got me to the Trailways station in Kingston, where I took the bus to and from the city. My lives, for the most part, stayed separate, which, to my mind, was the best of all possible worlds.

CHAPTER 12

My fourth-floor walk-up studio apartment in NYC's Upper West Side was small, you could say cramped, but it had what I needed. I built up along the walls with makeshift shelves for books, notes, whatever. The tiny closet was crammed with jeans, oversized tee-shirts (Always worrying about gaining weight, I liked them big to disguise whatever flesh was popping out.) and sweats. There were a few jackets and blouses and a couple of nicer tops and pants for professional meetings with an editor or an interview subject for an article, or few-and-far between dates. I could not even remember the last one, which, considering my unfortunate luck with men, was probably for the best.

I picked Wedgewood blue paint for the bedroom and bathroom and yellow for the dingy kitchen/dining area in an effort to brighten it up. There was plenty of room for my work desk and four-drawer file cabinet since cooking was definitely not my thing and never had been. There were the minimum basics for survival, meaning a microwave, tons of stuff in the freezer and magnets holding the all-important takeout numbers of local delis, Chinese restaurants, and pizza places on the refrigerator.

My digs were rent-stabilized, so I could more or less afford to live there. The neighbors were friendly, and the neighborhood was tree-lined and full of charm, with window-boxes and shrubbery blooming bright every spring. What was great was having two of my college friends in apartments just down the block, and a couple blocks away, a Barnes & Noble and Starbucks. Today I was going for coffee with my college friend, Wendy Chen.

It was only a few blocks' walk, and it was a lovely fall day. A light breeze was blowing, and the air had a note of the colder weather to come. I hoped not too much, remembering the last long, brutal winter. Down here in the city, the temps were mostly in the teens or warmer. It was much worse in the Catskills, where it could be below double digits. Sometimes, I could feel the cold reach down into my bones, and I thought I would never be warm again. I loved the mountains so much, though; I put up with it, but not without complaining, of course.

The good weather brought out the dog-walkers en masse. Unfortunately, this resulted in noxious smells. Luckily, these days, the walkers usually picked up after them. The *Curb Your Dog* signs must have worked, thankfully.

When I got close to Starbucks, I felt a chill down my back. I looked in a glass shop window and someone, I could not tell if it was a man or a woman, quickly moved away, disappearing across the street.

I ran inside Starbucks, where Wendy was waiting for me at a table.

"What happened? You're shaking." She got out of her chair and put an arm around me. "Come, sit down and tell me."

I told her.

Wendy was near tears. "Phil, I'm so worried about you. You need to be much more careful."

After we ordered our coffees, espresso for Wendy, cappuccino for me, I told her about The Murder Blog.

She shook her head. "Phil, you shouldn't be doing that blog. You're just tempting fate – posting about murders. It's bad enough that you dig up dirt on bad people for that magazine."

Tempting fate? Maybe if I ever stopped to think – or really cared – what happened, I might not be doing what I did. At least being an investigator helped people, even if it put me in danger, so I just kept plowing straight ahead, no matter what.

Wendy was on her lunch break. With her black hair smartly cut, navy suit and crisp white blouse, conservative navy pumps and Coach bag, she was the picture of quiet, professional elegance. As for me, I already had cappuccino drips on my purple turtleneck.

Scary-smart Wendy was now a criminal defense attorney, an excellent one, considering all the scumbags she saved from their just desserts. "Please," she said, biting her lip, "please try to be more careful. Can't you find something less dangerous to do?"

"Huh!" I said. "You should talk, with your job, dealing with the lowest of the low, turning them loose on society."

She made a face. "I know, I know, but these guys are grateful to me and wouldn't think of harming me. We're talking about *you*. You've already gotten death threats from doing those exposés."

I sipped my drink. "You're right, but the relatives of the victims of the criminals you defend are not your friends. Doesn't that worry you?"

Wendy sighed. "It's the dues I pay for doing what I do."

"So, why do you keep doing it?"

She finished her croissant. "Somebody has to."

"Touché."

After we hugged goodbye, I promised to try to be more careful – but I was not about to give up chasing down bad guys. Risk-taking was part of the job of an investigator, and I had to admit, crazy as it sounded, it made the whole thing more exciting.

CHAPTER 13

Who Killed Who?

The blog for those with an inquisitive nose ... for murder and mayhem

SAUGERTIES, NY: Kimberly Thomas, 18, of Saugerties, was last seen two days ago on her way home from high school with her friend, Suzanne Wilson. Kimberly is white, with blonde hair in a braid. She was wearing a striped jacket and black jeans.

If you have any information about this missing young woman, please call the toll-free number: 1-800-555-6453.

Philomena Wolff

UPDATE: Kimberly Thomas's body was discovered today in a wooded area near her home in Saugerties.

COMMENTS:

From RandyJ: Why isn't the school system doing something?

From ChrissyW: You're right, but what can they do?

From FrequentFlyer: Simple. Just install security cameras in the front, sides and back of the schools.

From ZackH: And put armed security guards inside and outside.

From ToryN: Cops would be better.

From AnnieL: Whoa. Slow down, guys. Do you really think it's a good idea for kids to see armed guards or police in and outside of their school? It could feel like a prison.

From Philomena Wolff: Are you people kidding? Nothing's going to do anything.

From the real Philomena Wolff: Ignore the post above. It's from an imposter.

CHAPTER 14

Lily finished up for the day, neatening the edges of the freshly dug grave. Perfect, she thought, saying a silent blessing for the soul of the deceased who would soon occupy it.

She started back toward her car, clutching her sweater tighter around her and shivering a little as the wind picked up. It seemed to be getting darker, much too early, she thought. Maybe there was a storm brewing. She shivered again.

She was terrified of storms. People would laugh at her if they knew. This woman worked in a graveyard, crawled into empty graves, and in her spare time, had visions, perceptions, and was deathly afraid of thunderstorms. She had good reason to be.

A day after Lily's 11th birthday, her mother told her to go get her big sister, to help give their little brother a bath. Lily knew Abby would be where she always was, in the backyard under the big old elm tree, reading and eating an apple.

Pretty, blonde, 17-year-old Abigail was reading one of her favorite books under the tree at the far edge of the yard. Lily knew that when Abby was reading, she did not notice anything or anyone around her. Rain was just starting to fall when Lily stepped out the door onto the porch and froze.

A strange man was bending over her sister. Abigail gave a little scream and then fell over, as if she were sleeping, like the baby doll Lily had that closed its eyes when she put it in her doll's bed.

"Shhh, don't wake her up. She's sleeping." The man kept his head down so Lily could not see his face.

"What are you doing here?" Lily screamed, as he picked Abby up and ran to his car. "Leave my sister alone!" She kept on screaming for help, as he drove away. The rain was falling harder now, and there was thunder and lightning. No one could hear her, with the noise of the storm.

Lily was terrified. She ran back inside to tell her mother what happened.

She cried for her sister every night. Her mother and grandmother were crazy with fear. The search went on for three weeks until Abigail's body was found in the woods behind the park.

Light and joy died for the family after that. Lily's grandmother would cry silently when she thought no one could see. Lily's mother, Rebekah, stopped speaking. Lily, too, was different after her sister's abduction, becoming quiet and subdued. She was not the same curious, trusting girl she had been.

A few weeks later, Lily's gift appeared – softly, gently, at first, just a whisper. When she woke up one day, everything around her was a little blurry. Her senses felt heightened. She could hear sounds she never heard before, like the singing of distant birds. Smells seemed to be stronger, too. The scent of just-budding flowers in a garden in the next street delighted her nose. What she could see now was even stranger. Slowly, a vision of a little boy who was crying after being knocked down by a bully came before her eyes. What was happening to her?

CHAPTER 15

Lily's mother, Rebekah, could not stop blaming herself for Abigail's abduction and murder. Lily and her grandmother tried very hard to help, to no avail.

Rebekah refused to leave the house. All day long, she sat in a rocking chair in the kitchen, next to the stove, huddled in a blanket. When Lily and her grandmother tried to talk to her, Rebekah's eyes would half-close, and she stared off into the distance. No one could tell what she saw there.

"Maybe she's trying to follow Abigail's journey into the wherever," Lillian whispered to her granddaughter.

Even when the little boy, Thaddeus, cried, Rebekah was not moved. Lily and her grandmother took over his care. Soon, Thaddeus was calling Lillian, "Mama." When Lily came home from school and relieved Lillian, he broke into a huge smile. When Thaddeus learned to walk and then to run, it was Lily he ran to on his chubby little legs, burying his downy head in Lily's knees.

Eventually, Rebekah began refusing to eat or drink. Lillian grew frantic, and tried to feed her daughter special soups, made to tempt a delicate palate. "Rebekah, darling, you always loved this soup when you were little. Please, just try to eat some," Lillian would plead. Finally, she called in the family doctor.

The doctor told Lillian that Rebekah had to go to the hospital. "Otherwise, my dear, your daughter will surely die. I know you've tried your hardest, but things have reached a dangerous state."

An ambulance carried Rebekah away, as Lillian, with Lily holding Thaddeus, cried and blew kisses.

Lily and Thaddeus moved into their grandmother's cottage. A few weeks later, Rebekah drew her last breath, with her family at her side.

"Why did Mama die?" Lily asked her grandmother through her tears.

Lillian said, "Sweetheart, she just couldn't keep on living, I guess. It was just too hard for her."

"But why couldn't she do it for us?" Lily asked.

Lillian hugged her granddaughter and grandson. "I'm sure she wanted to, but she wasn't able." Then she said, "Let's try to remember her the way she was before."

"Okay," Lily whispered.

Lillian put her arm around Lily, while holding Thaddeus close in the other arm. "Now let's go home. There's the cow to be milked and chickens to feed."

CHAPTER 16

"Don't go anywhere alone," Lily's grandmother warned her. "Don't talk to people you don't know, especially men."

Lillian made sure Lily knew how to take care of herself. She enrolled her in a kids' gymnastics class and, later on, it was kickboxing, karate, and other martial arts. She armed Lily with a whistle and pepper spray. By the time Lily graduated from high school, she was the strongest kid in her class, including the boys.

Lily's gift, her special ability, had become sharper. She could see people who needed to be found, both alive and dead. Something must have jarred loose during the "bad time," as she thought of it.

This was not so strange. Her grandmother Lillian claimed the women in their family were descended from a woman named Lilias, who lived in Scotland about five hundred years ago during the North Berwick Witch Trials. "They burned her at the stake as a witch, though no one had ever been harmed by her second sight, except those who needed to be harmed.

"It started with the Witchcraft Act, in the year 1563. Then, in 1590, the town elders gathered up all the older women they could find," her grandmother told her sorrowfully. "That's when the first Lilias was hanged."

"Did she do something terrible? Was that why?" Lily asked, wide-eyed.

Her grandmother shook her head. "No, she didn't. At least," she said slyly, "not to anybody who didn't deserve it."

"Well then, I don't think she shouldn't have been punished like that," Lily said.

Lillian smiled and gave her granddaughter a hug. "You're right, sweetheart.

The family named one woman in every other generation in the family for Lilias. Every woman named for Lilias was gifted with second sight. Curiously, though, none of them had ever been gifted as young as Lily.

Lily was happy about her gift when she found someone's lost pet. When she played hide-and-seek with other children, she always found the hiders. The others thought she must be cheating, not closing her eyes when she should. Then one of them stood next to her and watched closely. After that, the children grew frightened of her. Some of the older boys in the schoolyard teased her and said mean things.

"See anything, Lily? Woo woo!" They ducked behind a tree, calling, "I see you; do you see me?"

No one wanted to be her friend. She wished her gift would go away, but no matter how hard she wished, it was still there, stronger than ever.

One day, her little brother, Thaddeus, went missing when a thunderstorm was just starting. Thaddeus was only four. Lily thought about the bad thing that happened to her sister during a storm and shivered. Then she got hold of herself and sat down on her bed and waited.

Soon, an image of Thaddeus appeared, and she rushed out of the house, down the hill and over to the stream. There he was, wading in the water, trying to catch a fish, while the thunder and lightning began raging around him. The water was still shallow where he was, but further out, it was much deeper.

Lily grabbed her little brother and took him back home, scolding him all the way. Their grandmother was very grateful to Lily. For once, Lily was thankful for the gift, even though most of the time, she was not. She kept wondering why this blessing and curse was hers at such a young age.

When Lily was fifteen, she decided to ask her grandmother about it. Lillian and her grandchildren lived in the little blue-and-white cottage in the Phoenicia woods that Lily lived in now. Lillian disliked most people and certainly did not want to be bothered talking to them. Most people were afraid of her, though Lillian had never been known to harm anyone, except those who needed to be harmed, and she helped those who needed help.

After school, Lily rode her bike home. When Lillian opened the door, she gave her granddaughter a big hug.

Lillian wore a blue-and-white polka-dotted apron, tied at the waist, which served to cover her white blouse and ankle-length blue skirt. She was looking older these days, Lily thought. She was more stooped, her long white hair was thinning out and her cheeks were sprouting new wrinkles, but her blue eyes were as sharp and knowing as ever and she remained fiercely strong and independent. She never accepted help from anyone until her grandchildren came to live with her. She taught them how to weed the garden, milk her one (white) cow, feed the (white) hens and gather eggs. The herb garden behind the cottage gave off sweet and pungent odors: rosemary, lemongrass, mint, cilantro, and many other wonderful-smelling plants. Their little house was always clean and neat, except for the cobwebs.

When Lily asked her grandmother why she did not sweep them up, Lillian replied, "Because spiders in the house bring good luck, especially Daddy-long-legs." Lily learned in school that Daddy-long-legs were not exactly spiders, but Lillian called them that anyway. "If you sweep them away …" Lillian frowned.

Lily did not mind spiders. They made her think of *Charlotte's Web*.

"Your brother is napping, so we have time to chat," Lillian said. She made Lily cocoa in a white china cup and poured herself tea from a blue-and-white teapot. They sat down at the round table, painted blue, in the kitchen, which was the biggest room in the little house.

"I love a big kitchen," Lillian always said. She pulled herbal bread out of the oven in her ancient black stove. Lily could smell rosemary, thyme, dill, and some other things she could not name. Her grandmother cut Lily a thick slice and placed it on one of her white china plates. Lillian loved the colors blue and white. She told Lily she thought there was something magical about those colors, not knowing exactly what that was. "It's better to be safe," she said.

Lily finished her slice of bread, which was as delicious as everything her grandmother cooked or baked up. She drained her cup of cocoa and laid her arms on the blue table. Her grandmother did not mind elbows on the table. She believed people should enjoy their time at a table any way they wished. Then Lily said, "Lillian, (which was what her grandmother wanted to be called) why was I given the gift so early, so young? It's a burden I wished I never had, for sure." She sighed.

Her grandmother took a sip of her tea (peppermint, good for digestion, she said) and gazed at her granddaughter. "It was probably because of the 'bad time,'" she whispered. "Maybe it's to help you find ... him."

Lily stared at Lillian. "Why would I want to find that horrible man? I never want to see him again, ever."

Her grandmother stretched out her arm across the table to meet Lily's. "When you find him, you'll know."

CHAPTER 17

Who Killed Who?

The blog for those with an inquisitive nose … for murder and mayhem

NYACK, NY: Ashley Ford, 19, of Nyack, went missing two days ago. Ashley is white, with short, straight blonde hair. She was wearing a blue sweater and black jeans and was last seen walking home from her job at Roland's Bakery with her friend Sueann Hanson. Sueann told police that Ashley had wandered away, saying she heard a kitten mewing.

If any of you have any information about this missing young woman, please call the toll-free number: 1800-555-2444.

Philomena Wolff

After I posted this, I just sat in my desk chair, unable to move. Oh my God, I bet it was the same killer who killed my best friend and the other young women so long ago. Melanie told me she heard a kitten when we walked home from school together that day. According to friends who were with some of the abducted young women, several of them thought they heard something. He probably used the "kitten" trick every time. Okay, I have to find out about other cases, get onto the research, and post it on the blog. Hopefully, one of the readers might know about this.

He must imitate the sound somehow. Was it some kind of instrument? What could make that sound? I shook my head. No, not an instrument, that was not right. Maybe used his voice, somehow – a magician or a ventriloquist?

Ah, that made sense. It was someone who could throw his voice, imitate animal sounds, a performer.

Who Killed Who?

The blog for those with an inquisitive nose ... for murder and mayhem

We need to check out as many of the other cases as we can for the following: Find out if any of the missing young women were with a friend when they disappeared and if they told the friend they heard a kitten before they wandered off.

Philomena Wolff

UPDATE: The body of Ashley Ford was found this morning in a wooded area near her home.

COMMENTS:

From MarilynS: I blame the cops. What're they doing about this?

From CraftySue: They never do anything. Except go after people of color.

From GraceC: What they should do is check out all the perverts, the sex offenders, in the area.

From Dancingfool: Aren't they supposed to be registered with law enforcement?

From ConnieW: Yeah, but who knows if they all do?

From LennyK: Or if the cops follow through on checking them out.

From Philomena Wolff: Hold on, guys. You're making unwarranted assumptions about law enforcement. You don't know that they don't keep tabs on sex offenders, or that they're not doing that right now.

CHAPTER 18

Lily worried a lot about her little brother when he was growing up. Thaddeus, of course, could hardly remember their mother, who wasted away and died when he was a little boy, from what their grandmother said was a broken heart.

"She just couldn't go on after Abigail," Lillian said. "She blamed herself and she couldn't live with that."

Lillian did the best she could for her grandchildren. She loved them dearly and kept them well-nourished with fresh milk from her white cow and eggs from her white chickens, plus the fresh fruits and vegetables and herbs she grew in her garden. Once a week, they would have meat from the butcher shop in town. In the spring and summer, they went fishing in the Esopus Creek and sometimes, they brought home enough to cook and eat.

Lily thrived on her grandmother's food and nurture, but unfortunately, Thaddeus did not. He was a scrawny little thing, smallest in his class at school, and hopelessly un-athletic. This did not make him popular among the other kids, and they began making fun of him. Thaddeus also could not seem to learn his letters and got yelled at by his teachers. They finally diagnosed him as dyslexic.

"I knew all the time that you couldn't help it, that you were really trying." Lillian gave her grandson a fierce hug. "I'm glad everybody else knows it now, too."

Things got a little better after the school found Thaddeus help with his reading and writing, but he remained an outsider, a loner, among the other kids. They sneered at his pathetic attempts to join in the conversation, the laughter, the games, and he was still the smallest in his class. When they bullied him, he would fly into a rage and lash out, once sending another boy to the hospital. His teachers told Lillian that he was a troubled child and needed help.

"It's a wonder he's not worse, the poor, motherless boy," Lillian said to Lily, shaking her head.

Thaddeus seemed to calm down after weekly visits to a counselor, and eventually, the rages stopped. When he reached 15, he started to grow and fill out and his confidence grew, too. He joined a gym and began working out with weights, and soon the girls were paying attention.

"My, Teddy, (That's what he called himself, since Thaddeus was such a long, difficult name.), I swear you're growing up right before my eyes," his grandmother said, as Teddy was gobbling a large bowl of homemade soup and tearing off chunks of whole-grain bread.

Teddy grinned and held out his empty bowl. "I hope I'm not eating you out of house and home."

Lillian laughed and fetched him more soup. "There's plenty enough for all of us. Eat up."

Lily and her grandmother cried at Teddy's high school graduation. "Now I can rest easy," Lillian said to her granddaughter. "He's a fine young man. I did the best I could to raise him right." She turned to Lily. "You did, too. We did it!"

Now that her brother was grown up, Lily felt he deserved to know the whole story about what happened to their mother and their older sister. She knew he heard bits and pieces of it from the other kids. One morning, when they sat in the kitchen, Lily told him the story. She could see his face darken and his body tremble as she talked. She was afraid he would fly into one of his rages.

He did, his face purpling and the muscles in his arms shivering. "Why didn't you and Lillian ever tell me?"

Lily tried to soothe him. "Teddy, you were so little, we just couldn't. We wanted to wait till you seemed mature enough to handle all of it." She wondered whether she made a mistake in telling him at all. Then again, he already heard so much about it, she had no choice.

He stood up, still rigid with fury. "I know what to do! And I'm gonna do it!"

Lily chewed her lip. "What are you going to do? Teddy, please don't do anything rash."

He glared at her, then started out the door, slamming it behind him.

It was late that night when Teddy came back. He stood in front of his sister and grandmother in the living room.

"Teddy, are you okay? We were worried," Lily said.

"Where have you been?" Lillian patted the seat beside her on the sofa.

Still standing, Teddy said, "I joined the Army to learn how to fight. If I ever find that monster, I can give him what he deserves."

The night after Teddy left for his base in New Jersey, Lily had a terrible nightmare and started screaming. Lillian rushed into Lily's room, woke her up, and put her arms around her.

Tears poured down Lily's face. "I was dreaming that … that Teddy was …

"Shh, sweetheart. It was only a bad dream," Lillian said.

She did not tell Lily that she had the same dream.

Teddy wrote to them occasionally, and they were always glad to hear that he was doing well, that his superior officers liked him and thought he made a fine soldier.

Nine months later, they received a telegram saying that Teddy was reported killed in action by a roadside bomb in Baghdad.

"That's one more thing that murdering bastard has taken from us." Lily sobbed in her grandmother's arms. Then she wiped her eyes and said fiercely, "I'll get him if it's the last thing I do. That's a promise."

CHAPTER 19

I had to stop him, for Melanie's sake, and Lily's sister and all the other young women he destroyed. God only knew how many he murdered over the years. He must have moved around to not get caught, maybe even to different states or out of the country. He could have been in prison or a mental institution and just gotten out or escaped and started up again.

Why would he come back here, to the Hudson Valley? Maybe this was where he took his first victims, so, nostalgia?

Maybe he came back for me, whom he saw walking with Melanie all those years ago. He might think I saw him and came back to hunt me down – not knowing that I never really saw what he looked like because of the rain and fog, unfortunately for me.

I had the nightmare again tonight. Why am I still tortured by my mother, dead and buried for years? Why does thinking about her still hurt so much?

CHAPTER 20

My life alternated between writing for pay for a magazine and on the blog for fun – fun about murder? Puzzling out whodunit with Lily, that was the fun. I was also focused on my sex life, having more than my share of encounters with men, good, bad, or indifferent – nothing that ever meant anything.

It started when I was in high school. I ran with the baddies, the detention-sitters, the pot smokers, with a different boyfriend every week. Did I do that just to upset my mother?

I remember what happened one day after my last class. I always hated the idea of going home, but that day, I wished I could do anything else, be anywhere else.

There was a middle-aged teacher, not my teacher, who had a reputation around the school as a predator. He found his prey that day when I was lingering on the steps of the building. He gave me a sexy grin and asked me to go home with him. I shrugged and followed him onto the subway to his apartment. That was my first sexual experience, not even liking the man, not even finding him attractive. I felt absolutely nothing, except sore. I never thought about the horrible possibility that I could become pregnant, at 16. Years later, when I talked about it to my therapist, I said, "I think I went with him because I had nothing else to do that day, except go home, where I didn't want to be."

Something was always driving me toward taking risks. Even with a reckless lifestyle, though, I somehow managed to maintain my grades, to get and keep a scholarship through college.

I did not trust any man enough to get close to him. Maybe I felt abandoned by my father. Who knows? I left men before they could decide to leave me. One-night stands put me in control of the situation once I had my apartment in New York City. I picked men up in singles bars, went back to their place or a hotel (never my place; my space was off-limits to anyone else) and screwed their brains out, leave them wanting more. I was up and out the door without even a goodbye – just Wham, Bam, Bye. I never gave out my real name, address, or phone contact.

I always aimed to be super careful about disease and pregnancy protection, a diaphragm for me and condoms for them. When I tried the pill, I got a painful case of cystitis and ended up in the emergency room.

I was going along my merry way, until one night when the condom broke, just as we finished a hot and heavy session. I screamed at my so-called date, who kept apologizing, backing into a corner of the motel room, trying to get dressed as fast as he could. He looked so terrified, I thought he might pee his pants. I could be very scary when I was upset.

The next morning, when I checked my diaphragm, I realized that in my horny hurry, I did not put it in right. Six weeks later, my period was late. I always was dependably regular. What the devil had I been thinking? It was definitely not with the right part of my body.

My ob/gyn had just affiliated with a Catholic hospital, so what to do? I asked a woman I knew from the singles bar scene for the name of an abortionist. "He's good, and he's affordable," she said. "You'll be in and out real quick."

Affordable was mandatory since I was not exactly flush at the time. The waiting room seemed to be a regular doctor's office. So far, so good, I thought – piece of cake.

A nurse took me into the OR. Everything looked very clean. She gave me a needle in the arm, a local, something to take the edge off, she said.

Just as I drifted off, I caught a glimpse of a man coming into the room. He was wearing the usual doctor's garb, gown, gloves, and mask and was drunk as a skunk. I saw enough drunks at bars to know.

"No, stop!" I tried to move, tried to yell, but no sound came out. Then I lost consciousness.

The raging fever and infection lasted for days. They told me I should be grateful, that I almost died. When they said I could never have children, I cried myself to sleep.

I was far from grateful. I was furious at that drunken S.O. B, and very sad.

CHAPTER 21

A few months after the botched abortion, I met Barry at a singles bar in the Village. My friend Wendy, who lived on the next block from my Upper West Side apartment (in much bigger, nicer digs), dragged me to the bar under my loud protests: "I don't have time. I have a serious deadline."

"Don't make excuses, Phil. What you need is some serious fun," Wendy said, hustling me out of the apartment. Caroline, my other college friend, was meeting us there.

"Fun? What's that?" I had had my nose in my laptop for days, working on the article about baby-selling adoption lawyers.

When we walked into the bar, there was an absolutely gorgeous man standing near a table near the back, gazing at me. It sounds silly, but our eyes actually met across that crowded room. He had dark, curly hair, a sexy mouth, a lean body, and a hungry look in his dark eyes. They were aimed straight at me, as if he were devouring every inch of me.

I could feel myself growing hot and, to my embarrassment, wet between my legs. At the same time, something inside my head was sending out a warning: Oh, boy, here comes trouble, for sure.

Barry was a feature photographer for magazines, freelance, like me. Unlike me, he traveled a lot to wonderfully exotic places: Fiji, Kathmandu, Galapagos. "Someday, maybe I'll take you with me, if you want."

"I want, I want," I told him.

He often was not available, but when he was ….

My life had never been so thrilling, so dangerous, so risky. It was just what I wanted, or needed.

CHAPTER 22

I never would believe myself capable of doing these things with Barry, even with my penchant for risk-taking. I let him initiate all of it, losing control, giving it over to someone else. This was not me, I thought, but it was.

In the beginning, it was regular sex, lusty, salacious, voracious sex – still so-called "normal" sex. I soon found out that was just foreplay.

One night, he came out of the motel bathroom naked, except for four paisley silk ties around his waist.

I giggled. "Are those your new briefs?"

He smiled. "Wait," he purred. He untied them and climbed onto the bed. I loved the way his body smelled: rich, thick with sweat, male. "Lie still," he whispered.

Slowly, he slipped the ties around my wrists and fastened them to the bedposts. Then he tied the other two around my ankles.

The sex was amazing, stupendous. I was carried far away, into a wild and crazy world.

That was the beginning. Soon, it grew more and more violent. One night, he used handcuffs made of fur. Another night, he blindfolded me with a silk scarf, making tiny cuts on my body where it would not show, just before we came together, in perfect, lustful harmony.

"You're amazing," he said in my ear, the night he pushed a dildo into my ass while I knelt on the floor at his feet.

"So are you, my darling," I said.

Of course, he would not let me do anything to him without his permission. A sub doesn't impose her will on her dom. I never knew about such things before. This was a whole new world, an exciting, sensuous world, my new world.

All was well, until one night during sex, he pressed on the back of my neck, and I almost passed out. That was scary. "Stop!" I told him.

"What's wrong, baby?" He gazed into my eyes. "You're not afraid, are you? You're not afraid of me?"

I tried to smile. "No, no, it was just the sensation. It made me feel like I was choking. That's all." I couldn't admit that I felt a faint tingle of fear.

"You know I'd never do anything that you wouldn't want me to," he said, his eyes glistening. "You always love it, in the end."

"Yes. Yes, I do." I smelled his pheromones, whatever they were, and was instantly turned on.

"Let's try it again, please, Sir," I whispered

"That's my sweet sub," he said with a wicked grin.

In the rational part of my mind, of course, I knew he was dangerous, very dangerous. One day, he could push us to the edge where there was no turning back – but when I was with him, rational, sensible thought was nowhere to be found. There was no help for it. I was hooked. He was my drug, my fix, taking me to places I could not have dreamed of, ever. He made me feel alive in a way I never had before.

Was I self-destructive? Was I still rebelling against my unloving, hostile mother? Was there a better way? Maybe I was just too damaged.

My risky, dangerous life had included years of fascination with murder. Killers, especially serial killers, intrigued me. It was the way their mind worked, focusing all their energy on finding their next victim – plotting, planning, for that horrible end.

What goes into the making of a serial killer? Psychologists and criminologists have theorized about it for years. Was it a product of early trauma: a troubled childhood, bad mothering, bad fathering, no fathering, abuse? Then there was the element of genetics or chemical imbalance. What drove the serial killer to have that singular, laser-like focus, to seek out that next victim? It struck me that it could be called a quest – a perverted, horrible, sick quest, but a quest all the same.

Instead of a hero's quest, we have a twisted, reversed quest of not even an antihero, but a soulless entity without feeling, without remorse, without the normal emotions of a human being, a black, empty shell of a person.

How does anyone ever know what is inside someone else, what makes them tick, why they do the things they do?

What does it say about someone like me, obsessed with hunting down a serial killer? Would I, or anybody else with this preoccupation, have to have been damaged in some way, somehow? I knew that I had been, for sure.

Could filling your thoughts with the nature of evil also be considered a kind of perversion, or, at least, an unwholesome occupation? Maybe the killer and I were dealing with similar demons: rage, abandonment, loss. Both of us had lousy interpersonal skills and no impulse control, just plowing full steam ahead, no matter what. The realization that we were alike in so many ways was scary.

My own batch of personal demons had never led me to a homicidal lifestyle, only a risky, self-destructive one. After a few dangerous encounters, I broke down and realized there was no ignoring the crap in my psyche any longer and still remain more-or-less sane. Recently, I began to hopefully exorcise it with a therapist. Therapy might even help with the nightmare from my high school years and make it easier for me to sleep through the night without waking up drenched in sweat.

Therapy came with its own problems. I was afraid I would end up losing my edge, my passion for risk-taking. That was the point of the therapy, but it was also what made me a crack investigative reporter.

Like everything else in my life so far, it was complicated.

CHAPTER 23

I sprawled in the deep, soft chair, my usual posture here. At least I was not folding my arms across my chest and opening my legs (man-spread). That usually came later in the session, when we got to the things I preferred not to talk about or think about.

I looked around the room, one of my tricks to avoid getting into the heavy stuff. Boring landscape prints covered the boring white walls; why not blue? Blue was supposed to be calming for patients, right? The rug, at least, was a blue mix, an Oriental knock-off, I guessed. The chairs were a dark brown, maybe fake leather, and at least they were comfortable. The lighting was low, probably to lull the patient into spilling his or her guts.

I just started therapy. Gwen, my therapist, was supposed to be helping me with my so-called "risky behavior." We were in her office, a part of her house in Bearsville, a section of Woodstock. I finally gave in and started therapy after several too-close-to-call incidents following drunken nights in singles' bars in New York, not wanting to end up raped, knifed and dumped in an alley.

Gwen was a tall, slim, attractive African American woman, about my age, maybe a little older, and supposedly wiser. She was always beautifully dressed, though a little on the conservative side. I met her during intermission at one of the Maverick Concerts (our local concert-hall in the woods) last summer. She seemed understanding and nice enough, and she recently opened her office in Woodstock. I thought, if I have to get psychological help in order to try to stay alive and unharmed, why not her?

Gwen put on her granny glasses and opened a folder. My life was being laid out in the pages of a folder. What would anybody who did not know me think if they read it – a nut case, nasty bitch, a patsy, all three?

She cleared her throat. "Let's talk about the nightmare."

I looked down at the floor. "Uh, it's the same one I've had for years. I'm running away from a bad man in the woods who wants to kill me. I'm terrified that I can't run fast enough. When I finally reach my house, my mother smiles at me and locks the door so I can't get in. I wake up, shaking."

"When did it start?"

I took a deep breath. "When I was 17, there was a man who abducted and murdered young women in the area, including my best friend. I was scared he'd come after me and my mother made fun of me, saying 'Who'd want you?' That was the first time I had the nightmare."

Gwen looked up from her notebook. "What do you think the nightmare represents?"

She was seriously annoying me. "What do you think? My mother didn't love me, hated me, wished I was dead."

Gwen said, "Your mother had problems mothering."

She had to be kidding. I was getting furious. "No shit, Sherlock, she was definitely not Mother-of-the-Year." I was afraid I was going to hyperventilate, which sometimes happened when I got agitated.

"Do you need some help with your breathing? I have paper bags," Gwen said, getting up and going into a closet. She handed me a small brown grocery bag.

"I don't need…" My breathing was coming in gulps. I grabbed the bag and breathed into it, terrified that I was going to stop breathing.

"Take slow breaths, Phil," she said. "Take it easy now."

My breaths finally became regular. "Thanks."

Gwen said, "Can we talk again now?"

I nodded.

"Your mother might have been a depressive. From what you've told me, she was very unhappy with her life, and wasn't on medication. In those days, they either locked you up or left you to your own devices."

"Yeah, but that didn't give her the right to torture those around her," I said.

She nodded. "Your father and his family probably never realized what it was. They must've thought she was being moody, maybe missed being around her own family. You said that her family disowned her."

"She gets a pardon for the way she treated me, right?" I balled up my fists, ready to punch somebody out, no matter who, which was an old pattern. Whenever I remembered how terrible my mother had been to me, I got angry, very angry, angry enough to kill.

"Of course not, you didn't deserve that," she said.

"Damn straight, but she must've thought I did," I said fiercely. "Otherwise, why would she do that to me? You know, I used to wish I was adopted, and she wasn't my real mother. That could be the reason why she didn't love me. That she wanted to send me back to wherever she got me." I felt my eyes fill up and brushed it away quickly. *You are not a helpless little kid at her mercy anymore, you do not have to care about all that. Why does it still hurt so much?*

Gwen handed me a tissue.

I stuck my chin out. "I don't need that. I'm fine."

She looked me in the eye. "Phil, in order to get better, we need to deal with all that pain and anger. It has a lot to do with what's going on now, with your risky behavior. Why do you think you don't have a choice, that you're not in charge of your own life, that things in life somehow just happen to you?"

I shrugged. "I don't know. Plowing ahead without worrying about what could happen is good for my work. If I thought about what could happen when I was in some of these dangerous situations, I wouldn't be able to do what I do. It's made me an award-winning reporter." I shot back, "I've helped lots of people with my articles and the blog."

"Yes, that's true, but it's not so good for you otherwise."

The session was up, and I was relieved and sorry: relieved not to have to excavate any more of my crappy life, sorry that I had to leave that comfortable chair. I had to admit that it was not just the chair that was comfortable. I was in a non-judgmental situation, with someone who listened to my words, was focused on my life, me. It was a good feeling.

CHAPTER 24

Who Killed Who?

The blog for those with an inquisitive nose … for murder and mayhem

WEST HURLEY, NY: Molly Sorenson, age 18, of West Hurley, went missing three days ago. Molly is white, with short blonde hair and bangs. She was last seen on the way home from gymnastics practice. She was wearing a blue denim jacket, blue workout pants and blue-and-white sneakers.

If you have information about this missing young woman, please call the toll-free number: 1800-555-3232.

Philomena Wolff

UPDATE: Molly Sorenson's body was discovered last night near a playing field.

COMMENTS:

From ImissLondon: Blame God. After all, isn't He supposed to be in charge?

From JoyceD: In charge? Haven't you ever heard of free will?

From Iraqvet: God is dead. If He or She was ever alive.

From HelenA: What? You're both nuts!

From Elvislives!: Cut it out, people. We're talking about murdered teens, here.

From TinaZ: Where are the cops?

From AdamN: Out arresting African Americans and Latinos for driving while black and brown.

From GloriaI: Oh yeah? Then what about all the BLACK and LATINO cops who do the arresting?

From AdamN: They're part of that militaristic/police culture of discrimination, too.

CHAPTER 25

There were constant phone hang-ups, night after night. I was totally exhausted from lack of sleep – the bastard, the effing bastard.

Today, the cable TV stations were showing gruesome photos of the bodies of the murder victims and scenes of the crimes, the same with the tabloids. I had to look away. Why would they print such horrors and show the ghastly scenes on TV? Did people really want to see this, these poor, dead young women? It must be the case, otherwise, they wouldn't print it or show it.

At least the network stations were being more responsible and not showing photos of the victims' bodies, a small comfort.

The news cut to a huge protest in Washington. People were marching into the Congressional and Senate offices, yelling and screaming at their legislators. I applauded that, but was it going to do anything?

CHAPTER 26

When I opened my laptop, this was waiting for me.

My dear Philomena,

Being the curious sort, I'm sure you would like to know how it all began; my mission to save young women. It was because of my sister, Dolly, Dolly, who loved me so much. She was so sweet, so pretty, that my mother and I always called her our Dolly, our pretty Dolly.

When my sweet Dolly became a teenager, Philomena, I began to worry. She had definitely changed. She wore short skirts, which she said was the fashion, and her breasts seemed ready to burst from her sweaters. What would happen to her? She would become a vessel for male lust, a dirty thing, ruined forever. The thought made me ill. I felt nauseated, dizzy, and had to lie down on my bed.

I tried my best to stop thinking about it, but I could not. As the months passed, I grew more and more anxious. I could feel my strength ebbing away, almost to nothing every time she came into my room. I tried to stop her, saying I needed my privacy, and that she did, too, but she looked up at me with that sweet smile, shook her head, and hugged me, the way she always had. "You're my big brother and I love you," she said.

Oh, God, I thought. What can I do? I love her so much. I have to save her.

Then one day, she looked at me in a different way, not like a sister with a brother. Her eyes flashing, she took my hand and led me to my bed. "I love you so much," she said. I felt myself dying and being reborn in her flesh.

She was my first, Philomena, and my first save. I knew she had to die afterward, to keep her from a certain terrible end. I buried her deep in the woods behind our house, shoveling dirt over her, weeping. I kept one curl from her beautiful blonde locks, a memento, along with a picture of her before and after.

In the years since, this became my mission. I took pictures before and at the burial service that I and I alone presided over, respectfully, of course. I was the sole mourner, as was only right. I also took a memento of the tender youth that once was, that I preserved for all time. Sometimes it was an earring, or maybe a fingernail, or panties, never a lock of hair. That was reserved for my sweet Dolly.

When I came back to wherever I was staying, I placed the latest memento, together with the photos, reverently on the temporary altar I constructed before I could stash my trophies in their permanent place. That was my secret room, which I looked forward to visiting when I was near my home, where the altar and its objects circled the room. It was so full now that soon I would have to build more shelves.

Until next time, dear Philomena

Even though my gorge was rising, I forced myself not to respond. He wanted me to react to his horrible acts. He wanted me to know exactly what he was doing. He wanted me to know that nobody could stop him.

Stopping him was *my* mission.

CHAPTER 27

He could still hear his mother's screams and cries ringing in his ears all these years later.

"Somebody took Dolly! She's gone!" his mother wailed. "Sonny, you've got to help me find your sister!"

Sonny was not his real name, of course, but that was what his mother always called him: her Sonny, Sonny-boy, her darling Sonny-boy. His father died when Sonny was eight and his sister was six. His mother had taken him into her bed soon after that. How could he fight her? Maybe some part of him did not want to. He tried not to think about that.

Sonny always felt dirty and slightly queasy afterwards, but during "the act," as he thought of it, he felt excited and wanted. His mother had made him feel desirable, sexy, attractive.

"You're a real man now," she said. Still, he began to think of sex as something disgusting, a besmirching that needed to be purified and cleansed.

Thanks to him, now Dolly would be forever enshrined in Heaven as one of God's angels. He saved her, and her purity had been renewed. He vowed that he would make it his mission to go on saving as many young women as he could from a certain future of filth and degradation.

CHAPTER 28

For most of Sonny's childhood, his grandfather had been the only man in his life. George Aldrich, his mother's father, had spent his life as a restless, itinerant magician and ventriloquist, known as The Great Stepani. He married a sensible, practical woman, whose dearest wish had been to make a home for her family. The marriage did not last long. George stayed home just long enough to father Sonny's mother.

When he learned that he had a grandson, his grandfather traveled back to see him whenever his schedule allowed. George taught Sonny the tricks of his trade and was delighted that his grandson seemed such an eager, apt pupil. He was hoping Sonny would follow in his footsteps, take up the mantle of his legacy, which had been the chosen profession of the men in the family for generations.

Sonny's mother fought her father on this. "He needs a profession that will give him a stable life, a chance for a family." She glared at her father. "What kind of life would it be? Look at you, on the road all the time, always hustling for the next job."

Her son obeyed his mother reluctantly and stowed his magical talents away. He revived them again when he realized they could prove useful in his mission.

CHAPTER 29

It was around midnight, and I was working away on research for my magazine editor, Lourdes Cuellar. I was a night person and often worked very late, when I got my second wind.

I had all my articles and notes on the computer and a flash drive, but I felt more secure with a print backup, probably because of all the threats. I kept print copies in a bureau drawer.

I finished outlining the article for Lourdes, printed it out, pushed SEND, and sat back in my chair. It should turn out to be a great exposé of a nasty business. Of course, in the end, the editor's assistants could royally screw it up, or not. I shrugged, not being one who obsessed about how my articles appeared in print, but I always hoped for the best, which could bring in more freelance work. That would mean more cash in my not-exactly flush bank account.

I gazed at the wall to my left. There were no pictures of family or a significant other. Instead, the wall was filled with news photos of missing kids, homeless people living in the street, and victims of domestic violence who successfully left an abusive situation. This reminded me of what I was doing for so much time and effort.

The wall on my right held information on pending cases for "Who Killed Who?" I put up a whiteboard, where I scrawled notes on the dead teenagers, trying to find a pattern. The only link I could see was that all the young women were white and attractive with blonde hair.

I glanced out the window. It was black, very black outside. In the mountains, the dark swallowed up the night. There were no streetlights, no car lights, nobody around, dead quiet.

A hard wind was blowing outside, and cold air was seeping into the cottage. It was time to put more wood on the fire, I thought, pushing back the chair at my desk, and standing up. Then I heard it, breathing, behind me. I whirled around and everything went black inside.

CHAPTER 30

The pain was inside my head, on my head, around my head, and my face hurt badly, probably from landing on it. I wanted to howl like a wounded wolf.

Was he or she still here, getting ready to finish me off? I tried not to move or breathe. Lying still on the floor was easy, since it hurt so much, I had no desire to move. How was I supposed to try not to breathe, or at least not let on I was still among the living? I had to take shallow breaths and only when absolutely necessary.

I was someone who was the world's worst at improv, so pretending was not easy. It was necessary, though, if I did not want him – or her – to succeed. I figured I better try to make like an actor, hoping I could carry it off and convince my would-be killer that he or she had done the dirty deed.

After it was quiet for a while, I tried to get up, but the room spun around. I plopped back down on the floor again. I was still dizzy, but I made myself stand. I staggered to the door of my cottage and locked it with its flimsy lock, which would not stop even a preteen burglar.

As soon as I could, I better get myself to the hardware store for a secure lock system. I knew I could not afford one of those fancy alarm systems that people with money had. Up here in the bucolic Catskills, though, most people not only had no alarms, but hardly ever locked their doors. That was because often the break-ins were from black bears, hungry from winter sleep. All the locks in the world could not stop a black bear from raiding a cupboard or a refrigerator. You just had to give in and let them have their fill.

I reached up to touch my face and could feel it burning. I tentatively touched the top of my head, but even though I was gentle, that was a big mistake. Horrible spasms shot through my whole body, and I was afraid I was going to pass out.

Holding onto my desk, I sat down in my chair. That was another big mistake, since any slight movement made the agony worse. Should I take myself to the local ER to be checked out? Are you supposed to do that if you have a concussion? Did I have a concussion? Should I call the cops?

I had no description; I was not able to see a face or a body. He or she had not said a word, and there were no identifying smells. The only thing I knew was that I was hit on the head with a heavy object, which my would-be killer must have taken with him. This probably meant that he was smart enough not to leave incriminating stuff behind.

I opened my eyes and looked around the room as well as I could without moving my head very much. The only thing out of place was a tiny button next to a floor lamp that my potential assassin probably knocked over on the way out. I decided to leave it there in case the cops needed it.

There were no new footprints on the floor. It had been a rainy spring day and the ground outside would be muddy. He must have removed his shoes and come in barefoot, so as not to leave muddy footprints. That was another reason why I would not have heard him or her.

I slid on my shoes, trying not to bend down, and opened the door to look outside. There were footprints, all right, but smeared over. He obviously knew to cover his tracks; so much for any evidence I could show the cops.

I was already on their shit list because of all the threats I was getting, thanks to my investigative exposés and the crime-solving blog. The last time the cops had been to my house, after the latest death threat, one of them said: "You know, it would be easier on you, and us, if you left the detecting to us. If you keep trying to play detective, anything could happen."

There was no use trying to explain that I was not playing. I had been crime-solving for quite a while, quite successfully. I could not help it if I was gifted (?) with a nose for news of the infamous variety. Well, I better call the cops, anyway. So what if they were fed up with my sleuthing? I was calling them as a citizen, reporting a crime, right – two crimes, actually, a break-in and an assault.

Shortly after I made the call, there was a knock on the door. Before I could ask who, they announced themselves. I got to the door as fast as my poor head could manage and let them in. They shook off the rain from their clothes and scraped their wet boots on the mat.

I was well-acquainted with them both, unfortunately. The taller, nicer, Detective van Dijk, was from one of the old Dutch families around here. The other one, short and stocky Sergeant Jackson, and I, had had a few run-ins in the past and he looked totally disgusted.

"Sorry this happened to you, Ms. Wolff," van Dijk said.

"Thanks," I muttered.

Jackson nodded. "Okay, what happened *this* time?"

I started to relay the story of what happened, pointing out the button on the floor, which Jackson picked up with gloves and slipped into a baggie. Then I got dizzy and had to sit down. "Sorry," I said, "guess I'm still feeling the effects." I waved my hand toward my head.

"We get the gist, again," said Jackson. He sighed. "Why do these things keep happening to you? You think we've got nothing else to do but run over here every time you get into trouble?"

I gave him a mildly dirty look, not too dirty, since who knew when I might need them again?

Van Dijk poked Jackson on the shoulder. "Hey, c'mon, take it easy. She could be badly hurt." He added, "I think we should get you to the ER and have you checked out. A bash on the head could be serious."

"I understand," I said, nodding (Why did I do that?). Then I grimaced and tried not to scream. "I don't need the ER. I'll be okay, eventually." I was not going to wuss out and give in to the bastard. I was going to get even. That was my motto: *Don't cry. Don't scream. Get even.* The cops did not have to know that.

They looked at each other, and van Dijk shrugged. "Well, we can't force you to go." He asked me for more details, which I did not have. Then they looked around the cottage and went to check outside. When they came back in, van Dijk said, "We'll let you know when we can send somebody over to try to get prints, and a photographer. Please try not to touch anything in the area. We'll follow up. You should definitely get a stronger lock, or better yet, an alarm system." He gave me a pointed look. "This is not the first time we've been out to your place. We'd appreciate it if you could make an effort to be more careful and not put yourself in danger."

This time, I was careful not to move my head. "I'll call a locksmith and I'll try to be more careful. Thanks," I said, as they left.

CHAPTER 31

A good alarm system would not ward off a determined killer, hell-bent on coming back to finish the job. Speaking of said job – my demise – why the SOB never stuck around to hear me breathe my last, who knew? Was he or she frightened by a human, a bear? Was it possible that he was not trying to do me in, just trying to scare me off – off of what?

I was not going to the ER, but I definitely could not take a chance on a repeat performance, so, what now, go into hiding? I had it. I could not physically disappear into the ether. I had to leave the cottage if I did not want to sit and wait for my attacker to come back and finish the job. Hopefully, my friend Lily would agree to put me up.

Since one of the likely scenarios might involve the blog, I could disguise myself there by using a new name. I would also have to be super-careful when I was out and about, regardless of whatever part of my life had engendered such murderous rage.

The big problem was, there were just too damn many suspects. My near demise could be because of someone I exposed in a magazine article. My specialty was investigations of the sleazy, slimy and sordid; in other words, society's worst. There was the big-city mayor who lost his re-election bid after my article on the terrible living conditions in the buildings he and his slumlord partners owned. Another article resulted in the wholesale firing of the director and his staff of a group home for troubled teens, due to the gross mismanagement of the place.

My attack could be due to the murders of young women in upstate New York a long time ago. The killer may think I saw him when he abducted my best friend, Melanie, on the way home from high school. It could be the fallout from my testimony at a trial of a rapist/murderer during my college days. Maybe it was the result of one of the many dysfunctional romantic relationships I had.

How good would I be at solving my own almost-murder? After all, I had a reputation to uphold as the host of a popular crime-solving blog. I had my team of blog readers to help, plus my psychic friend and partner-in-crime-solving, Lily, and Lily's private investigator, ex-cop, boyfriend.

If the attacker was somebody familiar with my blog, the anonymity on the blogosphere would make it very difficult, if not impossible, to find out who he was. What I needed to do now was to use an alias on "Who Killed Who?" That was probably the best way to protect myself there. First, I had to inform my readers of my new situation, not give them the whole truth, just enough of it to cover myself.

I made my way to my laptop, wincing and groaning with every move.

Who Killed Who?

The blog for those with an inquisitive nose ... for murder and mayhem.

Some of you may have heard that our longtime host was brutally attacked recently. Everyone is hoping for the best, but it is touch-and-go at this time. Of course, she wants her valuable work to continue as usual. As a close friend, I am temporarily taking over as host of "Who Killed Who?" I plan to make every effort to proceed in the way she would wish.

So, as before, "Who Killed Who?" welcomes the participation of its readers. Send your questions, remarks, insights, news about cases, along to me. Thank you for your participation.

Miranda Grimaldi

One minute later, I got my first reply:

She deserved what she got.

The signature of the sender read: *Philomena Wolff*

CHAPTER 32

The SOB was out in the open. I was royally pissed. Never mind that for now – think, Phil, what does this tell you?

He or she is an arrogant bastard, for sure, confident, and sadistic. Someone who tries to murder me and uses my name for an alias – a killer, that was who. Somebody who thinks he can scare the life out of me.

Do not hold your breath, my friend. It was my turn now. Fighting injustice was my middle name, like my Aunt Oly, who never saw a good cause she would not take on. Here was a case of injustice, if there ever was one. The fact was that if somebody tried to bully me, I always bit back, no matter what or who, even if it scared the hell out of me. Fighting back usually got me into trouble and made me regret it later, but only a little.

I took a deep breath, which was a big mistake. I could not tell which part of me hurt the most. I definitely knew better than to take a look in the bathroom mirror. Seeing the damage would probably make me go ballistic.

That was enough of this, I thought. Right now, Lily was the only person I trusted to keep my secret: that I had not left town at all, it was still me on the blog and the attack would not stop me from hunting down the killer of young women and other bad guys on my radar – plus, of course, the SOB who left me for dead. It might be any one of them, or not.

I was afraid to tell anyone else, even my old college friend, Robin. The more people who knew I was still around, the greater the danger. Not being in hiding from my attacker, Lily could do a lot that I could not, and she was used to the death threats and weird goings-on. Maybe Lily could even figure out who tried to kill me. Still shaky but a little calmer, I picked up my cell and called her.

"Oh my God! What a horrible thing to happen to you!" Lily was shrieking in my ear. "You must be in such pain!" Then she said, "Come right over, now, and bring your stuff. I'll fix you up with my grandma's remedies. You definitely can't stay at your place, camp out with me. I'm glad you're eager to get back to work. After all, what better case for you to solve than your own?"

"Great, thanks! I'll be right over." I made my way over to my laptop and put it and my phone, charger, notes, clothes, and toiletries in a duffel bag. I dragged myself, slowly and carefully, wincing and grunting, to my car and drove to Lily's. The heavy rain had finally stopped, thank the gods.

CHAPTER 33

Lily opened the door, took one look at me, and gasped. "Oh, my God! This is terrible! Come inside, quick, I'll try to fix you up."

She did, with one of her healing herbal concoctions made into some kind of paste. After settling me in a chair, she lathered it on the top of my head so gently, it felt like a feather dusting. It had a strange, not unpleasant, foreign smell. I smiled at her. "I'm feeling better already."

I could use my friend's help in my own would-be murder case. Maybe she already tried to visualize the scene and the killer, and even succeeded. I had to ask.

"I just tried to see it before you got here, Phil, but for some reason, it didn't happen." Lily frowned. "I feel terrible, not being able to visualize who almost killed my friend."

I reached my hand across the table. "Don't feel bad, Lily. I know that sometimes it works, sometimes it doesn't."

She tried to smile. "I'll keep trying. Maybe if I just give it time, it'll happen." Then she asked, "Not to dwell on it too much, but why do you think the SOB didn't wait around to see if you were actually dead?"

"That's a good question. It could be that he, or she, just wanted to scare me off my game."

"Maybe he was scared off by somebody, himself." She stood up and went to put the bread away.

CHAPTER 34

Lily put me up in a cozy room in a section of her attic. I managed to fall asleep, even with the pain, because I was exhausted. Unfortunately, the nightmare woke me up, and I struggled to get back to sleep.

"Are you feeling any better?" Lily asked the next morning, pouring out chamomile tea.

I smiled at her. "Whatever you did, helped, thanks."

"I've been thinking," she said. "What about your neighbors? Maybe they saw something. You never know."

We were finishing a delicious breakfast of frittatas and homemade corn muffins. "I hardly have any neighbors right near me, just in that big old house down the road. The one that looks like nobody lives there, all overgrown and the shades are always drawn."

Lily nodded. "I heard the kids call it the ghost house. Nobody ever sees that old lady who lives there, right?"

"Only when she looks out the window and scares the hell out of everybody. Maybe she does it on purpose."

Lily laughed. "Maybe she's bored. Didn't you say you heard she's sick, so she doesn't get out? So, maybe she looks out the window for entertainment. Anyway, with all her snooping, she could've seen somebody at your house."

"It's possible, I guess, but I've never spoken to her. I don't feel comfortable about going over there to ask, not to mention that I want to stay off the radar at this point." I took another delicious bite of frittata. "She's a sick old lady, and she never goes out, or maybe she's a drunk. When I'm in town, I see her daughter buying booze at the liquor store." I shook my head. "That poor daughter. I don't think she even goes anywhere. It's as if she's a slave. All she does is go to work and go home and take care of her mother."

"She could be the one who drinks, the daughter, or she could be your attacker. Do you know her at all?"

I shook my head. "She's not outside to chat over the mail or the trash. I don't think it was a neighbor. Maybe it's something to do with one of my articles, or the blog. The daughter doesn't look like a drunk and she goes to work every day, somewhere. I see her driving off in the mornings. Her name's Claire. I heard somebody call her that. She always looked worn out, but not so much anymore," I said.

Lily put another batch of muffins on the table, along with a fresh pot of herb tea. "What's going on with her?"

"She's been fixing herself up and lost some weight. I saw her in Woodstock Design the other day, trying on a couple of nice outfits." I snagged another corn muffin and sipped my tea. Chamomile.

"Good for her, d'you think she's got a boyfriend?" Lily said.

"Who knows? If she does, I wonder how she sneaks away from that mother of hers."

"Maybe she gets her smashed, feeling no pain." Lily sipped her tea.

"I heard that the old lady is rich. Her husband was much older and left her lots of money when he died. So maybe Claire'll get lucky one of these days."

Lily shivered. "Don't say that. It's bad luck."

CHAPTER 35

Claire Castle was dressing to go out. She met a new guy, really good-looking and smooth as all get-out, last week at a bar with her girlfriends – Jerome, his name was. She liked the way it sounded on her tongue: Jer-ohme, Jer-ohme. She liked his looks even better: tall, with blond hair and a mustache, smooth. The fact that he was well-fixed didn't hurt a bit. When they met, he told her that he managed the family business, a diamond mine in South Africa. Fortunately, he only had to go there once in a while. Diamonds, she thought, how lovely.

She smiled and made sure he got a good look at her considerable cleavage when she bent down, supposedly to fix the strap on her stilettos. Jer-ohme, she thought, maybe you are The One.

Growing up, she always had a weight problem. Her mother had to buy her plus-sized clothes from the age of eight, all the while making fun of her.

"I don't know why you can't control yourself, Clairey. I certainly never had that problem. Look at yourself. You ought to be ashamed." Her mother would drag her, sobbing, in front of one of the store mirrors.

Her mother would dole out her food, tiny portions. Half-starved, Claire would sneak food from the kitchen when her mother was busy drinking and playing cards with her friends. She shoved the food in her mouth, anything and everything she could find. She ended up with a terrible stomach-ache every time, but she did not care. When her mother found out, she made Claire's food portions even smaller.

This went on until the day Jordan Wallace, the cutest boy in Claire's seventh-grade class, called her "lard-ass," loud, in front of everybody. Everybody laughed with him. Her face burning, Claire ran out of the room and hid behind the school building. She was afraid to go back inside and face her classmates and afraid to go home and face her mother's questions. She started to cry and could not stop. Finally, a teacher heard her, took her to the nurse's office, where she fainted.

When she came to and her mother brought her home, Claire made a promise to herself to be thin, even if she had to starve herself. At least *she* would be making the choice, not her mother.

She put on her new black lace lingerie set from Victoria's Secret and tossed her chestnut hair, smiling into the mirror. She loved looking in mirrors now, loved the way she looked. She shed the last 10 pounds she wanted to, and weight training had toned her. She had nice, regular features, a generous mouth and thick brown hair, which she wore long (sexier, *she* thought). A few hours on the tanning bed had topped off the image. Gazing into the mirror, she thought, picture-perfect, and now for the dress.

"Clairrey!"

Oh, God, what does the old bat want now? Whatever it was, she was not going to spoil my night out, come hell or high water. Claire hated that name her mother called her, Clairrey. It sounded like a bird's name. She had a perfectly good name that her mother made into a joke, the way she made fun of everything Claire ever did or wore. She had long since given up trying to win her mother's approval.

Her mother had married late, a man much older, for his money. She vaguely remembered her father, a nice man with thick gray hair and a beard, who petted her. This enraged her mother, who had all his attention before Claire was born. She only had a child to please her husband, she told Claire. When Claire's father died, that was the end of any love or warmth at home. As for the money, all Claire knew was that there was lots of it. Her mother never seemed to spend much and kept the money and its whereabouts secret. One of these days, Claire thought.

She threw on a robe. God forbid her mother would see her lingerie; she would either sneer or call her a whore, or both. She dragged herself into her mother's overheated bedroom. Her mother always complained of the cold, even in summer, when she was not complaining about everything else.

Her mother was propped up in bed, her long, white hair spread out on her overstuffed pillows. A half-empty box of chocolates and a nearly empty glass of brandy rested on her nightstand. She was clutching her head. "Oh, the pain. I can't stand it. Clairrey, please, another glass of brandy and water for my medicine. Why must I suffer like this?" Her voice was a thin, high whine.

Claire looked at her mother through narrowed eyes. You are so full of it, she thought, even the doctor thinks you are nothing but a selfish malingerer. "Okay, Mother, I'll bring it right away. Sorry you're feeling so bad." If her mother detected the sarcasm in her daughter's voice, she did not let on.

Goddamn lush, Claire thought, going into the kitchen to get the brandy and water. Maybe luck will be with me and one of these days, she will overdose on that mixture. Her medicine was insulin, for diabetes, brought on by obesity, definitely not to be taken with alcohol. Her mother knew that but was too addicted to stop. She could get so fat from all the booze and candy that she dropped dead of a heart attack, or a stroke, or complications from the diabetes.

She trudged back to her mother's room and poured out the brandy and water. Trying to sound casual, she said, "I'm going out. I'll check on you when I get back."

Her mother eyed Claire's robe, which had partially fallen open, and sneered. "Just where are you going, missy, with that whore outfit on? Spreading your legs for the first man you see?"

Claire gritted her teeth, then stopped herself. The dentist said she was wearing them down with all the gritting and grinding. It will be much better to get rid of the problem instead of her teeth, she thought. Someday could not come soon enough. The thought gave her some measure of satisfaction. She grinned as she left her mother's room.

CHAPTER 36

Claire was a happy camper these days. Jerome had been taking her out every Saturday night, calling every day, and sending a single red rose to her office on Mondays. He said it was a reminder of their time together, so she would not forget him – as if she could.

She made sure her mother knew nothing about him. Who needed the old bat carping and criticizing? She arranged to have him pick her up outside their house, saying her mother was too ill for company and should not be disturbed.

"You're positively blooming." Her friend and co-worker, Nadine, blonde curls bouncing, appeared at Claire's cubicle Monday morning, toting two cups of coffee.

"Me and the rose, I guess." Claire grinned, pointing to the flower in the vase on her desk. "Thanks," she said, when Naddy put one of the cups down. A photo of herself and Jerome, taken by one of those street photographers, sat next to the vase. Jerome had his arm around her and was leaning in to kiss her. A warm feeling came over her whenever she looked at it. He was The One, no doubt about it. It was high time something good happened in her life. Sometimes, when she was sure nobody was looking, she kissed the picture.

"You're a lucky lady," Naddy said, pushing her curls out of her eyes. "When do I get to meet Prince Charming?"

Claire smiled. "Soon, it'll be very soon."

"By the way, does he have a brother? They're rich, right? Did you meet his family yet?" Naddy said.

"Not yet," Claire said, "I gotta get back to work now." She was a little superstitious, so she kept quiet about the fact that Jerome already proposed. They were going shopping for a ring on the weekend, a diamond ring. She grinned. Soon she would have all the diamonds a girl could ever want.

His mother and father lived in South Africa, so no big wedding. She sure as hell did not want the old bat there, making her miserable. It would be just the two of them, and maybe Naddy and one of Jerome's friends. She could hardly wait: Mrs. Jerome Anderson, Mrs. Claire Anderson. She doodled the names on a memo pad.

CHAPTER 37

Who Killed Who?

The blog for those with an inquisitive nose ... for murder and mayhem

TARRYTOWN, NY: Julie Anderson, 18, of Tarrytown, was last seen three days ago on her way home from her job at the Rialto Movie Theater. Julie is white, with short blonde hair. She was wearing a purple jacket and blue jeans.

If you have any information about this missing young woman, please call the toll-free number: 1-800-555-7777.

Miranda Grimaldi

UPDATE: Julie Anderson's body was discovered today in a field near her home.

Miranda Grimaldi

COMMENTS:

From JordanY: Somebody's got to do something!

From HankL: Like who? If the cops can't find this SOB, who can?

From Lovemydog: Maybe it's up to us.

From MichaelV: You're kidding, right? How can we do anything?

From Lovemydog: We could organize. Protest at the Governor's office.

From SusieB: I'm in!

From JocelynM: Me, too!

CHAPTER 38

Who Killed Who?

The blog for those with an inquisitive nose ... for murder and mayhem

From Philomena Wolff:

My dear Philomena. Let me share the details about the latest young lady who had the good fortune to be saved by me. Julie Anderson was a feisty little thing at first, but so lovely. She had a golden cap of shining blonde hair, sky-blue eyes, and a bow-shaped mouth. Ah, she was such a beautiful young woman.

As always, I was slow and tender. I whispered in her ear, "Don't worry, pretty dolly. This is my gift to you, to keep you safe."

She needed me to protect her. The fact was that I, and I alone, could save her, which was my special purpose in life. The tender beauty had to die. She would be safe again, safe from becoming only a used thing, a helpless repository of unworthy male desire. My motives were of the highest, purest, selfless. Taking her and purifying her with my body and soul, then burying her in her purity so that she would be blessed forever.

When I first found her – Julie – I felt the blood growing hot in my veins, as always, eager to fulfill my divine purpose, my holy task.

Until the next time, dear Philomena.

I let out a stream of the worst curses I knew. Unfortunately, the horrible creep would not hear me. At least he would not have the satisfaction of seeing how angry and upset he was making me.

Wait a minute, Phil, nobody can make you angry or upset. Remember your mantra: *Don't get mad. Get even.* I will get him if it takes everything I have, and then some.

CHAPTER 39

I had a bad case of cabin fever. I worried about who might be out there waiting to do me harm, but I could not hide in Lily's attic forever. I told myself to be super careful before I drove into town to catch Robin at her shop. She was not only a good friend, but someone I could count on for wise advice, and whatever she said would be B.S.-free.

My college roommate and her husband owned Woodstock Design; a trendy women's clothing shop located across from Woodstock's Village Green.

When Robin and her husband, Mike, moved to Woodstock with their two little kids, they began selling children's jackets hung from a rack under a stairwell in their cottage. After they opened the shop, they added jeans and women's clothes.

Blessed with a keen sense of style, Robin and her husband Mike had made it the most popular women's clothing shop in the area and beyond. It helped that besides the fashion sense, Robin had a winning smile and gave her customers plenty of individualized care and feeding. I teased her about running a "walk-in clinic": for women on the verge of leaving their husbands; whose husbands were leaving them; whose grown kids were driving them crazy; or those who just needed a listening ear.

My face was still messed up, courtesy of my attacker. I plastered on a good amount of some old makeup I found in my dresser drawer before I ventured downtown to the village, the main section of Woodstock. When I checked in the mirror, it looked as if I had makeup slathered on bruises. I shrugged. There was nothing to be done.

I parked in the main parking lot off the Village Green. The weather was turning colder, but it was a bright, sunny day. The trees were showing off their reds, oranges, and yellow leaves. I especially liked the ones that had two or three colors on a tree. I said hi to a couple of shop owners and staff, street musicians, and homeless that I knew. People were friendly here, even to their exes, whether married, partnered, or un-partnered. It was a small town and if you wanted gas for your car, a prescription for your cough, you could not escape running into a living reminder of a dead relationship. You had to be friendly, even if you did not exactly feel friendly. Small-town life, even life in a famous small town, had its goods and its bads: people looked out for one another here, hosted benefits for sick people without insurance, celebrated holidays *en masse.* (Hallowe'en has been called Woodstock's National Holiday, maybe because the adults dressed up even crazier than the kids in the annual parade.) The downside was that the people in a small town knew things about you that you would rather they did not.

When I walked into Woodstock Design, Robin, wearing black as usual, was handing a well-dressed and well-coifed woman a tissue. "You'll see, it'll all work itself out," she told her. When my friend saw me, her eyes widened, and she put her hand over her mouth. She shook her head and signaled me to wait. Retail being one of my therapies, I was happy to wander around and check out the new outfits, especially if they were colored purple, fuchsia, or blue. The clothes in my closet could blind you. I gravitated to bright clothes, maybe because my mother had touted the virtues of subdued colors.

"The women in our family have always set an example by looking ladylike," she'd say. "Subtlety, Philomena, subtlety." Subtlety was definitely not for me.

Just as I was about to try on a smashing fuchsia top, the customer left. Robin motioned to one of her staff to take over so we could go to Bread

Alone, a local coffee, pastry, and more hangout. Another of my therapies was their great cappuccinos.

It was jam-packed as usual, but the wait staff moved everybody along quickly. We found seats at a long table. People at the table were busy with their phones or laptops, so we could talk with relative privacy. I tried to talk as quietly as I could, not wanting people around me to hear, and God only knew where my attacker was. He could even be nearby. I shivered.

"Okay, what happened?" Robin blew on her milky coffee to cool it down.

When I started telling her about the attack and the murder blog, she rolled her eyes. As I went on, her face darkened. "Phil, this is insane. You're insane. What's the point of doing this murder blog if you end up getting murdered yourself?"

"Somebody's got to do it, to get the bad guys," I said. I should know by now that would not work with my sharp-brained friend.

"Bullshit!"

"Somebody has to ..."

"It doesn't have to be you." She put down her cup and ran her fingers through her short, purple-streaked hair. "The cops can take care of the murderers, so you don't have to."

I sipped my drink, pretending to ignore what she said. "Mmm, this is delicious."

Robin was not a woman to be deterred. "Maybe you need to get a dog or a gun."

"I hate guns." I shuddered. "Knowing me, I'd shoot myself in the foot, or the arm, or the whatever."

"You're not funny. Okay, how about a dog, then, a big, nasty one?"

I laughed. "I don't like nasty dogs, but I can't even have a nice one. What would I do with it when I'm in the city? They don't allow dogs in my building."

She sighed and finished her coffee. "Well, let's go to Jean Turmo and get you some stuff to cover up those awful bruises."

Jean Turmo was a local shop next to Woodstock Design, specializing in handmade beauty products, yummy teas and elegant household objects, run by a mother-and-daughter team. I drained my cappuccino cup, got up, and followed my friend out and over to the shop. Between Jean and her daughter, Rebecca, my face would be in good hands.

CHAPTER 40

My cousin Elana's baby shower was scheduled a few days later. Before I left for my aunt and uncle's house, I did a fair job of covering the nastiest of the bruises with Jean Turmo's makeup. Unfortunately, it was not enough to evade Aunt Oly's eagle eye. The minute I got there, I knew she and the rest of the family would carry on mightily. It was a hopeless task to try to hide anything from Aunt Oly. That was why I never even thought of making an excuse to not be there.

When I moved back to Woodstock after college, one of the perks was renewing my relationship with my father's family. Here, I felt that I belonged. I was part of them, their tribe.

My father died when I was 18, the year after the attacks on young women. My aunt, my father's sister, had been my refuge. I could run to her, well, drive actually, whenever I felt especially lonely, or sad about losing my dad, or when life with my mother had gotten too much to bear, which was often. Though as I got older, my mother mattered less and less, except in my nightmare.

No storm had been predicted, but the cold air felt as if it were going to snow. I was not exactly the most intrepid driver. In fact, you could call me a wuss about driving in bad weather. The local garage guys laughed when I asked them to put on snow tires. Why would I need them when I would not get in my car when I saw a few snowflakes?

I worried a little about the drive, since Aunt Oly and Uncle Gus's farmhouse was in Delaware County, north of Woodstock, which got more snow.

This was where the clan gathered – uncles, aunts, cousins, cousins-in-law, the works. It was always somebody's birthday or anniversary, baby shower, or graduation.

As soon as I got in the door, Aunt Oly took one look at me and gasped, and started yelling. "What happened to you, your poor face? Oh, my God!"

I was in for it, for sure. Everybody swarmed around me, pointing, clucking and, of course, yelling: "What happened to our Philomena? What kind of animal did this?" and so on.

I was forced to tell them all what happened. After the ohs and more clucks, my aunt shooed them away. She sat me down on the living room sofa and fixed me with a look, a fierce, Aunt Oly look. Her dark eyes bored into mine.

"What kind of trouble are you getting yourself into? I never saw such a one for getting herself into the worst possible situations." She shook her head, her thick gray curls bobbing. "It's that dangerous job of yours, that reporting. It always gets you into trouble."

I looked down at my lap. What could I say? She was right. "Aunt Oly, it's not that bad."

"Philomena, you are not fooling me for one minute." She folded her arms across her considerable chest.

It would take someone a lot more clever than me to fool her, for sure. I tried a different tack, something she could appreciate. "It's what I'm good at. It's my passion, to help people, to make a difference." This, of course, was true.

She pulled me close, enveloping me in a giant hug. "Chip off the old block, huh?" Then she drew back and frowned. "Still, I worry about you, Aunt Oly's sweet girl. You take such chances."

I kissed her cheek. "I'll try to be more careful, Aunt Oly."

She took my hands. "Try harder."

CHAPTER 41

Who Killed Who?

The blog for those with an inquisitive nose ... for murder and mayhem

RYE, NY: Chelsea McKinnon, 17, of Rye, went missing three days ago. Chelsea is white, with long blonde hair in a French braid. She was wearing a denim jacket and blue jeans. She was last seen after getting off the school bus.

If you have any information or ideas about what happened to Chelsea, please call the toll-free number: 1-800-555-4141.

Miranda Grimaldi

UPDATE: Chelsea McKinnon's body was recovered yesterday near the school bus stop where she was last seen.

Miranda Grimaldi

COMMENTS:

From GaryF: You know, young women can be provocative. You can't always blame the man.

From MarthaN: You're kidding, right?

From CupcakeLady: How could you say such a thing, GaryF? Are you a pervert, making excuses for your own behavior?

From GaryF: How could YOU say such a thing, CupcakeLady? I'm just saying that young women, teenagers, go around in those sexy outfits, skin-tight pants, low-cut tops.

From GoYankees: And don't forget those teeny, tiny bikinis ....

From EllenH: You guys are totally disgusting.

From IreneM: Ditto. Go Yankees and GaryF, you should be ashamed of yourselves. We're talking about young women, not even out of their teens.

Then this appeared:

From Philomena Wolff: You just think you're safe.

I was just going to have to bite the bullet (pun intended) and deal with my fear of guns.

Tomorrow, I was definitely going to sign up for a gun safety course. I was also planning to report the latest threat to the police.

After I calmed myself down, I turned on the little TV in Lily's attic to hear the news. Not only were parents, teachers, and others in an uproar, they were protesting outside the governor's office in Albany. Smaller protests were being held in towns in Westchester, Dutchess and Ulster counties.

The protesters were calling for a Special Task Force, and more police on the streets, especially near schools – good.

Hopefully, the governor was listening, and a Task Force could help.

CHAPTER 42

Night after night, there were phone hang-ups. I was totally exhausted from lack of sleep. The bastard, the effing bastard, just when, thanks to my therapist, the nightmares were slowing down a little. Now I had a new bad dream to deal with, one that was only too real.

Albany finally seemed to be paying attention. The governor organized a Special Task Force on Missing Young Women and put more cops on the streets. The DA's office was upping its efforts to catch the killer. As the governor put it, "focusing like a laser."

Maybe all this will help, and maybe help me, too. I could only hope.

My gun safety instructor said I was doing well. I was proud of not having shot myself in the foot yet. Seriously, though, I was feeling a tiny bit more confident about being able to defend myself – a tiny bit.

CHAPTER 43

"What's going on?" My therapist looked up from her notebook.

"Well, I'm working on a new assignment for my editor, chasing down sleazy adoption lawyers in the baby-selling business. The blog is going well, which is good and bad. Bad because it's dealing with crimes; good when it can help solve them." I put the cup down on a little white side table next to my chair. I should tell her about the gun and Barry, I thought. "I, uh, bought a gun. A .22-caliber pistol." I looked at her. "Before you say anything, I've been taking a gun safety course and I have a permit."

Gwen put down her pen and gazed at me intently. "You're taking shooting lessons and bought a gun. I thought you were afraid of guns because of what happened in high school."

I could feel myself getting defensive. "With everything that's been happening, being attacked, getting death threats, don't you think I needed to protect myself?"

"Yes, of course." She paused and waited. She did a lot of that, waiting. She evidently did not feel she had to fill up the space while a patient was gathering her thoughts.

I blurted, "I met a new guy." I could feel my face getting warm as I described my relationship with Barry, speaking of risk-taking. "After all I've been through with guys," I made a face, "I was worried you'd be upset and tell me to take it easy, go slow."

She looked up from her note-taking. "That would be what, making you think about this? Telling you not to go ahead?"

I felt myself getting warmer. "No, no. I didn't mean, no, you don't do that. But ..."

She gazed at me again. "You know, Phil, nobody can *make* you do something, *make* you think about something." She paused. "People can only suggest, toss ideas out to you. What you do with them, you do with your own free will."

I felt like a first grader, being admonished for talking in class, tossing spitballs. I said as much to her.

She just listened. Then she said, "Why do you feel the people around you are in charge of your life?"

I looked down at the floor. "I don't know," I whispered. "I always worried about what other people think of me and tried to be what they wanted, thinking that maybe there was no real 'me', there. I was just a shell, waiting to be filled by whoever came my way. I used to think of myself as a chameleon – there was no there, there – changing my colors to fit whoever and whatever situation I was in. I even tried to talk like they did and mimic their opinions."

Gwen stopped writing. "Do you think there might've been a reason for that from early on in your life?"

"Oh," I stared at her, "I just always thought ..."

"What did you think?" she peered at me over her glasses.

"I don't know. I guess I just thought it was about trying to fit in."

Gwen scribbled some notes. "Did fitting in mean you had to erase your real self?"

"Not exactly, because I didn't think I had a real self." I thought for a moment. "You know," I said slowly, "maybe it was because I only knew what my mother told me about myself; ugly, bad, not loveable."

"Do you think she said those things because she was unhappy and didn't want you to be happy, either?"

I stared at her hard. "Uh, I never thought about that."

"Why would you? You were just a child, accepting what your mother told you. You don't have to accept that anymore." She smiled at me.

CHAPTER 44

Who Killed Who?

The blog for those with an inquisitive nose ... for murder and mayhem

GLOVERSVILLE, NY: Caitlin O'Brian, 17, of Gloversville, went missing two days ago. Caitlin is white, with long, blonde hair. She was last seen on her way home from gymnastics practice, wearing a blue hooded sweatshirt over navy blue leggings, and blue sneakers.

Her friend, Morgan Mahoney, who was with her, said that Caitlin thought she heard a lost kitten.

If any of you have any information or ideas about this missing young woman, please call the toll-free number: 1800-555-7373.

Miranda Grimaldi

COMMENTS:

From FrancesL: Oh, no, not another one. Why can't the cops find this monster?

From GregH: I've got a gun. Think I'll go hunting.

From Miranda Grimaldi: GregH, please, please don't do that. You could be in serious danger. Or be arrested. Leave it to the authorities, please.

From GregH: Ha! And what've they been doing to solve this?

From Vinyl lover: Nothing. Absolutely nothing.

From CarlaM: Maybe we ought to take things in our own hands. Nobody else is doing anything.

From AnglerF: Damn straight!

From Miranda Grimaldi: Guys, please, listen to me! This person is very, very dangerous. He's killed God knows how many people. You don't want to be his next victim.

CHAPTER 45

Finding a murdered young woman, yet another one, ate at Lily's insides. She always threw up afterwards. She was embarrassed and tried to apologize to the cops, but they understood.

"Ms. Maccraw," one of the officers told her, "please don't apologize. One of our new guys over there is doing the same thing. It's understandable at times like this." He gestured to a spot a few feet away, where a white-faced young man was wiping his face. "Thanks to you, her parents will be able to give her a decent burial, and hopefully, someday, have closure." He patted Lily on the shoulder.

"Well, I'm glad of that, at least." She wished she were anywhere but at the site of Caitlin O'Brian's remains. It was her horrible burden to bear, but she had no choice. She could no more not be there than she could turn off the vision she had of where the poor victim lay. This young woman should be alive, wishing, dreaming, looking toward her future, living with her family, hanging out with her friends.

This 17-year-old would not have a future. That made Lily not just sad, but full of fury for the monster who took a living, breathing daughter away from her parents, from her life. The way that monster who took Abby from us did, she thought, clenching her fists, the bastard.

Caitlin's parents were standing with the cops. Lily tried not to look at the sobbing couple, not speaking to them because what could she possibly say? How could she provide them any comfort? She shook her head, said goodbye to the cops and headed for her car.

CHAPTER 46

Jack was the first guy to not be scared off by Lily's gift. It did take him a while, though, to get used to it after she fell into a trance on their first date. She sometimes did that without planning to, which could cause no end of problems.

He took her pulse and checked out her breathing. Once he realized that she was, indeed, alive, he gently carried her – she fell forward in her chair – to her bedroom and laid her on the bed. Covering her with a blanket, he pulled up a chair next to the bed. There he sat, with anxious eyes, watching and waiting till she woke, stretched, and smiled at him, as if nothing at all had happened.

"Lily, what is it? What happened to you?"

She could hear the fright in his voice and sat up, reaching for him. "Oh, I'm so sorry. I should've told you."

"Told me what?" He hugged her tight. "Are you sick? Was it a fainting spell?"

Lily grinned a mischievous grin. "You just might wish that was what it was when I explain."

"It's not funny. I was very scared." He frowned.

She patted his arm. "Sorry, again." She told him the whole story, from the beginning, from way back in Scotland, to when Abby was murdered and after she received her gift. She had planned on telling him in bits, so as not to frighten him off.

When she was done, she took a deep breath and crossed her fingers. She stole a sideways look at his face, hoping he was not frightened enough to quit on her, as all the others had been. Then again, he was a former cop, and now a private investigator, who went after criminals – not a weak sister, for sure.

He did look a little dazed and confused, she thought, but still, not scared out of his wits.

"Ah," he said, leaning back against the sofa cushions. "Oh." Then he sat up. "Of course, that's all it was. I should've recognized it." He hugged Lily again.

Now Lily was the one who was confused. "Huh?"

"My great-aunt, I was told, fell into trances. What she did with it was to make dire and doom pronouncements about the family, like Cassandra, in the Greek myths." He shook his head. "Which, unfortunately, sometimes came true."

"Worry not," Lily said, giving him a kiss. "I use my ... gift ... to help people. Mostly, to help the police find missing people, or dead ones."

"That sounds dangerous. You could get hurt, seriously."

She smiled at him. "I'm careful. When I work with the cops, they keep my name out of the public eye." Then she said, with a serious face, "It's important that I do this, Jack. I have to use my gift to help people, especially for Abigail." Her mouth quivered.

He hugged her tight. "Just promise me that you'll try to be careful."

CHAPTER 47

Lily upped the tension on her spin bike. She worked out regularly at MAC Fitness in Kingston to keep up her strength, as her grandmother had taught her. She could barely hear the instructor over the pounding music.

"Hey, take a look at that!" Carolyn, the woman on the next bike, puffing away, was staring at a couple a little distance away.

Lily looked. Carolyn was talking about Andy. The new, very muscular, personal trainer was smoking hot in her opinion – not that she was interested in any guy except her Jack.

In full view of everybody, Andy's muscles, and probably everything else, were being exercised by an attractive woman with flaming red hair. Lily recognized her from the shops in Woodstock. What was her name? Gretchen, that was who she was, Gretchen the shopper. The woman was forever loaded down with bags from the shops in town and anywhere else she could spend her husband's money, according to local gossip. Gretchen was standing so close to Andy that Lily had to look away.

"Gretchen Hardesty is sure flexing her, his –" Carolyn giggled – "muscles."

Hmm, Lily thought, Gretchen was evidently not worried about what people think, or whether it gets back to her husband.

Lily had a flash, almost falling off the bike. Regaining her footing, she shook her head, thinking about what she just visualized – not good, she thought.

CHAPTER 48

Lily and I were relaxing on the sofa by the fire in her living room, enjoying wine and apple muffins and the peace and quiet. That was until we heard the rumble of trucks coming from a couple roads over down below.

"What's that?" I asked her, between mouthfuls of apple and spices.

"Remember that old hotel, built in the 1920s, I think? People with lots of money bought it and are renovating it."

"Well, people need more places to stay in the area," I said, after swallowing a chunk of muffin, "but I saw the inside when they used it for a benefit a while ago: tiny rooms, plumbing and wiring way out of date, not to mention heating problems. It would cost a fortune to fix it up. They might as well tear it down and build a new place."

"It's not going to be a new hotel," Lily said. "They're making a stage. Wiring it up, fixing whatever is necessary and bringing in musicians, making a performance place." She groaned. "There goes the peace and quiet in the neighborhood."

"People with enough money to do whatever they want, regardless of the effect on their surroundings." I shook my head. "No thought for the people and environment around them, just how much money they can make. Can you imagine the effect on the water, the traffic, not to mention the noise?"

"Unfortunately, they just don't care," Lily said, pouring another glass of wine. "Anyway, the guy seems nice, though, but the wife is awful. Actually, I know who they are. Well, I know who she is. I've seen her at the gym and in the shops in town, Gretchen Hardesty. She's rude to everybody she deals with. When she goes into a shop, and she's always shopping, she'll push ahead of everybody else and demand to be waited on. That's no matter who else is already there, or how busy the salespeople are. She's even worse when she goes into Bread Alone for coffee. She'll stand there and say, in a loud voice, 'Are you people asleep up there?'"

"I wonder how she treats her husband if that's the way she treats outsiders. Too bad that the nicest guys sometimes ..."

"End up with the most awful women," Lily said, taking a sip of her wine. "I bet she made her husband buy that property. Maybe he thought it would give her something to do besides shop. Could be that he's tired of her just blowing all his money on herself. Anyway, I think he goes along with whatever she wants, except ..."

"Except what?" I snagged another muffin.

"Well, guess what, she's probably got a boyfriend. When I was at the gym, I saw her with the new personal trainer, getting very, very personal, if you know what I mean. Maybe she wanted a private place where she could entertain her boyfriend."

"Who knows? It's too bad about the building." I poured another glass of wine, to fortify myself for what I knew would be coming when I told Lily what was on my mind. "Uh, I've got something to tell you that you probably won't like."

"Oh, oh."

"I've been taking gun safety lessons, and I bought a gun."

"What? You hate guns. You're scared of guns. You told me about your terrifying experience in that shooting at your high school. What changed your mind?" she said, wide-eyed.

I told her about the latest death threats on the blog. The phone hang-ups in the middle of the night. The fact that the police still had no clue who my attacker was. "I've got to do something before I go nuts. I can't sleep. I keep looking over my shoulder, especially when I'm in New York. I'm sure I saw someone following me when I was there, but I couldn't see who it was. When I turned to look, they were gone, disappeared into the crowd."

"Oh, my God, Phil, I had no idea," Lily said, with a horrified look.

"I didn't want to worry you," I said.

She let out a little scream. "Of course, I worry about you! You should've told me before this got ... how long has this been going on?"

"Actually, probably since I started focusing the blog on the uptick in murdered young women." I put down my glass, thinking.

"What is it? Tell me." She leaned forward.

"You know," I said slowly, "I think the threats could be connected to the killer."

CHAPTER 49

On hearing her husband's car in the driveway, Gretchen Hardesty said goodbye to her lover and clicked off her cell phone. She checked herself in the full-length hall mirror, liking what she saw: an attractive redhead, with even features, perky breasts, a tight tummy, and long legs. All those gym workouts had done the trick. She turned away from the mirror and plastered a ready smile on her lips, wishing for the day that he never came through the door again.

"Hi, darling," she purred, giving her husband a hug. Seeing his shoulders sag, she murmured, "Bad day at the office?" When he nodded, she said, "Drink, coming right up."

Norman Hardesty sank into the sofa, stretched, and groaned. "The board is driving me nuts." He inherited a supermarket company from his father, an innovator who grew a little grocery store to a national chain. Unfortunately, Norman was the farthest thing from an innovator and the board was getting impatient with his lack of initiative. Lucky for him, the stores had been coasting along on their reputation. That, as the board members warned him, could not last forever.

Norman had been a reasonably nice-looking man when he was younger, but that was a long while ago. Now in his fifties, he had developed a paunch and his hair was almost gone. Recently, his hearing had started to go too, but he refused to wear a hearing aid.

Gretchen learned to speak loudly and enunciate clearly. Happily, her husband's hearing loss had a distinct advantage when she was engaged in planning a sexual encounter. She had been doing whatever she pleased, and with whomever, for a long time now, nothing ever serious.

A few months ago, she hooked up with Andy. Thinking about Andy made her feel hot, ready, and willing. Andy was a sleekly handsome personal trainer at the gym she joined. Very soon, he became her very own, very personal trainer. Thinking about his biceps, his abs, his ... made her crazy.

They had sex, amazing sex, two, three times a week, the best she ever had. Andy knew how to keep a woman satisfied, all right. Everything had been going swimmingly until he started going on about her leaving her husband and moving in with him. "What would we live on, sweetheart, your salary? Living in your one-bedroom apartment in that lousy neighborhood?" she said with a scornful laugh.

His eyes darkened when she talked that way. He accused her of not respecting him, not taking him seriously, not caring about their relationship, about him.

"Don't be a goose, baby," she said, "of course I care about you." She coaxed him back to bed, hoping he realized how impossible it was and forget about it.

That did not happen. She chewed a mauve fingernail. Stop it, she told herself, think about that lovely French manicure.

She had to deal with Andy's pushing her to leave Norman before it could ruin her marriage. She was not about to jeopardize the cushy lifestyle that she worked so hard for, so long for, and that she certainly deserved. She sighed, knowing she was weak where sex was concerned. She had to be strong, will herself able to give it up. Why was her life so hard? It just was not fair.

CHAPTER 50

Growing up in the crummy section of a middle-class town in New Jersey, Gretchen had to suffer the indignities of not only being poor, but names and taunts from the other kids.

"We ain't allowed ta play with ya, 'cause ya ma works in a bar." Mary Ann Bridges said, arms folded on her chest. Her minions, a half-dozen, nasty ten-year-old girls, shouted, "Yeah, bar girl! Go back to ya bar!"

Gretchen ran home. When she got upstairs to her bedroom, she threw herself down on the bed and sobbed into her pillow. After she cried until she had no more tears, she got up, wiped her eyes with a tissue, and went to her mirror. It was the one luxury she had: a full-length mirror on the back of the door. Her mother found it at a second-hand shop.

Gretchen stood there, lifting her chin, straightening her shoulders, and planting her feet apart. She narrowed her eyes and smiled in satisfaction. "Nobody will ever make me cry again, not ever again," she whispered into the mirror.

After that, she was a different Gretchen. She learned how to stand tall and fight when she had to. In school, she walked the halls between classes as if she owned them. Soon, nobody dared to call her names or make her cry. She would narrow her eyes and give them a death stare.

She determined, early on, to make a success of her life. For Gretchen, marrying a wealthy man was the key. She would live the life she was meant to live, not like her mother and her aunts, grubbing along, barely making ends meet. They married losers, drunks, abusive men, who never made a living, and expected their women to take care of everything.

That was not going to be her. She sniffed. She was going to find someone to take care of *her,* take *very* good care. She made a plan. She became a whiz at computer skills, learned how to dress for success, and developed a subtly flirtatious, perfectly ladylike demeanor. She got a job at a high-end company, after she researched the company's CEOs and other top corporate officers, as to whether any of them were single or divorced. It would be a little trickier to scope out whether they were straight, but she could figure it out. She developed a good sense about men, especially older men. Fortunately, she had always been attractive and knew how to play up to them.

That was how she landed Norman, easy peasy. She had been happily provided with the finer things of life ever since. Whenever she remembered the torture she went through from those nasty kids, she'd think: *If you could only see me now, you lousy snots. You'd eat your hearts out.* She was surrounded by furs, jewels, beautiful clothes, tons of shoes, a gorgeous house, a cook and a maid. Who cared if Norman was boring, boring, boring? She was not about to give all that up for a gym rat, no matter how sexy he was.

Thinking of Andy brought a pleasant warmth to her lower region. Hey, she was a healthy young woman with normal urges, so not her fault, right? She told herself that she gave Norman what he wanted, all right; a sexy, attractive, younger wife who looked great on his arm when they were out with his business colleagues. There was middle-aged Norman and a woman other men lusted after – with his blubbery stomach, pale skin, bald pink head, and boring conversation. Of course, she and Andy never had much conversation. She grinned to herself. That relationship did not need conversation. Anyway, she had always been great at compartmentalizing.

CHAPTER 51

Who Killed Who?

The blog for those with an inquisitive nose ... for murder and mayhem

CATSKILL, NY: Tracy Sanders, 19, went missing two days ago on her way home from Columbia-Greene Community College. Tracy is white, with curly blonde hair. She was wearing a dark blue hoodie and black jeans.

If you have any information about Tracy, please call the toll-free number: 1-800-555-8765.

Miranda Grimaldi

COMMENTS:

From JackieM: Oh, my God. That girl and her parents are my neighbors! I'm going right over there to see what I can do.

From PeteW: That's so terrible. Maybe you can find out if anybody saw anything.

From JackieM: Yes. I'll get some of the other neighbors together.

From RachelP: Hopefully, somebody saw something or somebody that shouldn't be there.

From MartyR: No matter how small or insignificant, it could be important.

UPDATE: Tracy Sanders' body was found this morning near her home.

CHAPTER 52

Lily and I were having brunch, which meant tea and whatever fresh delicacy she baked this morning. Today it was a mixed fruit bread, stuffed full of bits of orange peel, dried cranberries, dates, and raisins. I rolled my eyes. "Heaven, absolute heaven, you've outdone yourself."

Lily blushed. She was not great at receiving compliments. "Thanks, glad you like it."

In between greedy bites, I said, "Did you hear the latest about my neighbor?"

"What?"

"You know, the one with the controlling mother, Claire, Clare Castle? I heard from my friend Robin that she, Claire, I mean, got married." I sipped my tea, mint. "Robin recommended a bridal gown shop to her."

"Well, that's good news, for the daughter, I mean."

I scarfed down another slice of fruit bread. "Mmmm, yeah, but the not-so-good news is that they, Claire, and her husband, rented a small place practically in her mother's backyard."

Lily widened her eyes. "That sounds weird. I wonder why, especially since you'd think the daughter would be over the moon about finally getting away from her mother's clutches."

I put down my fork reluctantly, patting my stomach. I worried about gaining more weight, due to Lily's wonderful cooking. "Even more weird, she used to tell Robin how glad she'd be to finally get away from her slave-driver mother. She couldn't wait."

Lily said, "Hmm, do you know what makes her and her husband's whole move even weirder? Why would someone who's rich, whose family owns a diamond mine, for godsakes, choose to live in a small house? They could probably afford a mansion, or at least buy their own house somewhere." She got up and started putting things away.

"I know that place they're renting," I said. "It's nothing special, besides being small."

"It doesn't make sense, does it?"

"No," I said, slowly, "it doesn't, not at all."

CHAPTER 53

After their wedding (with just Nadine and a friend of Jerome's as witnesses), the couple settled into a small rental house near Claire's mother. Jerome had insisted on that. Claire had balked and was still unhappy about it.

"Honey, your mother is all alone, and she's not used to it. She needs your – our – company," Jerome said to Claire, who was brushing her hair at a mirror in their bedroom.

"Hmmph," she made a face, "she needs my company? There's no way in hell, babe. Maybe she needs yours." She turned from the mirror. "Why are you so palsy-walsy with the old bat, anyway? What's she to you?"

"Claire, sweetie, she's your mother. I'm just trying to be nice to her because of you." Jerome went over and hugged her. "Since I'm now part of your family, I want to be responsible about it."

That mollified her a little. He was her knight who came to rescue her, after all. That was what he did, right? Although, a tiny voice said in her ear, this house is not so great. Why not something better, with all those diamonds in his family?

When she asked him about it, or anything about his family and their money, he brushed it aside. "Don't worry, honey, this is just the beginning. It'll all be happening soon enough. It takes a while to set up the accounts from Johannesburg. Things like currency conversions need to be adjusted. Please, just be a little patient, okay?"

Then there were the trips he had to take, to the family's mine in South Africa. He was gone for weeks at a time. When she asked if she could come with him, he shook his head. "It's much too dangerous for you, sweetie, and I wouldn't always be able to be right there to protect you."

She bristled at this. "Hey, I'm not a helpless little flower, you know. I can take care of myself. I've been doing it since I was a kid. You don't think my mother was ever there to protect me, do you?"

He put his arms around her. "This is different, believe me. You never know what's going to happen there. Last year, there was a lot of trouble, people got hurt. We had to call in the local cops."

Then he made love to her, and she forgot all her doubts, but they kept creeping back, especially at night, like monsters in the shadows.

CHAPTER 54

I dreaded telling my therapist about my dom/sub relationship, but I knew I had to. "Barry tied me up, tied up my hands and feet, and covered my eyes with a soft, silky cloth. Then he beat me, lightly, with some kind of thin stick, but he made sure any bruising would be superficial."

Gwen looked me square in the eyes. "You allowed yourself to be tied up, blindfolded, and beaten."

When she said it, somehow it sounded shameful. I felt my face get hot. "That wasn't the way it was," I said petulantly. I felt as if I were a child, being chastised for bad behavior.

"Weren't you in pain?" Gwen said, looking concerned.

"I hardly felt it, and it wasn't the way you said." I jutted out my chin.

She scribbled something in her notes. "Okay, what was it, then?"

How could I describe the dom/sub relationship, so it didn't sound ... I thought for a minute. "He was gentle." I defended him, it, my actions, inactions?

"Then what happened?"

"He led me to his bathtub. He washed me very tenderly. It was almost a caress." I looked down at my lap. Why did it seem so awful, so sick, to talk about this? I felt as if I were going to throw up. It was all her fault. It was the way my words sounded in her therapist's mouth: a badge of humiliation. She was telling me that I was so stupid that I did not know any better, because I thought this was okay. Rage was building up inside my gut. Somehow, my hands balled into a fist, almost as if they had a mind of their own. I sputtered, "You think this is wrong? You think I'm stupid, or worse?"

Gwen shook her head, saying in that irritatingly calm voice, "I don't think anything about it. This is your life, your choices we're dealing with, and I definitely don't think you're stupid. Quite the contrary, you're an intelligent woman. But ..."

"But what?" My voice climbed up an octave. "You think I'm nuts, sick, crazy?"

Gwen sat back in her chair. "No, I don't think any such thing, but it seems that you don't think well enough of yourself. You don't realize what a strong, independent woman you can be. This sometimes gets you into risky situations that can end up being self-destructive."

"Are you talking about the situation with Barry?"

She nodded. "Your risk-taking is not all bad. For example, it seems to be helpful in your investigative work."

"What about my work?" Was she going to diss that, too? I tensed up, ready for a fight.

Gwen shook her head. "You're very good at what you do, because you've channeled some of that risky behavior into a positive, a positive thing for others and yourself, in that way."

I thought about that for a moment. She was right, at least about my work. I had not realized it, if I thought about it at all. If I did, I would assume it was due to my impulsive, headstrong, curious nature, a nature that just had to find out about everything, and about everyone. This did seem to piss off some people, and not just the ones with criminal tendencies, either. My friends sometimes got tired of my questions, feeling as if they were being interviewed, or, even worse, interrogated.

"Take some time to think about all the good you've been doing," Gwen said, leaning back in her chair. "I'm going to bet that you don't usually do that."

I had to admit it. "I guess I mostly just act, plunge right in, to whatever."

She nodded. "Well, that's a manifestation of your passionate nature, and why you're so good at what you do. It can even be good for you. But ..."

"But?"

"It also relates to your risky behavior, which is not so good for you."

I squirmed in my chair. Talking about this made me twitchy. Of course, she would say that was because we were getting to something real, something that I was resisting. I knew I was afraid if I tried to change, if I learned to pause, take a breath, maybe it would affect my work. Maybe I would not be able to summon up the necessary whatever to get into a story. It was the same passion, for good or for bad. I said as much to Gwen.

"Phil, that doesn't have to be the case. Eventually, you won't need that self-destructive way of acting, just the positive part, once you learn to appreciate yourself for the intelligent, warm, accomplished person that you are. You need to tell yourself that. Your mother never did that for you."

I could not resist saying, "No shit, Sherlock."

"When you begin to mother yourself, you'll start to see yourself, see the real you." She smiled at me. She had a warm smile, comforting.

"Exactly how am I supposed to do that?"

"We'll work on that." She smiled again.

CHAPTER 55

They said he was the worst of the worst. He was very proud of that.

When Judge Manfred ordered him to Springville, a group home for so-called "troubled teens," Manfred glared at him and said, "I would've opted for juvie, but the social worker seemed to think there was hope for someone even as vicious as you." He shook his head and pointed to the woman in the room with the swollen jaw and missing teeth. "How somebody could do that to this poor woman is beyond me."

Kenneth turned to the woman. "Ma'am, I'm so very sorry. I lost my head." Then he said, "Thank you, Your Honor, for your mercy." He tried to look humble. Inside he was thinking, they are so dumb, all of them, just like taking candy from a baby.

He just turned 17 and been caught in his latest B&E with his friend Robert. It was all because of Robert's stupidity, he thought, the moron who was supposed to check if a house was alarmed. The woman woke up and started screeching when it went off, and I had to knock her out. Robert took off and left me holding the bag when the cops got there. If I ever get my hands on him …

At least they could not pin the fire on me because I was so clever: no fingerprints, no evidence, nothing. Boy, did I play that one good. I came out a frigging hero, trying to save his mother, poor orphaned boy, ha ha. More important, this boy is much too clever to be stopped in fulfilling his mission of saving young women.

Well, now he was king of this frigging castle, all right. He terrified all the other kids into craven submission. They were so eager to do his bidding that it was pathetic, he thought, especially skinny little Jerry, who stuttered, sitting next to him in the dining room, spooning up the slop they called dinner.

"How d'you like your din-din-din, Juh-Juh?" Kenneth jabbed Jerry in the arm, hard.

Jerry looked down at his plate, trying not to cry, because he knew that would only make things worse. He tried to avoid Kenneth's jabs. They left painful bruises. "Uh, uh, uh."

Kenneth laughed. "I think your stutter is getting worse, Juh-Juh. You – you – you can't seem to-to-to- get out-t-t- your words-s-s to-to-to-day."

Everyone around them laughed and so did Jerry, too afraid to not.

Even the staff were uneasy around Kenneth. He was big and strong, after working out every day with weights, and there was an air of menace around him.

Jim, the staff worker in charge of the dining room, tapped a glass for quiet as the teenagers were finishing dinner. "Boys, we have a special guest coming later for a visit. You need to be on your best behavior."

As they were filing out, Kenneth grabbed Jerry and hissed in his ear. "Tell everybody to meet me in the exercise yard by the basketball hoop."

After they collected in the yard, Kenneth, standing with arms folded across his chest, said, "Okay, kids, somebody's coming to gape at the animals in the zoo. Let's freak 'em out!"

A cheer went up, but Kenneth made a motion for them to quiet down. "Sshh, d'you want our keepers onto us?" He spat on the ground. "Listen up. Here's what we're gonna do. Since they call us animals, let's act like 'em, okay?" He grinned and pointed, "Juh-juh, you're a tiger. Pimpies, a lion." Kenneth had a nasty nickname for all of them, pinpointing their weaknesses. Nobody dared to complain. "Pimpies" was Marty, a fair-skinned kid who suffered from terrible acne. "Fatty, a grizzly bear." "Bignose, elephant," Kenneth directed.

"Whaddya gonna be, Kenneth?" Marty asked.

Kenneth hissed and flicked out his tongue. "A very poisonous snake."

Late that afternoon, an elegant-looking, older man walked into the social room with Bill, the social director. "This is Dr. Abbott, boys. He came to visit with you today. Please be well-behaved and courteous."

Dr. Abbott whispered to the social director, "Who's the worst of the bunch?"

Without hesitation, Bill pointed to the scowling Kenneth. "I wouldn't be surprised if he ends up with a lethal injection."

Dr. Abbott shook his head. "Oh, no, no, no, I don't believe in writing a young person off. There's always a chance for redemption, don't you think?"

Bill shook his head. "Not always, anyway. Why are you interested in him for fostering? There's plenty of kids a helluva lot nicer here."

"I've always enjoyed a challenge, especially since I'm about to retire," Dr. Abbott said.

Then pandemonium broke out. The room was full of shrieks, howls and growls, chest-beating, jaws snapping. Bill looked terrified, but not Dr. Abbott. As Kenneth slithered toward him, hissing and spitting, Dr. Abbott just smiled.

"Okay, boy, you can get up now. That was a great show, everybody!"

Kenneth and the others looked stunned. "Who the hell is this guy? Maybe he's some kind of nutcase," he whispered to Jerry.

Next morning at breakfast, Bill called Kenneth to his office. "Dr. Abbott is interested in fostering you. He thinks you have the possibility of becoming an upright citizen."

Kenneth stared at him and burst out laughing. "You're kiddin', right, an 'upright citizen' – what the hell?"

Bill shrugged. "I agree with you. It's not in your wheelhouse. Anyway, that's what he said. So, what about it? It's up to you."

"What do I get outta it?"

Bill winced. "Kid, this is a brilliant man, a PhD scientist. He lives alone in a big place, and I guess he's lonely."

"Hmm, he lives alone. He's lonely. Doesn't he have his own kids, a wife or whatever?"

"He doesn't have children or a wife, as far as I know. Maybe he's been too busy all these years with his research, stuck away in his lab."

Kenneth scraped his sneaker along the floor tiles. "He lives in a big house, right? I'll have my own room, TV, Smart phone, tablet and all the rest? Oh, do I get a car, my own car?"

Bill said, "Don't see why not, after you get your license, but I'll check it out. Can I tell him you're interested?"

Kenneth grinned. "Don't see why not."

CHAPTER 56

OCTOBER 2011 A COLLEGE DORM IN THE HUDSON VALLEY

"Somebody's gotta do something," I said darkly, walking into my room.

My friends stared at me.

"There she goes again." Wendy said, pushing her long, black hair away from her face. Wendy was a slim, attractive, super-smart transplant from Taiwan, headed for law school. Sadly, that was her attorney parents' wish, not Wendy's, but she had always been a dutiful daughter.

My sassy, savvy roommate, Robin, propped on pillows on the sofa, rolled her big brown eyes, her chestnut ponytail spread out on one side. Robin grew up in the Bronx, with retail in her blood, helping out in her grandparents' clothing store on weekends. She was the best shopper in our crowd.

"Phil, someday that suspicious mind of yours is gonna cause a whole heap of trouble." Caroline shook her curly blonde head. Caroline was determined to shake off her old Southern family's prejudices. She was a real Georgia peach, with a face and skin to die for, but we liked her anyway.

"It already has. Luckily, nobody got hurt," Wendy said.

I grinned. "That's *almost* nobody, except Ron McCallister, that is."

Ron McCallister had been stealing laptops from the dorm on weekends and school vacations, for months, until he got caught, thanks to yours truly. He was dumb enough to be seen flashing money around and driving a fancy new car. That was after a series of laptops went missing. When mine was one of them, I went ballistic. I had to get it back, not having the money to buy a new one, or even a not-so-new one. I was lucky enough to retrieve it before he could fence it. Every time I used my laptop now, I felt a sense of virtuous satisfaction. The thought of McCallister spending his days in a cell instead of a dorm room added to the pleasure.

"Okay, y'all, what do we have to do?" Caroline said, reaching across the bed for the quilt.

"To whom?" Wendy said. Wendy was our grammar queen.

I aimed a pillow at her. "Don't tell me that you guys haven't heard?"

"Heard what?" She threw it back at me.

"There's a peeping tom peeping through our windows."

"Oh, that," Wendy said, stretching her long legs to inspect her newly pink toenails, "no sweat. Those ditzes on the first floor probably leave their shades up."

"Maybe on purpose?" Robin said, with a grin.

Caroline shook her head. "Don't think so, Rob. I heard the latest ones were Jen and Sara. Do you think they'd be that way, those prudes? God a'mighty, those two won't even walk around bare-nekked in the girls' locker room."

"I bet they keep their clothes on in the shower." Robin laughed.

"Okay, enough, this is serious business, guys. Do you want some jerk staring at us through our window?" I said, hands on hips.

"Not unless he was very cute." Robin ducked, as I tossed a towel at her.

Caroline frowned. "Hey, come on, y'all, Phil's right. Something's gotta be done about him."

"Right," I said, "so, who's with me?"

That was my first experience working with a team. Unfortunately, though, all our spying did not stop the peeper until much later. That was way after he graduated to rape.

We knew the rapist's pattern was prowling the campus grounds at night, looking for a girl who was alone, following her to her dorm and up to her room. We set a trap with another dorm resident, Janice, as the bait. Janice was cute and petite, with the face of an angel. The other thing about Janice, which most people did not know, was that she grew up wrestling down wayward calves and breaking horses on her family's ranch in Texas.

"You'll be the perfect candidate," I told her. We were sitting in a quiet corner in the student lounge.

Janice widened her eyes. "D'ya think I can do it? What if I can't fight him off o' me?"

"Don't worry," I said. "I'm sure you can handle him. Anyway, we'll be right there in the next room. As soon as you give the signal, we'll be all over him." I looked her straight in the eye. "Don't you want to stop him, especially after what he did to Vicky?"

She nodded. Vicky was her former roommate and best friend. She left school after her attack.

"Here's the plan ..."

After Janice wrestled Doug Dorgan, the rapist, to the ground, she hogtied him and roped him to the bed he tried to rape her on. We all ran into the room, and I poured ice water down his pants while he screamed.

Janice was very proud of the medal the college president gave her. A few years later, she became a champion on the women's wrestling team back home.

I had to testify at Doug's trial for multiple rapes and a homicide. (Yes, he killed one of the victims who fought him.) He trained his glare on me while I was in the witness box. It made me shiver and my voice was quavering.

When I stepped down from the witness box, sweat was pouring down the back of my neck. After the guilty verdict, he screamed that when he got out, he would hunt me down and kill me. Every time I heard a noise, thought that I saw something in the shadows, I was sure he was after me, somehow. I did not go to his sentencing hearing, not wanting to see his face or hear any more of his ugly threats. I was finally able to relax when I heard that he was safely confined for 25-to-life in a prison in upstate New York.

CHAPTER 57

PRESENT DAY

My radio alarm woke me up to the news: *Dangerous criminal escapes from the Clinton Correctional Facility in Dannemora, in upstate New York. Douglas Dorgan, a convicted serial rapist and murderer, dug himself out of prison, with the help of a female corrections officer. Local, county and state police are patrolling the area around the prison and beyond. Dorgan is in his mid-30s, with medium-height, dark brown hair, blue eyes, and tattoos on both forearms. If you see this man, notify authorities. Do not confront him. He is armed and considered extremely dangerous.*

I thought back to that day in court when he promised to kill me after he got out, and now he was out. Shivering, I picked up my cell and called the DA's office. They were supposed to let me know if he was on the loose.

I reminded them that he threatened me after the trial and yelled at them for not letting me know that he escaped.

This was their response: "We're sorry, Ms. Wolff. Guess it must've fallen through the cracks."

Somebody had to give me protection. I was a sitting duck, and I did not want to be a dead one.

These law enforcement officials were supposed to protect the public from dangerous criminals. Instead, what I got was: "We can't do anything unless (until?) he threatens you." Of course, he already did that at his trial, loud and clear, in open court.

CHAPTER 58

I told myself that I was being paranoid. Just because that SOB murdering rapist had ranted at me in court, that did not have to mean anything. It was so many years ago, he could have forgotten about me. He was probably busy drooling about more women to rape and kill.

Who was I kidding? Not only was I the chief witness that landed him in prison (most of the other women were too afraid, too embarrassed, too whatever, to testify), I had to do a lot of arm-twisting to get the few who would. They were hesitant, tentative, soft-spoken, unlike big-mouth me.

Plus, of course, there was the ice-water-down-the-pants incident. Grinning, I opened my laptop to my blog. There it, he, was.

"To Philomena Wolff: Every time I remember what you did to me, I breathe fire, thinking about putting you through the same kind of torture. You know who I am. Soon, very soon, you'll know pain that you've never experienced before. Pain so bad, you'll pray for a quick death. Yours in hell."

He must have Googled my name and come up with the blog. Why waste time and energy on me when he was trying to outrun the cops? Was he too dumb to realize I would tell them about him? Of course, how could he know the cops were tired of my cries for help and not necessarily come running?

Was he just thoughtless? Was he so consumed with hatred and revenge that I was his number one priority, no matter the cost? I shuddered. Then I wrote:

Yes, I know who you are. But you don't know who I am now. I have a gun and I know how to use it.

He answered: *Ha. Ha. Ha. We'll see who's the better shot.*

CHAPTER 59

I was doing some last-minute grocery shopping near my apartment on the Upper West Side, grumbling to myself as I maneuvered my way down the always-jammed aisles. Did everybody in Manhattan have to shop at this store right now? It was my own fault, I thought, grocery-rush-hour. I re-solved, yet again, to go during the middle of the day next time.

I felt calmer when I finally reached the snaking line at checkout and looked out the store window, smiling as I inched my cart along.

As I went out with my bags loaded with staples, I stopped for a moment to appreciate the pink-and-blue Maxfield Parrish colors in the sky before a passerby nearly ran into me. I apologized, and, humming to myself, started back to my apartment. What was that tune? I wondered, and why was it in my head?

Practically dragging the cumbersome bags, I was happy to finally get to my building. Putting the bags down, I opened the door and pushed the bags and myself inside. Then I had to negotiate the flights upstairs before I could drop the heavy weight. After I unlocked my door, I shoved the bags inside with my foot, shut the door and went into the bedroom-living-room-dining area. Then I screamed, "No!"

The room had been trashed. Sofa pillows were slashed, newspapers and books ripped and thrown on the floor, lamps smashed, curtains torn. Some-thing was glaring at me from the wall above the little white desk in the corner. Trembling, I made myself walk over to it. A block printed message in red paint said: *IF YOU THINK THIS IS BAD, JUST KEEP DOING*

WHAT YOU'VE BEEN DOING. IT'S GOING TO GET A LOT WORSE. THAT'S A PROMISE.

I sank down against the wall onto the floor. I'm not paranoid, I whispered. It's real.

CHAPTER 60

This was in my mailbox downstairs: *SHUT DOWN THE BLOG OR ELSE*. It was printed in big letters in something that could be blood. I sniffed it. Ugh, putrid. It stank like hell. It could be animal blood or some other disgusting substance. I could not tell. Maybe the cops could.

I showed the letter to a sleepy-looking detective at the local police station, whom I hoped was actually paying attention.

"Do you think it could be the same vile being who trashed my apartment? Same mind-set, right?"

He shrugged. "Ma'am, we'll check it out. What's the blog this guy is talking about?"

I did my best to explain.

He snorted. "Maybe you should leave the detective work to the detectives. You could be getting yourself in real trouble, you know?"

I snorted back. "You think this isn't already trouble? What about my apartment being trashed? That wasn't trouble, either?"

He sighed.

"Don't I deserve protection from the police? I'm a citizen. You're supposed to protect the public, right?"

He sighed again. "Ma'am, we try to do just that. But ..."

"I don't have a right to write a blog, or whatever else I choose to? It's called the First Amendment, right?" I was royally pissed.

This time he yawned, mouth wide open, no manners. "Yes, you do, but you're making it hard for us to do our job of protecting you from whoever is threatening you." He got up from his chair. I guessed that was the signal for me to leave, with no satisfaction – shades of Mick Jagger. "So, what are you going to do?"

"We'll check out this note, as I said. We're trying to find whoever trashed your place. And I hope you'll try to be more careful about your, uh, blog."

"Hmmph." I left in a huff.

When I got back to my apartment, there were a dozen messages on the blog. Thankfully, no more death threats. The posts were about whoever was appropriating my name. They also asked, was it me, was I still around and, well, pranking? I replied, assuring my readers that the poster was not the longtime host of "Who Killed Who?" She was indeed away for a rest. Someone, not Philomena Wolff, was playing a horrible joke, pretending to be her. Someone who should be ignored. I figured nothing upset the person who was doing this more than being ignored. He craved attention.

Besides worrying about myself, I could not stop worrying about more murdered young women. I needed to do something, but what? I made a note: talk to Lily, see if she discovered anything.

Now it was time to get back to work. Then I had a thought: Who knew if my readers, those who used names or initials, were even who they said they were? Not having the nerve to ask, I figured it was their business, right? Unless ... unless, of course, they had something to hide, but everybody, including me, seemed to have... something. If I were being honest, that was the case even before I was pretending not to be me.

CHAPTER 61

The next day, after I got off the Trailways bus back to Woodstock, I stopped into Woodstock Design to see my friend Robin.

Robin asked one of her staff to take over the shop so we could go to Pearl Moon, a local restaurant that made great omelets, yum. Their yogurt and granola bowls, veggie burgers, and other stuff were excellent, too.

"What's up?" she asked, after we ordered.

I sipped my coffee, heavy on the soymilk (lactose allergy). "Uh, remember Doug Dorgan, from college?"

Robin's eyes got wide. "That ... I try not to remember him. Why?"

"He just escaped from prison."

"OMG. How do you know?"

"It was on the radio, a BOLO – be on the lookout, armed and dangerous," I said. I looked down at my coffee. "He sent me a death threat on the blog."

Robin blew out her breath. "Phil, if that doesn't scare you ... You've got to stop doing that damned blog. You're putting yourself in a very dangerous place." She was looking at me as though I lost my mind.

I leaned across the table and lowered my voice. (That was hard to do since I was cursed with a loud one, which got me in trouble when I talked to my friends in school. The teachers always heard my voice above all the others and said: *Phil-oh-mee-na, stop talking.*) "I think somebody's been following me, stalking me." Saying it aloud to my friend made my stomach clutch.

Robin said, "Oforgodsakes, that too? Did you have your locks changed? You should get a good alarm system."

She did not know about my temporary living arrangements or the break-in at my studio apartment. "I got a locksmith to put in strong locks at the cottage. I'll think about an alarm system, but I have an awful feeling that something bad is about to happen," I said, trying for a quiet voice and not succeeding. "I can't seem to shake it off."

She stared at me. "You're serious."

I nodded.

She put her hand to her mouth. "Who do you think it is? What did they do?"

I took a swallow of my drink. How do you explain a bad feeling? "It's just weird. I mean, sometimes, I can feel something, a presence."

She laughed. Robin had no patience for superstition, ESP, things in the ether, whatever. I learned long ago not to discuss Lily's visions with her. She thought it was all B.S.

"Phil, you know that's just bullshit."

I sighed. Hopefully, I would have better luck with Lily and her visions.

CHAPTER 62

"I have something to tell you, actually, a couple of somethings." I began.

My therapist picked up her pad and pen and waited.

I told her about the escaped convict, and the break-in, and the warning. "See? I told you I wasn't imaging things. Somebody is after me, for sure."

"I never thought you were dreaming it up. You always seemed to not be sure. You were the one who didn't trust your own thoughts." Gwen scribbled on her pad and looked up again.

"I know. You're trying to help me with that, trusting myself." I sighed.

"What did you do after you saw what happened?" she said.

"Called the cops, of course." I grimaced. "They weren't exactly helpful. Oh, they said they'd make out a report, see what they could do, whatever. I don't expect much."

"You thought they didn't take it seriously, that they didn't think it was very important?"

I nodded. "As soon as they left, I called the super. He's sending somebody to take care of that horrible stuff on the wall, and I had the locks changed." I twisted my fingers together. "I never thought I'd say this, but I'm scared. Even though I have a gun. I'm not sure I'd be able to use it."

Gwen looked at me. "You also have your brain, and you know how to use that."

CHAPTER 63

Who Killed Who?

The blog for those with an inquisitive nose ... for murder and mayhem

KINGSTON, NY: Stacy Corliss, 18, of Kingston, went missing two days ago on her way home from Ulster County Community College. Stacy is white, with medium-length straight blonde hair. She was wearing a checkered flannel shirt and black jeans.

If you have any information about Stacy, please call the toll-free number: 1-800-555-8765.

Miranda Grimaldi

COMMENTS:

From JerryY: That's so awful. My daughter is a classmate of hers. I'll ask her if she saw or heard anything.

From SusieR: My friend is a teacher at the college. I'll get in touch with her right away.

From PeterM: This was supposed to be a safe area, a safe campus. Where were the campus police? The security guys?

From MaryanneG: Nothing is safe anymore.

UPDATE: Stacy Corliss's body was found this morning near her home.

CHAPTER 64

Life with Clarence Abbott was good, if boring. Kenneth figured out how to manipulate his foster father right off the bat. Be polite, make like you care for the old fag, be helpful around the house. Though there was not much that needed doing around this place, with Nelson, Clarence's creaky retainer tiptoeing around: "Do you need anything, Master Kenneth?" "Can I help you with anything, Master Kenneth?"

It took everything in him to not break out in a snarl. Nelson was a smarmy kiss-up, pretending to treat him with respect. He knew damn well that Nelson thought he was riffraff, dirt, garbage. Well, he would show him. He would show them all, alright.

The only problem was that Nelson was always hovering. It made it very tricky to get out without the old servant checking up on him, asking about his activities. Then again, he was a clever, clever boy, right, as his mother always said? Stop it, he told himself, stop thinking about the old whore.

To get around that snoop Nelson, he invented a friend. "I'm going over to George's place after school to study," he'd say. "There's a pile of home-work and an exam tomorrow." He'd let out a groan, laughing inside.

Clarence would give him a fatherly smile. "That's good, son. Hit those books. It'll pay off for you, you'll see, the way it did for me."

The first thing Clarence did when he brought Kenneth home from Springville was to show the teenager his state-of-the-art laboratory. "Are you interested in science, my boy? It's a fascinating world. You could work with me in the lab if you'd like, that's if you're science-minded." He smiled at Kenneth.

Kenneth knew he was supposed to look impressed with all the chemicals, containers, sterilizers, and other tools for research. "Wow! This is awesome, Dr. Abbott, sir." He widened his eyes and gazed around the room, acting intensely interested.

Clarence clapped Kenneth on the back. "Glad you appreciate it, son, but none of this 'sir,' or 'Dr. Abbott' stuff. Call me Clarence."

Kenneth grinned. "Yes, sir, I mean, yes, Clarence." In like Flynn, he thought, and just make very sure that we get along, play the dutiful foster son. I am not about to pass up the chance of easy living. This could be all mine someday if I play my cards right. Maybe not that far in the future, too, especially since it looks like the old guy is not in such great shape.

Most days, Kenneth's foster father was shut up in his lab, absorbed in his latest project. It turned out that was how he became rich, very rich, all because of dozens of patents, mostly on cutting-edge chemical compounds. That left Kenneth to his own devices, which suited his purposes beautifully. The fewer eyes on him, the better, he thought. This left him plenty of room to pursue his secret mission. What was even better, Clarence's apartment building was just blocks away from a local community college.

About six months later, Clarence told Kenneth that he wanted to adopt him. "If it's agreeable with you, my boy." Clarence peered at him over his bifocals. "It has to be what we both want."

Kenneth had to restrain himself from shouting out, "Yes!" Clarence disapproved of showy demonstrations, preferring quiet decorum. "Yes, Clarence, I'd like that very much, thank you." Kenneth gave Clarence a beatific smile, summoning up a tear in his eyes. God, I should be in the movies, he thought, not for the first time. I am so damned good at this.

After the adoption was completed and Kenneth was officially an Abbott, Clarence said, "This is the happiest day of my life. You've brought me much joy, son."

Kenneth made himself look too overcome for words. Finally, he was able to tell Clarence how meaningful it was to be his adopted son. Clarence said he was changing his will. "I'm making a very generous provision for my son," he said, beaming at Kenneth.

Meanwhile, Kenneth hooked up with another friend, Henry, a cohort for increasing his income. Though Clarence provided Kenneth with an allowance, he was not satisfied, but he knew better than to seem ungrateful and ask for more.

Kenneth got his friend to ask his parents to buy their son a car, supposedly so Henry could get a job. Henry was 18, and was the only son of doting, well-off parents. Clarence thought Kenneth was too young for a car and would not have allowed him to even drive one. Besides the car, Kenneth wanted, no, he *needed*, a nice little gun, a couple of switchblades, and fine burglary tools. He and Henry could get by doing B&Es in wealthy neighborhoods.

He found Henry, who was not too bright, but with plenty of muscle, hanging around the nearby schoolyard, shaking down little kids for their lunch money. He motioned Henry over to a corner of the yard.

"Hey, I got an idea that'll get you a lot more than that," he said.

Henry was all ears.

Henry got the car, an older one, that his parents said he could use as a "starter" car. Kenneth and Henry began burglarizing homes that looked promising, in terms of wealth, far enough away from the neighborhood, so they would not be suspects. They were careful to only steal money, which could not be traced, as jewelry and antiques would. It was up to him to do the thinking for Henry, but that was fine. Henry would provide the muscle, if and when it was needed.

It was not long before they amassed enough cash for the car, the gun, the switchblades, and more. Since Henry had no brain for figures, Kenneth had an easy time cheating him, being careful not to push it too far. Henry had a temper.

Kenneth hid the weapons and money in a storage locker he rented and parked the car in a garage. The next job they set out on was a rambling old mansion that belonged to an elderly widow.

Unfortunately for them, the old woman had a strong young grandson staying with her. He held the two at gunpoint while he called the police. Henry's parents and Clarence Abbott arrived shortly after the two were taken to the police station, booked, and fingerprinted.

Kenneth could tell that Clarence was not in a forgiving mood. He would have to work the old guy hard to be able to keep his cozy lifestyle. He got down on his knees.

"I'm so very, very sorry, Clarence. I won't blame you for wanting me out of your life. It was a horrible mistake. I can't ask you to forget, but maybe someday, you'll be able to forgive me." Kenneth made himself bring tears to his eyes by thinking of all he could lose. He looked up at Clarence beseechingly, a true penitent. "You can lock me in my room till you trust me again."

Clarence looked at his adopted son with tears in his own eyes. "Please, Kenneth, my boy, get up, get up off that filthy floor." He put his arm around Kenneth and helped him up. "It's all right. I know you aren't like that anymore. You made a mistake. I forgive you. I'll pay the bail and we'll go home."

Kenneth and Henry were put on probation. After that, Kenneth lay low for a long time, regularly reporting to his probation officer, making sure Clarence was not suspicious anymore and trusted him again. He still managed to sneak out now and then. There were young women to save.

Eventually, he began going stir-crazy, feeling as if he were in a gold-plated prison. He had to get out. Kenneth looked up his friend Henry, who was also itching to do another job. They decided to rob a large house on a hill a few towns away that Henry had already scoped out. He told Kenneth, "This one should be easy. I heard a neighbor saying the couple was staying at their beach house."

However, the owners came back as the two were trying to open the safe in the master bedroom. All hell broke loose. Henry beat the man to the ground and started after the woman, who ran into another room and called the police.

"Henry, make tracks!" Kenneth shouted, running down the stairs and out to the car, a 10-year-old yellow VW bug. Henry jumped in and they roared off as the sound of the sirens grew closer. It was the chase of their lives, skidding downhill, sliding onto the nearest highway, faster and faster. There were three police cars chasing them, sirens wailing and lights flashing.

Speeding along the highway, Kenneth lost control of the car. It crashed into the cement barrier, bursting into brilliant orange flames.

CHAPTER 65

I thought about not seeing Barry anymore, after being a little freaked out by our last encounter, but I was too hooked on him and the wild new world I discovered. Maybe I was just careless, or self-destructive, or whatever. Being on the edge, skirting danger, outwitting death, had always thrilled me.

I rented a car, since public transportation was difficult from my apartment at night to the East Side. All the way there, Gwen's voice buzzed in my ear: *Don't go there, don't do it, take care, watch out.* I swatted it away like a fly. Hey, what do you know about what was good for me? I can take care of myself, the way I always do.

This time, Barry led me to his soundproof, secret hideaway in the basement. "It's my man-cave," he said, with a laugh. "Wait till you see all my goodies."

I did not know what I expected to find, but this was definitely no ordinary man-cave. It was a dark room, lit by candles, seemingly 100s of them, all along the walls. That was not the only thing lining the walls. Handcuffs, leather straps and whips hung from hooks screwed into the bricks. A huge incinerator roared in the back of the room.

The absolute scariest was a large snake, sticking its horrible head out of its basket, flicking its horrible tongue. I was terrified of snakes. One winter day in Port Authority, I saw a kid on the escalator in front of me wearing something around his neck. When I realized it was no scarf, I jumped off and nearly got myself run over by a bus. I told Barry the story at some point. Why was he doing this to me? Was he testing me?

I froze. This was more than too much. I had a strong urge to turn and run. Why did I stay? I would probably never know and maybe nobody else would, either. This could be the last decision I ever got to make. "Barry, that snake ... "

"Oh, Sheba won't hurt you. Isn't it time you got over your silly fear?" Barry was at the built-in bar, wearing a black silk shirt and tight pants. "What's your pleasure, sweetheart?" he asked.

I sank into a chair as far away from the thing in the basket as possible. "Uh, just something light, okay? A glass of white wine?" I figured anything stronger could cause me problems. Lady, you just landed in a huge, steaming pile of problems, scary ones. I eyed the snake, which still had its terrible head out, tongue flicking, moving around in the basket. I started to shake. I better get hold of myself, I thought. Being a sub meant that a dom could do whatever he liked, do anything to me, make me quiver, shake with fear. The best way to deal with it was to act as if nothing bothered me. This I knew from previous experience with Barry.

He brought my drink and his, sitting down next to me. I could see that his pupils were dilated. His eyes looked huge in the candlelight. God, he was probably on one of his uppers, I thought. Brace yourself, Phil. Drink slowly, take it easy. Do not let him see you sweat or shake. Act calm. Remember, you could be overreacting. It was not as if he was a stranger, on a first date. Besides that, who knows, it could end up being a very exciting night. I looked at the basket again. It was quiet for now. Maybe it went to sleep or died. Please God.

He sipped his drink. What it was who knew, but not something light. With every sip, his fingers gently fingered my thigh, crawling toward my underpants. Then they were inside them and inside me. I was getting hot, and my head was kind of fuzzy.

Barry evidently put something in my drink. "Did you put anything in my glass?"

He smiled, actually baring his teeth, and whispered in my ear, "It's just to take the edge off. You seemed a little anxious. Don't worry, sweetheart. You're going to have the experience of a lifetime, something you'll never, ever forget."

CHAPTER 66

When I woke up, I screamed. I was naked, bound and lying on my stomach near the incinerator. That horrible snake was slowly making its way to me, trying to avoid the flames, which were reaching out toward my skin. I stared at the thing, terrified. "Please, get it away from me, please, please!"

Barry laughed. He had taken his clothes off. "She won't hurt you unless you disobey me, my sweet." He made a clicking noise, and it slithered back to its basket. He edged me even closer to the fire, licking at my backside, tonguing me roughly, and parting my legs. All the while, he was thrusting and moaning. "Ohhh, isn't this absolutely exquisite, my sweetheart? Are you in heaven, too? Ohhhhh." I felt him burst inside me and collapse behind me on a fur rug. He wrapped himself in it, still moaning.

I was ready to beg, plead, whatever it took. "Please, get me away from here, Barry!"

He opened his eyes and gave me a long, lazy smile and stretched. It made me think of some kind of feral animal. Then he laughed up at me, obviously in no hurry. "Aw, is my sweet little sub getting anxious?" This made him laugh even harder. "Hey, c'mon, I already put Sheba back in her basket. There's nothing to be afraid of now."

Never let him know you are frightened out of your mind. "I'm not afraid." I stuck my chin out. "I'm roasting. Please untie me. I have to go to the bathroom." I managed a weak smile.

He laughed again, and got himself up, saying, "Okay, my sweet." Shaking his head, he said, "I thought you were so tough, so adventurous, hmm?" He undid the leather straps, and I flopped down on the floor.

"Eventually, a girl has to go to the bathroom," I said, jumping up, "even an adventurous one." I managed a giggle.

It turned out that he put my clothes in there. I quickly threw them on, flushed the toilet, and splashed water on my face. I took a few deep breaths to try to calm down. It was not easy, but I was able to make myself do it, somehow.

When I walked out, he was back on the rug, beckoning me to join him. I gave a huge yawn, not hard to do after whatever he put in my drink. "Oh, sweetheart, I'm so tired and I'm on deadline with an article tomorrow. I'd better be getting home." I blew him a kiss and slipped out the door. I managed to walk, not run, to my car.

He was up and in the doorway in a flash. "Don't you dare!" he roared. "How dare you leave without my permission? You'll pay for this, my sweet!"

Trembling all over, I was able to start the car and drive off. After I was on the road for a few minutes, I had to pull over. I could hardly breathe. I reached over to the back seat and fumbled around for a paper bag. I breathed into it, slowly. I never had panic attacks this bad.

You win, Gwen. No, *I* win. *We* win.

CHAPTER 67

I kept shaking till I got on the bus back to Woodstock and made an emergency appointment with Gwen. Thank God she was available.

I sank into my usual chair and took a couple of deep breaths, hoping it would not lead to hyperventilation. "Thank you for seeing me on such short notice."

Gwen looked at me. "Not at all. You're obviously upset. What's going on?"

I looked down at my lap. "Barry," I whispered. "He..."

"Take it easy, Phil. Just let it happen." Her voice was kind.

I took another deep breath and told her about my horrible experience, finishing with, "I think, I hope, I've learned my lesson. You were so right on target about my risk-taking." I gave her a shaky smile.

Gwen peered at me over her glasses. "Never mind about my being right. It's important that you realize how dangerous some of your choices could be. It sounds like this person is very sadistic and could do you real harm."

"I've never been so frightened in my life, especially that horrible snake rearing its horrible head." I shivered.

"I imagine that he knew about your fear of snakes."

I nodded. "Yes, he even mentioned it then, saying it was time I got over my fear."

She looked at her notes. "Why would he want you to be frightened like that? Why do you think?"

I looked down at my lap. "Uh, I guess, because he thought ... he thought I was weak and wouldn't fight back, and it made him feel good."

She pounced. "Why would that make him feel good, to intimidate another person? Someone whom he supposedly cares about?"

I shrugged. "Who knows?"

She shook her head. "I think you know."

"He's a sadistic bastard." My lips twisted. "I should've brought my gun, but who brings a gun to a date?"

Gwen nodded. "Yes, why would you need a gun on a date? Maybe a better question is, why do you think you have a relationship with a sadistic bastard?"

I whispered, "I guess I think I deserve it. After all, my mother ..."

She sighed. "Isn't it time you got your unloving mother out of your head? The fact that she was that way had nothing to do with you. She wasn't capable of love. No matter who you were, she would've been the same uncaring, bitter person. She couldn't love herself, so she couldn't love anyone else, especially a child who was as unlike her as possible."

I stared at her. "You think so?"

Gwen stared at me, long and hard. "You're nothing like your miserable mother. You have a ton of courage, you're loyal and kind to your friends, and you're a good person. Someone who's been getting herself into terrible situations all her life, to reenact what her mother told her she was. You don't have to do that to yourself anymore."

I definitely never thought about all that. I smiled at her. "Now, if I can only do that..."

"Of course you can," she said firmly.

CHAPTER 68

My writing career began after college, when I decided to try my hand at journalism and eventually became an investigative reporter. It seemed to be a natural fit, given my fascination with crime: why criminals behaved the way they did, what made them that way, how crimes got solved, how the bad guys got caught. This meant dealing with the who, what, where, when and why of a case, whether it was corruption, child abuse, domestic violence, rape, even murder.

My nose was good at sniffing out news. After a while, my reputation grew, and people contacted me with the inside story of something I was usually happy to pursue, such as the scammers whose specialty was fleecing elderly people, and the corrupt owners of a nursing home where patients were being abused and neglected.

Constantly chasing stories (and hosting the blog) had not left me much time for extra-curricular activities, such as serious relationships with guys. At any rate, my self-esteem about my looks and everything else had always been in the toilet, thanks to Mommie Dearest.

The sooner my mother and I parted, the better. After college, I moved into an apartment in the city. When my mother died, I went back to Woodstock for the funeral. I signed up tenants for the house, rented a small cottage for myself not far from that for weekends, and reconnected with my father's family. My aunts and uncles and cousins welcomed me back with eagerness, and I felt surrounded by love and warmth.

Once I started spending more time upstate, I began to wonder about my mother's family, the venerable Abbotts. When I went into town and walked down the main street, I glanced at people I passed to see if they resembled my mother. I knew she had a sister and a brother, who possibly had families of their own, and that her mother and father, my grandparents, were long dead. My mother never talked about her estranged family, so that was all I knew. I never even saw any pictures of them when I was growing up.

Should I try to connect with the people who rejected my father and disowned my mother? It was, after all, a whole other side of me, my heritage, my genes. Then I thought, why bother, they would probably reject me, too, or be such awful people, I would reject them. This would usually be the end of my speculation.

That was until Henry Bradshaw, the Abbotts' family lawyer, contacted me. It turned out that my mother, and now, I, had an inheritance, some of which had originated from my grandparents, who made their money in real estate. The rest of the family's money came from my mother's other brother, Clarence, whom I never knew existed, who died just after my mother. He had a brilliant, lucrative career as a scientist. He was gay and never had a permanent relationship. Evidently, even though my maternal grandparents cut my mother off when she ran away with my father, her brother Clarence had tried to make up for it.

"Your Uncle Clarence was a good person, Philomena," Henry Bradshaw told me. Bradshaw was balding, paunchy and had a ruddy complexion. "Late in life, he adopted a son, Kenneth, whom he met as a patron for a center housing at-risk teenagers. He chose the most troubled of these troubled young people." Bradshaw shook his head. "There was a bad history there. This young man was too smart for his own good, very arrogant, thought he was too good to work or obey any rules. He'd already had several brushes with the law – armed robbery, burglary, assault. He was even a suspect in a fire. Whatever he did, he always managed to get away with it by blaming it on someone else. Unfortunately, all the good your uncle tried to do with this young man didn't take. He continued in his no-good ways, causing his adopted father no end of grief. Needless to say, your Aunt Martha and Uncle Lucius were not at all happy about this turn of events."

Poor Uncle Clarence, trying to do the right thing. "What finally happened to Clarence's son?"

Bradshaw sighed. "He came to a terrible end. He and a criminal cohort were involved in a car chase with the police after an armed robbery. The car exploded and both young men were presumed dead. There were no remains because of the intense heat."

The whole idea of their brother adopting a teenager with problems, in addition to Clarence's being gay, must have freaked them out. Not only that, it meant instead of the family money being divided in half (for just the two of them), each one only got a third.

Bradshaw continued, "Clarence designated one-third of his estate to his adopted son. After the son was killed in the car fire, that share was bequeathed to your mother and now to you. Martha and Lucius are furious about having to share what they consider their rightful inheritance with you, so they're contesting Clarence's will."

We were sitting in his office in uptown Kingston, about 20 minutes from Woodstock. It was the county seat, so the city was where most of the area lawyers' offices were. As was the case with a number of these buildings, it was once an old clapboard home, listed on the National Register of Historic Places in Ulster County. Kingston had plenty of history. It became New York State's first capital, in 1777, and was burned by the British in October of that year, after the Battles of Saratoga.

"What happens now?" I asked him, sitting back in the soft leather armchair.

He peered at me over his bifocals. "We'll have to wait till everything is resolved, one way or another. Frankly, I don't see that they have a case. Your uncle was of sound mind when he made out his will and I checked it over carefully." He closed the file on his desk and got up. "He was very determined that his share should go to your mother and then to any of her heirs. I'll keep in touch with you about it. I don't see that there's anything to worry about."

I leaned across his desk, shook his hand, and thanked him. As I left his office, I wondered exactly how upset these people were, and just what they would do if they lost their case.

CHAPTER 69

He changed his name, took up a sensible profession, married a sensible woman and began raising his own family. His wife was not happy. He never touched her after the children were born. When she questioned him, he called her a whore.

"You're a mother now," he said. "That should be enough." The idea that his wife, now a mother, should want, need, that kind of dirty, animal relationship, repulsed him. It made him think of his mother and what she did with him when he was a child. A mother should be chaste and pure, he thought.

"There won't be any more kids," he told his wife after the twins were born. "Two is enough." He was grateful every day that they were boys, who would not need to be saved.

CHAPTER 70

Who Killed Who?

The blog for those with an inquisitive nose ... for murder and mayhem

WOODSTOCK, NY: Sylvia Castle, a wealthy older woman, was found dead, possibly from a heart attack, in her Woodstock home yesterday. According to the Ulster County Sheriff's office, there is a question of whether Mrs. Castle died of natural causes or as the result of foul play.

If any of you have any information or ideas about the death of Mrs. Castle, please call the toll-free number: 1800-555-8000.

Miranda Grimaldi

COMMENTS:

From SallyY: Wow! When a rich old lady dies, 10 to 1, it's foul play. Just wait and see.

From JerryB: I wouldn't jump to conclusions, but ...

BonnieG: I agree with SallyY. Who are the relatives? Who inherits?

JoyceA: And how much $$$.

PaulM: Sounds like a lot. I agree with SallyY and BonnieG. Follow the money.

CHAPTER 71

Lily and I were sitting in her kitchen, working on the death of the old woman, my neighbor, Sylvia Castle.

"So, if it's murder, let's think about who might have done it. We know that Mrs. Castle always drove her daughter crazy. Besides the daughter, who else could have done it?" I said, sipping my rosehip tea.

Lily put her heavenly carrot cake, fresh from the oven, on a pretty blue-and-white plate. She knew better than to expect me to bake anything edible. My idea of preparing a meal was PB & J or ordering takeout. I was usually so caught up in my regular (for pay) writing job, let alone trying to solve murders online, that sometimes I even forgot to eat. This sounds great for someone short, like me, who was always fighting the weight battle and losing (no pun intended). The problem was that when I missed a meal, I more than made up for it by gorging on junk food later.

At any rate, in addition to being a good friend and great partner in crime-solving, Lily's excellent cooking and baking skills were a bonus.

"Hmmm, maybe it could be the latest nurse's aide. The old lady must've been awfully hard to deal with, whining, demanding. Her daughter said her mother wore out the aides quickly." Lily sliced the cake. "She said the agency was threatening to stop sending any more of them because of all the complaints."

"Yeah, I heard they had a lot of turnover." The carrot cake tasted as good as it smelled. "Is there any way we can find out who's mentioned in the will, besides the daughter, I mean?"

Lily smiled. "I'll see if Jack can find out." Jack Roberts, a private investigator, former cop and Lily's longtime boyfriend, had helped us out on a lot of cases. He was a great guy and more important, very good to Lily.

It took Lily a long time to be able to open up to a serious relationship, after the terrible tragedies in her family. Lily was a strong person, but I knew she was still very tender on the inside, and maybe always would be. She didn't talk about it, at least not to me. I hoped that Jack could help heal her sore heart.

I made myself stop musing and get back to the murder. "Maybe there were other relatives – hers or her late husband's – as beneficiaries, too, waiting in line for the old woman to die. Maybe some of them had children," I said, scarfing down the moist, sweet goodness of the cake.

"That's something we have to dig out, if the woman or her husband had siblings. If they were anywhere around when – if – she was murdered."

"Another thing we need to know," I said, gladly accepting another slice, "is how much money there actually was, and where it is: stocks, bank, whatever."

Lily poured us more tea. "Hopefully, it's somewhere safe and accessible."

I thought for a moment. Between bites, I said, "You know, we should ask Jack to find out who the family lawyer is and when the will's going to be probated. We need to know who gets what, how much, and when."

"By the way, how's your target practice coming? Much as I worry about it, I do believe you that it's necessary."

I sipped my tea. "Well, I haven't shot any part of myself yet. Seriously, though, my instructor thinks I'm doing very well."

She sighed. "I have to say, I had my doubts, but I guess you're doing the right thing, as long as you're careful and don't take chances. Jack always says about carrying a gun, 'It's a lethal weapon. Don't ever forget that.'"

CHAPTER 72

Who Killed Who?

The blog for those with an inquisitive nose … for murder and mayhem

ACCORD, NY: Tiffany Carson, 18 years old, from Accord, went missing yesterday. Tiffany is white, with long, blonde hair. She was last seen walking home from school, wearing a blue jacket and blue jeans.

The only witness, so far, is a homeless woman who was rummaging through a dumpster near the high school.

According to police, the woman thought she saw Tiffany start to walk down a side street.

"She was lookin' down that street as if she seen somethin' or somebody." She shook her head. "There was a car parked on the main street." The woman could not give much of a description of the car, except to say it was a sort of tan.

When the police asked her if she saw the driver, she shook her head again. "I couldn't see nobody. My eyes ain't too good lately and my rememberin' ain't too good, neither."

The cops told her to let them know if she remembered anything else, but they were not holding out too much hope.

If any of you have any information, please call the toll-free number: 1-800-555-1212.

Miranda Grimaldi

UPDATE: The homeless woman who saw Tiffany before she went missing was killed in a hit-and-run an hour ago. She was on the way to the police station after she called them, saying she remembered something else about the incident.

CHAPTER 73

Tiffany's body had been found lying in a shallow grave. Lily was a hero again. She had a clear vision of where Tiffany had been laid to rest after the snow had melted. Once she told the police, they knew where to look.

I worried about the publicity, even though the police always made sure Lily's identity was kept a secret and referred to her as a helpful volunteer. "What if the killer figures out who you are and gets nervous about your next vision?" I told her, over lemon tea and wonderful fresh-baked zucchini muffins in her kitchen. "You need to be careful." In my opinion, what she was doing was very risky, putting herself in danger. I knew she felt that it was her mission, her calling, to do this, as her ancestors had for ages.

Lily just laughed. "How's he gonna do that? The cops know not to mention me by name. I think I'll be fine. Don't worry."

I was doubtful. This killer had not escaped detection all this time to let himself be caught out by a psychic.

CHAPTER 74

He was dripping with sweat, aching all over, especially his right hand. Digging in the frozen ground had taken every bit of strength from him. Trying to bury her was a big mistake. He should have just left her hidden in the woods near the park.

He could not bear to look at her again. Her looks were deceiving. Though Tiffany fit his requirements: a pretty, blonde, young woman, he was fooled into thinking she was delicate, since she was small-boned. He had no idea how strong she was. She put up such a struggle he was forced to subdue her any way he could.

It was all because of his stupidity in not testing out the new syringe. It snapped in two when he tried to inject her with the tranquilizer.

She kicked and scratched and then bit him, hard, on his right hand. That startled him, and he automatically swung his arm around, smashing her across the face. Of course, this ruined her before he could save her.

The pain in his hand was horrible. He put ice on it, tied a clumsy wrap on it, and gobbled down some aspirin. He could stand the pain if it did not become infected. He heard that human bites were even more lethal than dog bites. He shivered. He told himself that it was best to lie down and get some rest before going out trolling again.

CHAPTER 75

Having to use both hands to swerve into the old woman caused him such agony, he was in danger of passing out on the road. Before he drove back to the motel, he stopped at a large pharmacy chain store for the strongest pain-killer he could find. He had to force himself to stop shaking when he paid at the counter.

By the time he walked in the door of his room, he could feel his body burning up. He got a bottle of whiskey from his supply in the cabinet, poured himself a large glassful and swallowed it down with a couple of the painkillers. He wished he were home in his own bed, with his family, but that would have to wait till he felt better.

It was a good thing his job required a lot of time on the road, so he could cover his excursions. He deliberately sought work that let him travel and be on his own schedule. He told his wife it could not be helped, especially since it paid more.

Soon he felt his vision growing blurry and the pain dulling a bit, hope-fully, enough for him to fall asleep. Tomorrow, he thought, as he sank into feverish sleep, he would find a doctor, preferably at one of those drop-in emergency centers. A place where nobody knew who you were, and your identification could be faked.

At one point, he woke up from the sweat-drenched sheets with a start. Did he remember to check the young woman's teeth before he buried her? Oh, God, he thought, she could have the tiniest bit of flesh, my flesh, in her teeth – maybe even enough for DNA identification.

Wait a minute, my DNA was not in the system, he realized. This meant even if there were some tiny bit of flesh, nothing would match it. He was always very, very careful. That was why he was never caught and never would be. He was just too damned smart, of course, so much smarter than any stupid cops. He chuckled.

He got up to pour more whiskey and down more painkillers. Sick and exhausted, he crawled back into the lumpy bed, not even bothering to change his sopping clothes.

CHAPTER 76

Around the time Tiffany's body was found, the killer had been worrying about something, namely, this psychic, whoever she was. I better check her out before she sees me in one of her spells, he told himself. Then he chuckled. Who cared what this crazy person saw, or thought she saw? Not only that, she seemed to only have hallucinations about dead people, not live people.

That was except for the fact that she was able to find places where bodies were or had been, he remembered.

He needed to find out more about her. That could help him forget the horrible pain in his hand. First, he better take off the dressing to see how bad it was.

He shivered. It was because of the wound, he thought, not fear. It could be infected. The pain was getting worse. He undid the dressing slowly and carefully, so as not to hurt himself more than necessary. Then he gasped, sickened by the sight. The wound had definitely become infected. I have to get this taken care of, dammit, he thought, but not around here. He had to find a place way out of town, use a fake name, and pay in cash, so there would be no record.

For now, he had work to do, going over to the bed where his newest angel lay. She was so quiet and peaceful, her blonde locks spread over the pillow, her blue eyes closed, with one red-painted toenail removed.

He had to hurry and bring her to her resting place, before that damn visionary honed in on his sanctuary. Wincing with pain, he wrapped her as best as he could in a cheap, mass-produced blanket, one of many he bought for this purpose, and carried her out to his car.

This time, he did not even try to dig a grave. He left her in a wooded area and covered her with leaves, whispering, "I'm sorry, angel."

After driving home, he went to his laptop. Using his good hand, he Googled the names of the surrounding towns, then typed in "area psychics." He grunted when he saw the list: three so-called "mediums." None of them advertised that they helped police find bodies. He tried another tack, looking up articles on bodies recovered in the area, narrowing it down to young women's bodies.

Then he struck gold. One of the stories had a quote from a police sergeant: "With many thanks to the volunteer whose insight led us to the body." Another article also cited the help of the volunteer.

All I have to do is keep an eye on the cops, he thought, and see who leads them to the next body. He chuckled again, then groaned from the pain.

CHAPTER 77

Lily and Jack were having a beer at Cucina, a posh restaurant in Woodstock. Drinks at the bar, however, were not too pricey. That worked well on a gravedigger's (even the head one's) salary and that of a P.I.

As a former cop and investigator in the Ulster County Sheriff's Department in Kingston, Jack still had a good relationship with the local force. They knew he would not do anything to screw up a case they were working on, and he tried to help whatever way he could. This was especially the case when it came to children who died. His own little sister had been a victim of a drunk driver when she was a teenager. He and his mother had never gotten over it. When he was barely of age, he rushed into a disastrous marriage and was long divorced. There were no children.

Jack asked the police lab for the results of the test on Tiffany's teeth. "The test on the girl's teeth just came back," Jack told Lily, between sips. "But …"

"But?" She and Phil hoped the test would give them the identity, or at least, a clue, to the killer.

Jack shook his head. "Unfortunately, the perp's DNA was not in the system."

Lily sighed, but she vowed not to ruin their evening with her disappointment. They never managed to have much time together between their schedules. As a P.I., Jack was out and about, traveling quite a bit. Lily's job at the cemetery sometimes caused her to be called in without much notice.

Tonight, they were snatching a few hours, which Lily was hoping could turn into longer, later at Jack's place.

CHAPTER 78

The antibiotic they gave him at the Emergency Care Center had done a good job of bringing down the swelling and pain in his hand.

He went over to the rickety pressed-board desk in the grimy motel room. A new plan was what I need, he thought, one that definitely could not fail.

Nobody, not the blogger bitch, not the cops, would be able to figure it out or be able to stop it. The devil himself would not be able to stop it.

Nobody can touch me except for that cursed psychic. He had to take care of her ASAP. He howled with delight and stopped himself. You do not want to call attention to yourself. Nothing must stand in your way.

Oh, I am so, so clever, he sang softly, such a clever boy. Mother always told me so. He snarled. Do not think about Mother, the whore, the beast. I slayed the Gorgon, the awful Dragon-Lady. I set her and her house on fire and got away with it. The thought of his mother's fiery corpse made him laugh aloud. You burned to a nice crisp, Mother Dear, a real crispy critter.

He looked down at the small, blonde figure on the bed, removed a glittery pink fingernail and tenderly placed it on his temporary altar.

How still she was! It was sort of a shame. She had so much life in her, before. He reminded himself, wagging his finger above the body, that now she will be pure forever. His own personal sweet angel was soon to join all the other sweet angels. They were a band of angels and they all belonged to him.

What a prince I am! he thought to himself, a savior, like Jesus Christ Himself! They will call me the Savior of Young Women. The world will praise me once it is revealed. Maybe they will even worship me, like the original Savior. Hey, He has nothing on me, performing miracles wherever I go, many more than He ever did, so many miracles that only I can perform.

He grinned into the stained mirror on the wall.

CHAPTER 79

Who Killed Who?

The blog for those with an inquisitive nose ... for murder and mayhem

ESOPUS, NY: Jasmine Donaldson, age 19, of Esopus, went missing three days ago on her way home from Ulster County Community College. Jasmine is white and has curly blonde hair. She was wearing a red-and-white sweater and white pants and red sneakers.

If you have any information about what happened to Jasmine, please call the toll-free number: 1-800-555-4545.

Miranda Grimaldi

COMMENTS:

From Christy'sMom: When will it stop?

From GerryW: I'm driving my daughter to and from her classes now.

From HappyMan: Smart woman. My wife is doing that too.

From WendyP: Me, too.

From TomY: I gave my daughter Mace to carry.

From ILoveDogs: I got my kids martial arts and kickboxing lessons.

UPDATE: Jasmine Donaldson's body was found today near her home.

CHAPTER 80

Lily finished up for the day, tidying the edges of the freshly dug grave, and sighed in satisfaction. Now she could sit down under her favorite shade tree and read Phil's blog post about Mrs. Castle's murder again. She was trying hard to visualize the murder scene, but with no success so far. Digging out her Android, she scrolled to *Who Killed Who?*

WOODSTOCK, NY: *Sylvia Castle, 65, a wealthy widow, was recently found dead in her bedroom in Woodstock, NY. She leaves a daughter, Claire Anderson, and son-in-law, Jerome Anderson.*

The county medical examiner diagnosed her death as insulin poisoning. Mrs. Castle had been in ill health for a long time. She suffered from diabetes, which could make it hard to tell if her death was caused by a mistaken overdose or foul play.

Miranda Grimaldi

Lily put down her phone and closed her eyes and waited. She had to be patient. Sometimes it did not work, no matter what.

Just as she was about to give up and go home, it happened. It was a picture. It was pretty dark. She could barely make out the figure of an old woman in bed. Sheets and blankets were pulled up around her. Was she alone? No, Lily could make out a shadow of someone near the bed. It was dark on that side of the room and whoever it was and whatever he or she was doing remained fuzzy and dim.

Come on, Lily thought, I need to see you. Throw a little light on yourself, please. The person remained hidden, unfortunately. Frustrated, Lily opened her eyes and stood up. Well, she thought, at least it was a start. I have to let Phil know. Know what – that I had a fuzzy vision of somebody in the dark with the old woman? She sighed. I just hope things are clearer next time. She started back home, thinking about what she saw and did not see.

CHAPTER 81

In bed with Andy, Gretchen glanced over at her snoring lover. She thought, how romantic can you get – wham, bam, thank you ma'am. Not even waiting for her this time, the pig. She was getting damn sick of this.

She jabbed him with an elbow. "Hey, wake up, sleepyhead."

"Whuzzat?" He rolled over and opened his eyes. "What?"

She bit back a smart remark. "I'm hungry, starving. Let's get something to eat."

Andy leaned over and started nuzzling her breast. "There's enough food right here, doll."

She moved away impatiently. "I mean real food, guy, okay?"

Andy groaned and pointed to the tented sheet. "But I'm ..."

She laughed. "You're always like that. Listen, though I'm tempted, I gotta eat, now." As they left the motel, she thought, I want lots more than this, a helluva lot more.

On her way home, Gretchen said to herself, why am I spending my time with a crude muscleman? I can do lots better. She smiled, thinking of the new guy she met "accidently-on-purpose" at the local Starbucks. She eyed his good looks as she waited for her order, noted with satisfaction there was an empty seat at his table in the crowded café, and asked him, coyly, if she might sit there. Luckily, she just had her hair done and was wearing a becoming (as in very tight) sweater and jeans, both of which looked glued on. She was gratified by his appreciative gaze, which was followed by a long conversation and exchange of cell numbers.

He was married, but so what? She had no intention of giving up her very comfortable lifestyle, no matter what it took. Hell, she could handle Andy, and Norman, and Charles.

Charles Simmons, that was his name. She could handle all of them, anything that came her way. After all, she grew up in a bar. She laughed. She never thought her crappy background would serve her well.

Charles seemed extremely intelligent; she could tell. Most important, he was very sexy, in a classy way. I sure deserve a guy like that. She sighed.

Just tell Andy to fuck off, she thought, but not that way. Who knows how he will react? She knew the result of Andy's temper when he got upset. He was strong, very strong, with all that weightlifting and bench presses. He was bulking up even more lately, planning to enter a body-building contest.

I better do it on the phone. Hopefully, that should give him a chance to cool off. She scrolled down to Andy's number on her cell. When he picked up, she said, "Oh, Andy, the most awful thing."

"What's the matter, doll? Are you okay?"

"No, I mean, I'm not hurt or anything, yet." She was thinking fast, winging it.

"Whaddya mean? What's going on? I'll be right there, okay?" His voice was full of concern.

"No, no, no, you mustn't. That'll make it much worse." Boy, am I good, she thought. "It's Norman. He's very suspicious. I heard him on the phone with a detective. I'm afraid, Andy." She actually thought that Norman had been getting suspicious lately, so she only had to lie about the detective.

"He wouldn't dare hurt you! I'll, I'll …!"

"Andy, Andy, listen to me, please! It'll be all right if we stop seeing each other, just for a while."

"No, we can't! You're mine, you're my doll!" He sounded hysterical, she thought, forgodsakes.

"Sweetheart, listen. Believe me, I don't want to do this either, but I don't want to risk your life or mine. It's just for a while, Andy. Let him cool down and start trusting me again. I'll do my best to convince him."

There was silence on the phone. "Andy?"

She heard muttering, then, "Okay, for now, for a little while." He grunted. "*Just* for a little while."

That sounded kind of menacing, she thought, after she clicked off.

CHAPTER 82

Norman Hardesty was on the phone with his younger brother, Fred. "Hey, it's a good thing I've got fast reflexes, bro. The brakes failed on the Thruway, of all places."

His brother asked him how that could happen, since Norman just had his car checked out, including the brakes. "Don't know. Guess the new guy at my garage isn't so good. Anyway, luckily, I managed to pull over to the side and called the state cops. They called a garage and got it fixed up temporarily, and I got home in time for the 11 o'clock news." He laughed. "Sorry, no, I don't think it's funny. Yes, I'll try to be more careful, and I'll get a new mechanic."

He clicked off and poured himself a drink from the supply in the liquor cabinet. Taking a sip, he turned to his wife, who just came in from a shopping trip, eyes wide, hovering as he finished his conversation.

"Norman, what the hell happened? Are you all right?" Gretchen, wearing one of her new purchases, a powder-blue designer dress, and a worried frown, threw her arms around him. "You're scaring me. Tell me, quick!"

Norman kissed her forehead. "Nothing to worry about, hon. Everything's fine, now. Sit down, have a drink, and I'll tell you all about it."

Gretchen gave him a weak smile, poured herself a glass of wine, and went to the sofa in the living room. Oh, God, now he will launch into one of his god-fucking-damn endless stories. Okay, kid, man, uh, woman up; time for earnest looks and a worried frown. She patted the seat next to her.

As Norman droned on, supplying every last detail that could be wrung out of the story, Gretchen snuggled closer to her husband, softly patting his knee with her finely manicured fingers. All the while, thinking, damn, this might have been a lucky accident, with that lousy mechanic. I mean, anybody else would be roadkill with brakes failing on the Thruway. Then I could have the stocks and the life insurance, and no boring Norman. Just my luck. He has great reflexes. Well, maybe another time, another accident, or whatever.

Much as Norman enjoyed talking to and being cuddled by his wife, lately, she felt that he acted a little uneasy about her. There were times when she was not reachable on her cell, which she knew annoyed him. Of course, she always had a good excuse. He told her that he depended on his world to be orderly. Not only that, but he and she seemed to be out of sync recently.

He always claimed not to mind her buying sprees. He liked seeing her in nice things. After all, he said, she deserved them for putting up with an older man. (which, of course, she agreed with) She could have had any number of younger guys, which he realized long ago. She knew he felt a certain satisfaction in being able to sweep her off her feet, or so he thought. They had a whirlwind romance, were married before he knew it, and had settled down to a comfortable country life.

When Gretchen met Norman, he was divorced and lonely. Before the divorce, he and his wife had been estranged for years. He told Gretchen that his wife had poisoned his children's minds against him, and he missed them. He fell hard for Gretchen. She was young, beautiful, and, though he could hardly believe it, she told him she loved him back. His only regret, he always said to her, was that there were no children. He was hoping to start a new family with her. Gretchen told him, before they were married, tears raining down her cheeks, that she was unable to have kids. She said she was happy just taking care of him.

Unknown to Gretchen, the reason Norman and she seemed to be out-of-sync was that one day, he discovered her packet of birth control pills while looking for a bottle of aspirin. He had a splitting headache and was trying to head off a possible migraine. The bottle in the bathroom off his bedroom was empty. He went to the bathroom in her bedroom – they had separate bedrooms because Gretchen complained about his snoring – to look. He fumbled around in her dimly lit bathroom cabinet for a few moments, unsuccessfully. (She knew that dim lighting was more flattering.) Holding his forehead in agony, he pushed aside a couple of the expensive creams, hoping there was something behind them. There they were, birth control pills.

That was the beginning of his migraine and his uneasiness about his wife.

CHAPTER 83

Who Killed Who?

The blog for those with an inquisitive nose ... for murder and mayhem

SCHOHARIE, NY: Olivia Sadler, 17, of Schoharie, went missing three days ago on the way home from high school band practice. Olivia is white, with short, wavy blonde hair and was wearing a dark gray woolen sweater, blue jeans and white sneakers.

If you have any information or ideas about what happened to Olivia, please call the toll-free number: 1-800-555-4000.

Miranda Grimaldi

COMMENTS:

From CherylY: I'm the mother of two teenage girls and I'm scared to death.

From WinnieS: I've been taking my daughter to martial arts.

From JimH: My girls are going to kickboxing.

From GeorgeM: Karate for my daughter.

From Miranda Grimaldi: This all sounds great, guys, helping your kids defend themselves.

UPDATE: Olivia Sadler's body was found today near the high school.

CHAPTER 84

I told Lily about my mother's relatives after we sat down for lunch. "I want to get acquainted with the Abbotts."

"That doesn't sound like such a good idea," Lily said, taking a cheese strata from the oven. "Remember what the lawyer told you about their being furious over the will?"

"I think it's worth a try. What can it hurt?" The smell was delicious. As soon as it was on the table, I grabbed a piece without even a potholder. "Ow!"

"I told you it was hot, but you couldn't wait." Lily rolled her eyes. "Anyway, didn't your family lawyer recommend against that? From what you said, they could be nasty."

I blew on my strata and dug in – heaven. "Well, I want to see what they're like, out of curiosity, if nothing else. Who knows, maybe I could get them to like me, with my winning personality. You think that could be enough for them to stop fighting my inheritance?"

Lily poured us tea. "You need to be careful, okay? Oh, I forgot to tell you, I've got news. You know my neighbor, Norman Hardesty? I heard that he was in an accident on the Thruway that could've killed him."

I put down my fork. "What happened?"

"The brakes on his car failed. Fortunately, he was able to pull over to the side somehow," Lily said, cutting more slices of strata. "He was lucky, just bruised ribs where he landed on the steering wheel."

"That sounds scary," I said, taking a sip of tea. "Wait, what if it wasn't an accident at all?"

Lily widened her eyes. "You think?"

CHAPTER 85

After Phil had gone upstairs to bed, Lily began thinking about the Castle murder again. She lay down on the living room sofa and pulled a quilt over her. As she quieted her breathing, her eyes started to close.

Soon, a vision of the old woman came to her. Someone was standing next to the woman's bed, holding a syringe, and speaking to the old lady. The person was saying, "Don't worry, this will make you feel better."

The old woman smiled up at the person, saying, "I never worry when you're taking care of me, Jerome, honey."

The man smiled, patted her hand with one of his, then swiftly plunged the syringe directly into the old woman's heart. She opened her mouth and froze as her heart gave out.

Lily came to with a start. "Oh my god, Phil was right! I've got to tell her, and call Jack, and the cops." She ran upstairs to the attic.

CHAPTER 86

I decided to check out the Abbotts on Google. I was good at finding out about people, so why not my own people? It would be helpful to know what I was getting myself into – well, probably trouble. However, I was a bona fide member of the family, so I had a perfect right to make myself known to them. It might also help lessen the blow about the will. I could always hope, right?

Start with my uncle first, I thought. I was young, reasonably attractive, and relatively presentable. I would have to dig out the clothes I wore when I met with my editor about an assignment. This would be my blue, at least not electric blue, more of a mid-blue suit, my only suit. I had a sky-blue blouse to go with it and I owned one pair of pumps, black. This was my grudging bow to respectability – and discomfort. I heard my mother's voice in my head: subtlety, Philomena. I told the voice to shut the hell up.

I got the lawyer to give me Uncle Lucius's and Aunt Martha's addresses and phone numbers. Uncle Lucius lived alone in an apartment on Sutton Place. He was divorced, with two sons who lived out-of-state. Maybe he was lonely, I thought. I might be able to soften his heart with my charming company. I seemed to be his only niece, at least, his only blood-related niece. Aunt Martha, a widow, lived on the Upper East Side. Her only child, a daughter, had died of leukemia.

I Googled Lucius Abbott. He had been a renowned lawyer, a partner at the New York City headquarters of a prestigious law firm. Retiring a few years ago, he took a pricey buyout. His sons were moving up the ladder in branches of the same firm. Uncle Lucius was a patron of two conservative art galleries and a chamber music group and had established a scholarship at a minority-serving college. All this was a good sign. Evidently, Uncle Lucius was a man with a conscience – unless it was just for a tax write-off.

I could manage a conversation about chamber music. To talk about art, though, I would have to fake it somehow. What I knew about art could fit in a thimble.

I picked up my cell and punched in his number.

CHAPTER 87

I decided to combine a trip to Uncle Lucius the same day of a lunch meeting with my editor about an upcoming assignment.

Lunch with Lourdes was always a treat. She was about my age, with short, dark hair, beautiful brown eyes, a terrific figure, married with two kids. She was also smart, no-nonsense, and a genuinely nice person. Imagine that, an editor of a major magazine who was nice. We connected several years ago, after an intro from my friend Wendy.

After the waitperson took our salad orders, Lourdes opened her briefcase, grabbed her iPad and a file, and shoved her glasses onto her nose. "Kudos on the Internet scammers piece." She high fived me, beaming. "Now, how about an article on something illegal for a change?" She gave me a knowing look.

Just about everything I ever investigated dealt with something illegal or scary-dangerous or both.

One of those was the story I did on teenagers selling drugs to elementary school kids. I had gotten a tip from an informant about who, when, and where. Needless to say, it was dicey, and I was lucky to not end up dead. The drug-dealers, happily, ended up in prison.

There was my interview of convicted child molesters who never admitted wrongdoing. "She made me do it, she led me on," one guy said, talking about his 13-year-old stepdaughter.

Another time, I spoke to wife-beaters who attended court-ordered group therapy at a mental health facility. At least the child molesters were behind bars. All there was between me and these guys was a social worker. I felt them eying me as if I were a fresh piece of meat.

I looked at Lourdes. "You're talking about illegal in terms of ...?"

Our salads arrived, and we dug in, not slowing down the conversation. "I'm talking about illegal adoptions, sleazy lawyers snatching babies from poor women in Asia. They auctioned them off to unknowing wealthy American couples in a bidding war for higher and higher amounts of money. These are desperate people who don't ask too many questions about where their baby came from."

I stopped chewing. "Wow!"

She handed me the file to get started on. "I know you'll dig it out and do a great job, as usual. Also, as usual, I'm warning you to be careful."

"I can handle it. Hey, the bad guys haven't done me in yet." I grinned at her.

Lourdes frowned. "I'm serious. These are very bad people, so please, take care."

"Okay, okay, I promise." I tried to look solemn as I tucked the file into my oversized handbag.

At least the first part of my day in the city was a positive one. God only knew how part two, the meeting with Uncle Lucius, would end up. He did not sound bad on the phone, only a little stuffy, so I had hope.

CHAPTER 88

Uncle Lucius's apartment was awesome. It was in a beautiful old building, with marble floors in the lobby, and manned by a uniformed doorman. The apartment itself had high ceilings, wide oak floorboards, and soft lighting streaming from recessed sconces on the living room and dining room walls. It made me think of a Gilded Age apartment. I almost wanted to call the living room a parlor or a drawing room and leave my card, in my white-gloved hand, in a silver tray on a table in the entrance to the living room.

The man himself reminded me of those old earls, dukes, or lords, in a Victorian TV drama on PBS. He wore a dark suit, a discreetly patterned shirt, and, would you believe, an ascot? His looks matched his attire: thick silvery hair, ice-blue eyes, a lined forehead with patrician features, tall and slim, well-tanned from, I guessed, outdoor activity – tennis, anyone?

When he spoke, even his voice was cultured. With almost a bow and an outstretched hand, Uncle Lucius grasped mine. "My dear niece, it's so good to finally meet you." He guided me to a large sofa set on a gorgeous oriental rug at the far end of the room. It faced a concert-sized grand piano.

"Who plays?" I burst out. My parents had never been able to afford anything except an old upright for my weekly lessons. All my life, I longed for a grand.

Uncle Lucius gave me a small smile. "I did, my dear, a long time ago." He held up his hands, which were terribly knotted. "Arthritis."

"I'm so sorry," I whispered, reaching out to pat the crippled fingers that could no longer make music on that beautiful piano. He drew back, stiffly. Okay, Phil, do not presume.

Remember, this is the Other Side of your family. I had a quick flash of my Uncle Gus, enveloping me in a bear hug whenever I came to visit.

"Are you hungry, my dear?" Uncle Lucius said, seemingly recovered from my inappropriate behavior. "I can ring for tea or coffee, and sandwiches."

Ring for tea and sandwiches? Delivered by a butler? There was probably a cook and a maid, to boot. Well, it was a large apartment, and he was not exactly a young man. Stop being so judgmental, Phil, just because these people left you and your parents to eke out a living, while they …

"Thank you, but I've just had lunch, Uncle Lucius." I gave him a wide smile. "I'm just happy to be here, to get to know you."

He gave me another small smile. I wondered if the effort made his jaw ache. "I, too, am glad you're here. Tell me, what shall I call you? Philomena seems quite a mouthful for such a little lady." He grimaced.

How patronizing could he get – Little Lady? The man was a relic. Another minute and I was going to hurl. "Call me Phil," I said, offering another wide smile.

He made another grimace. I guess that was not appropriate, either, but what could he do? Was he just going to call me, "Niece"? At least he was not suggesting I adopt a new name, right?

"Oh, dear," he said, frowning. "That sounds so …"

"Tough? Lower class?" I said sweetly. I had a sudden urge to do something disgusting, like fart or scratch my ass.

I could see him trying hard to ignore my sarcasm. Clearing his throat, he said, "I think Phyllis would be a more appropriate name, for an Abbott, that is." Icy eyes stared me down. "Don't you?"

Well, if I was going to find out what he was up to about the will, I had to suck it up. "Okay, Uncle Lucius, that will be fine." I gave him a sweet, placating smile.

"Good girl." He seemed to be thawing. "What made you decide to get to know your long-lost relations? Of course, I'm glad that you did, for whatever the reason." He gave me a searching look, as in: exactly what was the reason, hmm?

I might as well come right out with it. He was obviously too damn intelligent for any subterfuge on my part. I counted to five in my head, my method of easing into a difficult situation. Sometimes it worked, but mostly not.

I related the conversation with the lawyer about Uncle Clarence's bequest and how disappointed I was that he and my aunt were contesting it. "I thought that getting to know you and Aunt Martha..." I gave him my most ingratiating smile.

Those eyes turned to ice again. He sat back against the couch pillow. "You thought that might settle everything amicably." I could hear the sneer in his voice.

I nodded, trying for a demure look, and failing. "I was hoping."

He made a point of looking at his watch. "Well, it's getting late," he said, getting off the sofa and walking toward the front door.

It was three in the afternoon. Okay, that was it, for now.

CHAPTER 89

Aunt Martha was as bad as Uncle Lucius, but in a different way. Not even bothering with a phony veneer of politeness, she was just downright vicious.

She made me think of what my mother might have been as a bitter old woman, soured by her pinched life, showing her true colors.

Nasty was written all over her face. Her thin lips seemed to be curled in a perpetual expression of disgust. She looked down at me (She was a tall, skinny woman.) as if I were something to wipe off the bottom of her shoe. She did not invite me to sit down. She probably thought I would pollute the place with my Jewish-Greekness (Greek-Jewishness?).

"Well, you're here now." She sniffed. "We might as well talk." She wagged her finger at me. "Don't you think you're going to put anything past me, young lady."

"But ..."

"Your father was a dirty foreigner who never took care of his family, and you're his mongrel child." She sneered.

I felt as if she punched me in the stomach. Then I wanted to punch HER in the stomach. I started trembling.

She noticed and laughed with her hands on hips. "Good, you're afraid of me. You should be. I'll drive you and your lousy crappy claim away so fast you won't know what hit you."

I laughed. Me, afraid of this disgusting old woman? I thrust out my chin and moved toward her. She actually backed up a few steps. Who is afraid of who, Auntie Dear? "That's fury, you see, Aunt Martha, that I'm trying to control. You're just not worth it."

She opened her mouth and shut it again.

I slammed out of her apartment, breathing hard.

CHAPTER 90

Gretchen was worried. Lately, she had a feeling that Norman actually was getting suspicious. She was afraid he was checking her phone calls or her texts. What if he hired a private detective? Was someone tracking her movements, following Andy and her to their motel dates? That would be a fate worse than death. She could not let Norman catch her out and divorce her, she told her friend Rachel, when they were toweling off at the gym.

Rachel turned from the mirror, frowning at her uncooperative, curly brown hair, comb in hand. "Why would Norman do that? You said he's not the suspicious type, right?"

Gretchen put the towel down. "Oh, whoever knows about somebody else? He's been moody lately and giving me funny looks."

"Do you think he's been checking up on you? Do you think he knows about you and lover-boy?" Her tone was heavy on the sarcasm as she glanced in the mirror again. "Ugh, every time it rains, I turn into a frizz ball."

Rachel was not fond of Andy. Gretchen thought it was because he had not given her a second look, even though she came on to him. Rachel seemed to be especially pissed that being divorced, she was much more available and her life much less complicated than Gretchen's.

"Why do you suppose he's so into you?" Rachel had sniffed after Gretchen and Andy first started up. "What I mean is, after all, you've got a husband to deal with." She gave Gretchen an apologetic smile.

Gretchen had just shrugged. "Guess he thinks I'm worth it, for some reason." At the time, she missed the black look Rachel gave her.

She never tried to hide their relationship from Rachel, or from anybody else within ear and eye shot at the gym. The mutual attraction had been obvious from the get-go, and once they got going… she grinned.

Now, Gretchen worried that it might end up being obvious to her husband, which would be a freaking disaster, for sure. She did not think it could ever happen, since she always was so careful, so discreet – outside of the gym, that was.

Then she thought, maybe it was someone at the gym, maybe Rachel? She knew Rachel was jealous. Maybe she put a bug in Norman's ear, and he hired a detective to follow her. Rachel was her friend, or was she? Maybe she was just pretending to be her friend all along. How could you ever know about someone else, especially someone who wanted Andy for herself?

Gretchen gave Rachel a sidelong glance. Could she trust her? She was sympathetic to Rachel's situation. Nobody had handed her anything, either. Rachel was divorced and got absolutely nothing out of that marriage with her loser ex. She had to drudge away at her lousy, boring job, barely making ends meet. Gretchen and Rachel had worked together before she married Norman.

"You should try to find a rich guy, to take care of you," Gretchen told her. "Then you'll be set for life."

Rachel moaned. "There sure aren't any at work, you know that. They're losers, every one of them."

After one of their conversations, Gretchen ended up feeling apologetic about her good fortune and cast away any doubts about Rachel's trustworthiness.

CHAPTER 91

Who Killed Who?

The blog for those with an inquisitive nose … for murder and mayhem

ELLENVILLE, NY: Melissa Parsons, 19 years old, of Ellenville, went missing yesterday on her way home from Ulster County Community College. Melissa is white, with ash-blonde hair and green-framed glasses. She was wearing a pink jacket, blue jeans and pink-and-white sneakers.

If you have any information about Melissa, please call the toll-free number: 1-800-555-9876.

Miranda Grimaldi

COMMENTS:

From ScoobyDo: I'm praying for those parents.

From MyraP: Are you kidding?

From Rock'nRollForever: What are you, a lousy atheist! You're going straight to hell!

From MyraP: After you, sweetheart!

From FrankL: Stop it! More important to try to catch this killer, people!

From ZumbaLady: Damn straight!

UPDATE: The body of Melissa Parsons was found near her home last night.

CHAPTER 92

Of course, that was not the end of it. I should have known, Gretchen thought bitterly. Andy was not about to let go without a struggle. She was so sure that she could handle him, unpleasant though the conversations had become.

That was until their conversation that morning, after Norman drove off to work.

When Andy called, he sounded strange, she thought. "Doll, how's that husband of yours? What a shame about his car accident." He laughed, a high-pitched, disturbing laugh.

Stunned for a moment, she finally said, "How did you know about the accident? It wasn't in the papers."

He giggled. "Who says it was an accident?"

She gulped. Quick, she thought, you have to stop him, or get blamed for it. You know how it is. The spouse is always the logical suspect, especially with all that money to be had if he died. This was my fault. How many times have I told Andy that I wished Norman was dead? If I was not accused of murder, I could be stuck with Andy forever. If I tried to get rid of him, he could blackmail me, bleed me dry. She gritted her teeth. This is not going to happen, with all the effort I put into my marriage, all the boring, mind-numbing years I endured. You have to talk him out of it right now, sister.

"Andy, love, I know you don't want to hurt anyone, even Norman. Please, I'll be the first one they suspect. You don't want to see me in prison, do you?"

He let out that creepy laugh again. "Who says I don't? I got nothin' without you, anyways."

"You know you've always got me, sweetheart. I think about you all the time. Just try to be patient for a while, please, for me? You'll have me back in your arms in no time."

He giggled. "You'll be back in my bed, right?"

Gretchen let out her breath. "Yes, sweetheart, I'll be right back in your bed."

"That's where you belong, with me."

She said goodbye and clicked off, trembling.

CHAPTER 93

"I've got a plan," Gretchen told Andy.

She could never trust him not to do something stupid about Norman, something that would get the cops onto both of them, especially since he already tried once, with Norman's car, goddamn it. Not only was Andy dumb as a rock, but reckless as well. Who knew what he might do next? She had to head him off. If she did the thinking for both of them, it could all work itself out in the end – for her, that was. She grinned. That would be two birds with one stone: a rich, boring husband, and a poor, stupid-as-dirt boyfriend. All that money would be just for me.

"What's the plan, doll?" Andy was practically breathing in her face. They were sitting in his car in a supermarket parking lot.

"We do it on a Saturday night, preferably one that's rainy or cloudy or both. I tell Norman that I'm feeling romantic, that I'd love to go 'parking' with him the way we used to when we were dating."

Andy grunted and made a face.

"I tell him to drive to that dead-end lover's lane we used to go to and that I'll meet him there later. With a big surprise." She smiled at Andy. "The big surprise is you." How clever I am, she thought.

Andy giggled. "Then, boy, does he get surprised! Bye-bye, Norman."

This was perfect. He was practically salivating at the idea, the moron.

He kissed her and grabbed at her nearest breast. "Don't you worry about a thing, doll. I'll take good care of you."

You bet your well-toned butt you will, she thought.

CHAPTER 94

Who Killed Who?

The blog for those with an inquisitive nose ... for murder and mayhem

WOODSTOCK, NY: Dara Williams, age 17, of Woodstock, was last seen on her way home from high school basketball practice two days ago. Dara is white and has short, straight, blonde hair. She was wearing a red jacket, blue jeans, and red-and-white sneakers.

If you have any information or idea about what happened to Dara, please call the toll-free number: 1-800-555-5666.

Miranda Grimaldi

UPDATE: Dara Williams was found in a wooded area near her home.

COMMENTS:

ModelT: We've got to organize! More petitions, protests, sit-ins in Albany.

MarcyH: Right!

ModelT: Meet in front of the governor's office this Saturday, 2 pm, everybody.

FashionistaG: Yes!

ChrisL: Yes!

LisaE: I'll be there!

CHAPTER 95

I was standing outside The Pub, a popular bar and grill in Woodstock, wondering if I should turn tail and head back home. A fix-up date was something I vowed never to do. I had quite enough of scary dates with Barry, thank you. Just thinking about that last night with him and that horrible snake made me shudder. I was still wary about the possibility that he could come after me again, so why did I need any more problems?

"I'd rather have my wisdom teeth pulled," I said to Robin the week before, after takeout drinks (coffee for her, cappuccino for me) at her place.

Robin was in her best cajoling mood, finding all sorts of reasons why I should meet her husband, Mike's, friend, Elliott Fisher.

"You two have so much in common," she said, sipping her coffee. "He's always reading, and he loves mysteries, especially ones that take place in England. He goes to classical music concerts. Besides that, when's the last time you had a relationship?"

If she only knew. Well, maybe what I was doing, including with Barry, would not exactly count as a relationship, but I definitely did not need a serious involvement with a guy, any guy. That would mean I would have to trust him. He would get to know the real me, whoever that was. I was so busy trying to dodge flying attacks from my mother when I was growing up, I never had a chance to figure out who I was.

I ignored her last comment about my relationships and sipped my cappuccino. I needed a new relationship the way I needed an extra head. "Mike said he was a computer geek. I don't speak geek, so why is he for me?"

She smiled. "That's just his day job. At night, he's working on a novel."

In spite of myself, this piqued my interest. It would be a nice change to meet somebody who actually liked to read, and write, too. Presumably, he was able to use actual words, instead of grunts or words that did not relate to football, hockey, or basketball.

"Okay, okay, I surrender," I told her. "Wait, what does he look like? Is he cute?"

"He's adorable," she said.

I tried to shake off my doubts and headed into the restaurant. There they were, at a table for four. I stole a look at my date. Robin was right. He was definitely adorable: curly red hair, reddish mustache, wire-framed glasses. I almost giggled as the thought came into my head – what if his hair was red all over? Save that for later, Phil. He was not handsome, but he looked intelligent and sensitive, and unless he had tiny legs, he was tall.

I smiled and walked over to the table. Elliott gave me a warm smile back.

CHAPTER 96

Elliott's teenaged mother abandoned him when he was a baby. He told me the horror story that had been his childhood in the group home.

"They'd lock me in the cellar if they thought I did something wrong. It was dark and scary. I could hear rustling near the walls, sure it was rats." As he told me all this, he was trembling violently.

"That's terrible. I'm so sorry you went through this," I soothed.

He was still shaking. "I was terrified of rats, of any kind of animal, actually. They snuck up on you and weren't to be trusted. They could attack you in your sleep, with their teeth and claws."

The other kids in the group home tormented him, he said: "Scaredy-cat El-li-ott, afraid of spiders, afraid of rats, afraid of worms." They shoved a spider or a worm onto his shirt and laugh when he screamed and wet his pants. Then they told the couple who ran the group home, who would shame him and lock him in the cellar. Even Tommy, another boy the other kids made fun of, the boy he thought was his friend, eventually joined in Elliott's torture and humiliation.

"What that taught me was that you couldn't trust anyone. Anyone could pretend to be your friend and then become your enemy. I promised myself I wouldn't let anybody get close to me again." He sighed. "I hope it'll be different with you."

I gave him a hug.

CHAPTER 97

From the beginning of our relationship, Elliott had always been very secretive about his novel-in-progress, which irked me no end. You know me, I had to know everything, otherwise, I got very anxious. An anxious me was not much fun to be around.

That was what I told him later on. First, I said, "Sweetie, what are you writing about? Is it fish or fowl, animal, vegetable, or mineral?"

Elliott smiled at me from the chair at his desk. "I can't tell you yet."

I crept up behind him and ran my fingers around the back of his neck, tousled his hair and even stuck my tongue in his left ear.

He stood up, grabbed me, and led me to his bed, which was fine. However, that was not exactly what I had in mind.

"Elliott," I said, afterward, "come on, can't you tell me? Pleeeze?" I ran my fingers down his chest, which was remarkably hairy for a redhead. They were curly, red-gold hairs, the same all over.

He gave me a hug. "I'll tell you in due time."

"Due time?"

He rolled over and got up and started getting dressed. "Yup. Now let's get a pizza, okay? I'm starving."

That was the end of that, until he stopped working on his novel, at least while we were together. I asked him why, not that I minded. I found it flattering that he wanted my company so much.

"It's because, darling, I want to be with you whenever we're together. When we're not, all I do is think about you." He made a rueful face and wagged his finger at me. "You, my dear, are bad for my writing."

"Oh," I said, "I don't want to be the cause of not-writing," I said. "Your work is important, and you shouldn't let anything, even me, get in the way." I laughed.

His answer was to cover me with kisses.

That was the way it went until I began getting swamped with deadlines for articles from several magazines. This, of course, was a good thing for a freelancer. What made things even more crazy, at the same time, the cases on the blog were heating up.

Elliott got impatient. He watched me scribble notes on a legal pad, looking sheepish. I tried to placate him whenever I could.

"Phil," he'd say from the other side of the sofa (mine or his, it did not matter), "our relationship is the most important thing in my life. I don't know what I'd do without you, and I'm afraid you don't care."

"Of course I care," I said, soothingly, "but I have to meet my deadlines, and the blog means a lot to me." I felt I had a calling, a mission to help find out what happened to the missing and the victims of violence. I tried explaining it to Elliott.

"Sweetie," I said, sliding over to give him a hug, "you know I can't help the deadlines. That's the price of being a freelancer. If you don't make the deadline, you're dead." I tried to laugh, but when I saw his expression, I stopped.

He was glaring at me. "Okay, I know about deadlines, but the blog? C'mon, you can't be serious about that. It's just a hobby, right? All this murder and mayhem stuff sounds like kid stuff to me."

I stiffened. "It's not a hobby, and it's not kid stuff. It's very serious. We're talking about missing young women, murdered people. It's very important."

He sighed. "Okay, okay, but why you? Who appointed you Batwoman, Superwoman, a crime-fighter, whoever? What's more important, our relationship or chasing criminals?"

It was my turn to sigh. "I care about our relationship, of course, but I care about what I'm doing, too. After all," I said, "you have your writing, about whatever." I gave him a sly grin, hoping a little humor would help his mood. "What *is* it about, anyway?" I tried changing the subject, not to mention that besides that, my curiosity was killing me. (Do not use that word, Phil.)

He shrugged. "It hasn't been going well, which is one reason I stopped working on it. The other, of course, is our relationship." He gave me a pointed look.

I squeezed his arm. "I know, dear." I smiled sweetly at him, "What's your book about? It *is* a book, right?"

"It's a mystery novel, actually, a mystery within a mystery." He sat back against the sofa pillow and closed his eyes.

"Oh, that sounds intriguing. Tell me more." I snuggled against him.

He sat up and shook his head. "You might get upset."

I laughed. "Don't be silly. Tell me, please."

He looked down at his lap. "Uh, it involves a man, a writer, who writes a mystery after his fiancée leaves him, for no good reason. So, he writes a mystery, plotting it out."

"Whew! Then what happens?"

"He, uh, kills her." Elliott was looking at me oddly, as if he were not actually seeing me.

Something cold crawled down my spine.

CHAPTER 98

On my way to my therapist's the next day, I told myself I was being silly, which is what I said to Gwen.

"Why do you think you're being silly to worry?" Gwen balanced her notebook on her lap as she took a sip of tea. Today she made a pot of Darjeeling for us.

"Well," I scrunched down in the soft fabric chair, "after all, this was Elliott. It was a novel, fiction, not real."

She looked up from her notes. "It couldn't be real, you're saying?"

I sat up and took a sip of tea. "I mean, even though I guess I'm narcissistic enough to think everything is about me," I grinned, "sometimes, it's just not. Sometimes, a novel is just a novel, like a cigar is just a cigar."

"What happened after he told you about the novel?" Gwen tapped her pen on her notebook.

"Well, we didn't talk about it again. Since he said he stopped working on it, what was there to worry about?"

She frowned again. "So, why do you think you had that scary feeling?"

I looked down at my lap. "Uh, I don't know. Maybe you can tell me."

She shook her head. "That's not the way we work, Phil. I can try to help you, but in the end, you're the one who needs to figure it out."

"Do you think I should worry? After all, this is Elliott, who loves me, who can't live without me, he says. He's so intense." I made a face.

Gwen regarded me thoughtfully. "The intensity sounds like it's making you uncomfortable."

"Uh, I guess so." I took another sip of tea. "Sometimes it seems sort of overwhelming. I mean, it's kinda nice being someone's be-all and end-all, but ..."

"But sometimes it can seem a bit too much?"

"There are times that I feel I'm being, I don't know, maybe, smothered," I whispered. "That's kind of silly, right?"

CHAPTER 99

Elliott and I spent time with each other whenever we could. He was a computer consultant at a local community college, and his schedule was fairly flexible. His technical expertise meant he was also in demand as a troubleshooter at a number of colleges, hospitals, and other non-profits. His actual love, though, he said, besides me, was poetry. We spent hours reading poetry by Emily Dickinson, Edna St. Vincent Millay, Elizabeth Browning, and others. A man after my own heart, he would lie down on my sofa, with his head in my lap. I ran my fingers through his thick red curls while we took turns reading aloud to each other.

The first time we made love (love, not just sex) at my cottage, I felt something inside of me burst open. I did not feel closed up, locked up, anymore. I loved him without reservation. He made it easy.

"I want to be with you always," he said, pulling me close in bed, my bed. He was the first guy I let into my sanctuary. "I need you."

I was happy to be needed, to take care of him and have him take care of me. It felt more than good. My life had meaning. For a while, everything went swimmingly. I was loved, cherished, appreciated. What more could I want?

He told me he wanted all of me, every last bit. To prove it, he said, he was going to do something he thought I never experienced before, and he was right.

That night, monthly bad cramps and a particularly messy period had left me curled up practically in a fetal position on the bed. He crawled in beside me.

"Careful," I said, "it's pretty yucky down there."

He grinned. "Not for me." He started licking my toes, moving up my legs, ignoring the blood, and plunging right into it all, lapping away, draining my fluids.

When he lifted his head, his face was a gruesome sight. Even his teeth were stained with blood, my blood. It felt invasive, even creepy. I wondered if he had a blood fixation. I heard of such barbaric practices, almost resembling human sacrifice. With all that blood being swilled down, I was repulsed.

Cuddling next to me, he said, "I want to drink in every bit of you." He grinned, showing his bloody teeth.

I tried not to shudder, but being so observant and sensitive, he caught it. "Look what I did for you. Isn't that proof of how much I love you?" He was teary-eyed and his face looked so sad. I felt terrible for hurting his feelings. After all, he was only trying to please me.

I hugged him and told him I was just a little overwhelmed, that was all, but it was not true. I realized he was very needy, needed me so much, it was overwhelming. I was not sure I was up to that, up to being what he wanted me to be: his all, his everything. He said that his life depended on me.

His clingy ways began to grate on me. When I was working on a story, or the blog, trying to concentrate, he sat on the sofa and pouted.

"Hey, c'mere, I miss you," he'd say.

I laughed it off. "How can you miss me when I'm right here?"

"Can't you leave it alone for a while? You've been at it for hours."

"Sweetie, just let me finish up this section," I said, smiling at him, trying not to grit my teeth. "Remember, when you were working on your novel, I didn't interfere."

"After we got close, I gave up working on it when I was with you. It was worth it, I thought." He was sulking.

Sulking was not something I wanted to put up with in a relationship. To me, it was a mark of immaturity, but I bit my tongue and hoped it was just a momentary lapse.

The little cottage I rented in the country had always been my salvation for peace and comfort. When Elliott insisted on staying there on weekends, instead of at his place, it was no longer a refuge. He wanted all my attention, all the time. There was no getting away from him and I needed breathing room. I began feeling trapped.

What finally did the whole thing in was when he started talking about us having a family. I never told him about the botched abortion, the raging infection afterwards that almost killed me, and the hysterectomy. Then there were the one-night stands in New York, and my dom/sub relationship with Barry. I thought I could keep some parts of my life to myself. I let him think I was too busy hustling for work to do much sleeping around. In his fantasies, he probably thought I was pretty naïve, just waiting for him to come around and enlighten me. I managed to keep up with the pretense, acting thrilled to learn new things about lovemaking from him.

Finally, I told him I thought we needed a break from each other. Things were getting too serious too fast, I said. "I love you madly, but I think I need a little time for myself. I'm not ready yet for a real commitment, and that's not fair to you." I gave him a big hug. "Okay? It's just me. It's got nothing to do with you, okay?"

He pulled away so hard, I almost fell backward. "No, it's not okay, not okay, no."

The look in his eyes frightened me. It was dark, angry, not-quite sane. "You know I can't live without you. You know that." He started toward me.

CHAPTER 100

I finally managed to calm Elliott down for the moment by pretending to faint.

He caught me as I was falling to the floor and picked me up, cradling me against his chest, depositing me on my sofa. All the while he was mumbling, "I didn't mean to frighten you, please, darling, believe me."

I could feel his tears dripping down on my face. Ugh, the man was crazy. I wanted him out of my life now, but what was the best way to do it? I did not want to sweet-talk him. That would only start the whole thing up again. Think, Phil. I had it – my gun. It was in the bedroom, in my nightstand. If I could just get past him, I could run and get it.

Maybe I can try something else. All right, Philomena, get tough, Wonder Woman or whoever, here I come. I bolted up from the sofa, murder in my eyes, teeth flashing, looking as if I could bite him or shoot him. I actually thought I could if necessary. I could see him backing away from me. This was a whole new me, one that he never saw or heard.

"Elliott," I spoke slowly and distinctly, "If you don't stop this behavior, I'll get my gun. I'll use it on you if I have to."

He looked befuddled. "Wha –? Why are you acting like this?" He actually got down on his knees. "You know I didn't mean it, darling. You know that." He started crying.

I dug into my jeans pocket for a handkerchief and handed it to him. "Blow your nose and leave right now." I folded my arms on my chest and glared at him, hoping I looked fierce.

He scuttled out the door. I was quite proud of myself. Wait till I tell my therapist about my newfound guts.

A little voice in my head said this was not the end of it.

CHAPTER 101

No big surprise, Elliott would not, or could not, accept my feelings about our relationship. He called and texted constantly. When I tried, gently at first, to make him understand how I felt, it only made him angry, crazy-angry. Then he started showing up at my door. When I saw him outside, I tried ignoring him, to no avail. Finally, the noise was ruining my concentration, my work, and attracting the attention of my neighbors.

I made the mistake of letting him in, thinking I could reason with him, that it would make him stop. First, I got my gun and shoved it in my jeans pocket.

I felt bad for him. He was so pathetic. Unfortunately, letting him in encouraged him. "We can work things out. I know it. Just give us another chance. You know we love each other. We're soul mates." His eyes got weepy, and his mouth trembled. We were sitting on the sofa in my living room.

I took a deep breath. Try again, Phil, you have to make him understand. "Elliott, I care for you very much." Well, one small part of me still did. "At this point in my life, I can't be in an intense relationship, and I know that's what you want." I smiled at him. "We can still be friends, good friends, just not in that kind of relationship."

His face turned ugly, and he looked insane. "You, you think you can just push me out of your life, just like that?" He tried to grab me, whether to embrace me or attack me. Who knows? Whichever it was, it was not welcome.

I moved away from him and stood up, hoping he got the point and would leave. "I'm sorry. I just can't do this anymore. Please, I need you to leave now."

He just stood there, furiously shaking his head. "I'm not leaving."

Should I cajole or threaten? So far, nothing seemed to make a dent. Try again, Phil. You have to make him understand, somehow. Threatening him with a gun is not a great solution. "Listen to me, sweetheart." I tried not to grind my teeth. "I'm not talking about breaking up for good. I just need some time for myself, that's all. You're the first guy I've been with in such a meaningful, intense relationship, and it's a little overwhelming for me, that's all." I gave him my best smile.

He looked a little less angry. I let out my breath and bent down to give him a kiss.

Finally, he got to his feet and nearly crushed me in a hug that almost made me fall. God, I had no idea how strong he was. He was always so gentle with me. I better not poke the bear.

He let me go and pulled my face up toward his. "All right, because I love you so much, I'll give you your space, for now," he said as he went out the door.

CHAPTER 102

Who Killed Who?

The blog for those with an inquisitive nose ... for murder and mayhem

PHOENICIA, NY: Brianna Cole, age 18, of Phoenicia, went missing two days ago on her way home from basketball practice at high school. Brianna is white and her hair is in a blonde braid. She was wearing a pink-and-white jacket, pink jeans, and white sneakers.

If you have any information about Brianna, please call the toll-free number: 1-800-654-1234.

Miranda Grimaldi

COMMENTS:

From TracyR: I've been checking out my old neighborhood where that creepy guy used to live. Don't worry, I didn't go alone. I took my brother-in-law, an ex-soldier. Anyway, some people there remembered him. There was a fire in the house that killed his mother and some people think he did it.

From WallyM: Wow, TracyR! You did good!

From MarciaN: You're very brave, TracyR! Good on you!

From JohnnyY: So, what happened?

TracyR: Well, the last that people heard, he was in a group home for troubled kids, and he was adopted. Then he got killed in a burning car crash.

HarryG: Maybe he didn't. Maybe it's been him all along. He sounds crazy enough.

UPDATE: Brianna Cole's body was found last night near her high school.

CHAPTER 103

Sam Michaels, Jack's new P.I. associate, and I were on our way to New York City. Our mission was to catch a couple of sleazy lawyers in the baby-selling business, my latest assignment from Lourdes. We would pretend to be a hopeful adoptive couple, with plenty of money and desperation. Lily and Jack would be another pretend adoptive pair.

I was wearing a skirt and blouse for the first time in, who knows how long, with a strand of fake pearls, no less. I wore real shoes, instead of my regulation sneakers. (The advantage of working at home: undressing for success?) Sam, my supposed husband, ditched his jeans and flannel shirt for a jacket and tie and a nice pair of pants.

Even though he was always nice to me, I was a little nervous around Sam. It did not hurt, though, that he was a real hottie: tall, with dark brown eyes and hair, and an engaging smile. I was probably skittish because of Lily's reaction after she met him at Jack's office a couple of weeks ago.

I called Lily to make sure we were coordinated about our roles at the adoption agency. She started talking about Sam again. "Phil, I don't know, but there's something bothering me about Sam," she said. "I caught him going through files when Jack was out of the office. He looked embarrassed when he saw me. I don't want to say anything to Jack because it's just a feeling I have."

My nerves got even worse. "Uh, Lily, your feelings are usually spot on, though he *is* cute, and sexy. Why do you think you've got that feeling?"

She paused a moment. "I'm not sure."

"What d'you know about him? What's Jack told you?" I asked.

"Jack says he grew up in the Catskills, traveled around a lot, gets restless if he's in one place too long. Evidently, he had a tough life: a poor family, no father around. I suppose that could account for his strange manner." Then she said, "I know you have to work with him on the adoption case, but just be careful, okay?"

"Okay, but I'm not planning to marry him, even if we *are* going to adopt a baby. Gotta go, now, Sam's waiting for me."

Sam took my hand and flashed me a smile. (He had great teeth.) A tingle went straight up my arm. Please do not let me blush, I thought. We were shown into one of the lawyers' offices by a busty red-haired secretary. Were they even real lawyers?

"Come in, come in," the lawyer called. The name on the door said Robert Watson, Attorney-at-Law.

Watson had combed-over strands of graying hair, a thick neck, and fat cheeks. He beamed and shook our hands. His hand was moist and clammy, ick. I tried to wipe mine surreptitiously on my skirt as he motioned us to an enormous black leather sofa, surrounded by an Oriental rug that looked genuine. Watson took one of the black leather chairs opposite us. All was cozy and non-threatening, I thought, setting the trap nicely.

"Coffee, tea, or something a little stronger?" He winked.

"Tea would be great," I said, turning to Sam, who asked for coffee. We sat on the edge of our seats, looking eager and trusting, I hoped, with the right amount of nervousness for a prospective adoptive couple.

Besides the profusion of black leather, there was lots of glass in the room: a glass coffee table, a glass-topped desk, a huge mirror on one wall. The better to check out his comb-over? On another wall there were a couple of awful department store prints, big-eyed animals looking pathetic.

Watson opened a file and cleared his throat. "Well, Mr. and Ms., uh ..."

"Sally and Tim Morton," I said, with a smile.

"Mr. and Ms. Morton," Watson said. "I understand that you're interested in adoption."

"Yes," Sam said.

"Definitely," I added, "We've been, uh, trying for quite a while now." I shook my head.

"I understand," Watson purred, "but you want a child to complete your family."

Sam and I nodded.

Watson rubbed his hammy hands together. "There's a little girl, six months old. She's healthy and has had all her shots." He removed a photo from the file and pushed it across the desk.

"Ohhh," I crooned, hoping I sounded heartfelt, which wasn't hard to do about this gorgeous Asian baby. "She's adorable and so sweet. Look, Tim." After he made appropriate sounds, I said, "Why is her mother giving her up?"

Watson looked sorrowful. "It's a very sad situation. The father deserted the mother, and she just can't manage. She's only 15."

"How awful for her," I said, trying to look sad.

Watson said, "Yes, and she wants to see her baby in a good, stable home."

Sam smiled. "I think we can do that."

I nodded. Jack had a lawyer friend dummy up the necessary papers for us: fake IDs, credit reports, bank statements. We sent them to Watson ahead of our appointment.

Watson opened another file. "Hmm, yes, I see, good, good." He looked up. "You people are certainly financially secure. This brings me to another item. The poor mother, she's desperate." He shook his head. "Her family threw her out. She doesn't have a job, so she must have enough money to go on."

"Of course, I understand." Sam's voice was full of compassion.

Watson closed the file and beamed again. "That's good. She'll be needing about $60,000." He paused.

Sam and I looked at each other. I bit my lip, trying to look as if I did not expect it to be that much money.

"Of course, you don't have to decide right now," he said smoothly. "I must tell you, there is another couple who've expressed a lot of interest in the little girl." He flashed a sly grin.

I knew exactly who that couple was: Lily and Jack, playing the same game. Jack would be wearing the same kind of wire as Sam. We rehearsed it all several times.

"Oh," I said, "we don't want to lose out."

"No," Sam said, shaking his head. "When do you need to know?"

There was another grin. "I'd say as soon as possible." He leaned across his desk. "The other couple is very, very interested, so, I'd say, as soon as possible."

Sam stood up. "We appreciate you giving us a heads-up." He turned to me. "We'll get on it as soon as we can. C'mon, hon, let's go home and talk things over."

I got up to leave. "I'm sure we can work it out very quickly."

Watson rubbed his hands together again. "Good, good, give me a call as soon as you can."

"There's just one thing. We want to see the baby before we decide," I said firmly. "Right, Tim?" I knew Lily and Jack would be making the same request.

"Definitely," Sam said.

Watson looked irritated. "Well, I'll get in touch with the mother. There shouldn't be any problem, any problem at all. I'll get in touch with her right away and let you know when."

"I can hardly wait," I gushed, "a baby girl."

Sam gave me a hug. I felt like hugging him back, but I made myself stop. Be careful, Phil, I told myself, this man is practically a stranger. Who knows who he is? He could even be the killer.

"We'll be a real family," Sam said.

Watson beamed. "You two will be perfect parents, I'm sure."

CHAPTER 104

Who Killed Who?

The blog for those with an inquisitive nose ... for murder and mayhem

KINGSTON, NY: Brianna Cole, age 19, was last seen on her way home from her job at Adams Fairacre Farms two days ago. Brianna is white and has curly blonde hair. She was wearing a black jacket, black jeans, and black-and-white sneakers.

If you have any information or idea about what happened to Brianna, please call the toll-free number: 1-800-555-5666.

Miranda Grimaldi

UPDATE:

Brianna Cole's body was found behind a row of trees on the grounds of Adams Farms.

COMMENTS:

From MiraH: My daughter works there. I'll check with her to see if she saw anything.

From HeleneG: My son works there, too. I'll see if he knows anything.

From VincentO: I know the store. I'll check around.

From TerryP: That all sounds good, guys.

From Miranda Grimaldi: Good luck and be careful out there.

CHAPTER 105

When I got home, I saw a message on my cell from my illustrious Uncle Lucius. Ugh, well, I better call him back.

He answered on the first ring. Jeez, the old bastard must have been waiting with bated breath. "It's Philomena, Uncle Lucius, returning your call."

"Ah, yes, how are you, my dear?" Oozing, unctuous tones.

"I'm well, Uncle. I hope you are, too."

"Yes, I'm fine, thank you, fine."

I waited. I heard breathing and throat-clearing. Boy, this must be good.

Finally, he said, "I called you, my dear" – every time he called me that I wanted to hurl – "to, ah, discuss a financial matter."

What a big surprise. "Oh?"

"You see, your Aunt Martha and I have been trying very hard to make you feel included in our family. After all, you are an Abbott, even if only by half." He gave a small chuckle.

Is this a joke? "Okay."

"So, your aunt and I have decided, very generously, I believe, to offer you a financial interest in Clarence's estate."

Wow, was I wrong about them, after all? "That's great, Uncle Lucius. I appreciate it." I did not have to fake the warmth in my voice.

"I'm glad. We're happy to do our part to look out for your welfare."

Okay, cut to the chase, uncle dear. I was afraid that I said the words aloud. "Uh, could I ask what my, uh, financial interest would amount to?"

There was more throat clearing and a cough. "Ah, that would come to, ah, about $10,000, I believe. That is a very generous amount, considering."

"You're kidding, right?" This I said aloud. The lawyer had told me that the estate was worth several million., and a third of that ...

He sounded positively injured. "My dear, I'm shocked at your tone. Your aunt and I ..."

"Are trying to screw me royally. Goodbye, Uncle Lucius."

I clicked off, steaming.

CHAPTER 106

All his hard work had paid off. He was able to track that damn psychic down, even though his research had gotten off-track at times. His brain seemed to fog up now and then. Sometimes he thought he saw things, heard things, that could not possibly be there.

He staked out the path at the edge of the woods, where he laid his latest angel to rest; Brianna Cole, softly curly blonde hair, fair skin, delicate features. He sighed, remembering his delight in her. Now she was preserved in virtue for all eternity.

Wearing a Forest Ranger outfit that he purchased online, he stocked up on snacks and water, grabbed a flashlight and parked his car far from the scene. Then he hid in plain sight. He chuckled. In plain sight! He read up on a forester's duties, so he looked as if he was hard at work. He chuckled again. Smokey the Bear was at your service, folks.

Black clouds were threatening, and he felt a few drops that soon turned into a downpour. Trying to find shelter, he hunkered down in a clump of trees and dozed for a bit, snapping alert whenever he heard movement. Usually, it turned out to be a deer or another animal, browsing for food. When he heard yelling and gunshots, he bolted up. A couple of hunters, maybe poachers, had bagged some kind of animal. These were terrible people, he thought. Why would you do that to a defenseless animal? He shook his head.

He knew it would have to be a couple of days before they sent out a search party and notified the papers and that damned psychic. A long time seemed to pass, but there they were, at last: the cops, somebody taking photos, another person who must be the medical examiner, and someone else, a young woman. That must be the psychic! He practically jumped up and down before he remembered to be quiet, seemingly absorbed in his task of checking for dead trees. Only YOU can prevent forest fires! He carefully took note of the woman's appearance – red hair, generous mouth, sturdy figure, probably about 25.

Then he thought, of course! The psychic must be from that family of witches or Wiccans or whatever they were. Everybody in the neighborhood was afraid of them. We all called their house the haunted house. That was the house with a big tree in the front yard and underneath, that sweet little dolly was reading a book. How lovely she was. He remembered feeling lucky that the only witness when he took her was the little sister. She was probably about 11 or 12. I bet that was her, that psychic bitch, that he was going to take care of right now. Then she can practice her black arts in hell, not on him. He grinned.

When the group was thinning out, he got ready to move. The psychic bitch was the only one still there, sniffing, staring, making notes in a book, not even having enough sense to get out of the rain. You just think you are safe, but not from me, he thought. I will get you, my pretty. She would not be one of his angels. Oh, no. He would dump her in a landfill, maybe in a dumpster, a garbage heap, where she belonged.

He watched as she went back to her car and started to drive off. He wrote down the license plate, color, make, and model. As soon as she was gone, he scurried back to his own car and took off after her.

CHAPTER 107

A man in a car was following her. Lily was sure of that. Every time she tried to steer away from him, he crept closer and closer. She tried speeding up, though she was nervous about doing that in the rain. As she sped up, so did he. Then she felt a grinding, a thump, and another thump. He was trying to force her off the road.

She tried to see who it was, but his face was hidden by large sunglasses and the visor on his cap. Then there was the rain. Never mind that, she thought. Just try to control your car, grab your cell, and call 911.

Lily was dripping with sweat. They were coming to a sharp curve, and the road was flooded. She tried slowing down, but it did not work. Suddenly, there was a huge crash. Her little car went tumbling down the hill, turning over and over before it shuddered to a stop.

CHAPTER 108

He started down the hill, sliding in the mud. He needed to make sure she was dead. When he heard the wailing sirens, he scrambled back up to the top, racing to his car.

Driving off in the opposite direction from the approaching emergency vehicles, he let out his breath. That was a close one, he muttered. Then he chuckled – close but no cigar, ha, ha.

Even if she was not dead, she would probably be seriously injured and laid up for quite a while.

CHAPTER 109

Who Killed Who?

The blog for those with an inquisitive nose ... for murder and mayhem

YORKTOWN HEIGHTS, NY: Sara Denton, age 17, of Yorktown Heights, went missing two days ago. Sara is white, with curly blonde hair. She was last seen coming home from gymnastics practice with her friend, Alexandra Neiman. According to Alexandra, Sara said she heard a kitten mewing before she disappeared.

If you have any information about what happened to Sara Denton, please call the toll-free number: 1-800-555-4559.

Miranda Grimaldi

COMMENTS:

From Babyface: That's it. I'm organizing a sit-in at the Westchester DA's office on Monday, 2 pm. Who's with me?

From SusanP: Yes!

From Goodwitch: Yes!

From CharlieT: Yes!

From HallieN: Yes!

From IloveParis: Yes!

From Miranda Grimaldi: Great!

CHAPTER 110

When Lily finally woke up, her first view was of her left leg lifted high in the air, in traction. She looked down at her arms. They were covered in bruises, and one was connected to an IV. Monitors blinked at the side of the bed.

There was pain, horrible pain, in every part of her body. When she tried to move her head, she almost fainted.

She heard footsteps outside the room, and a nurse came in. "Wonderful, you're awake! That's great! Everyone will be so glad."

All Lily could do was moan. Finally, she was able to get out, "Where am I? What happened?"

The nurse, a plump blonde, whose name tag said Peggy, smiled at her. "You're in Kingston Hospital. You were in a terrible car accident. It was nothing short of a miracle that the EMS reached you when they did. Otherwise …" She shook her head. "They had to use the Jaws of Life to get you out of that car."

Lily tried to take it all in. "I … I don't remember. I don't remember what happened."

"Don't worry, it'll all come back. Just try to relax. Can I get you anything?"

"Something for the pain, please."

"Of course." Peggy left the room.

The exertion of talking left Lily exhausted, but she had to think, think about what happened to her. She closed her eyes, and a vision swam into her consciousness. She was in her car on a highway, being followed by someone in a car. It was tan, or beige, medium-sized, a few years old. She could not see the driver's face, because of the oversized sunglasses and the visor of his cap, pulled down low on his forehead.

Fortunately, she had the presence of mind to call 911, which probably saved her life, she realized. The man in the car had been pushing, shoving, bashing her car, over and over. Then came the sickening crash, her car rolling down a hill, with her upside down, sideways. Then, it was dead silence.

She opened her eyes when she heard Peggy return with her medication. "Thanks," she whispered, as she swallowed it with a cup of water. "Uh, there's some people I need to …"

"They've been waiting in the lobby, very worried, especially one young man." The nurse said, with a wink. "I'll let them know you're awake."

"Thanks." As soon as Peggy left, Lily tried to gather some strength. Jack must be frantic, she thought, and Phil, too.

Jack and I burst into the room, throwing kisses, carrying armfuls of flowers, magazines, and candy. He sat down on the edge of the bed, and I grabbed a chair. "We were so …" Jack and I both started. Then we laughed with relief.

"Worried," Lily said, trying to smile.

"You could've been …" Jack looked near tears.

I burst out, "Whoever did this to you is going to pay, big time."

Jack patted Lily's leg, the one that was not hurt. "I know the cops are already on it."

"We're going to do our part, believe me. As soon as you're up to it, we'll strategize, okay?" I said.

"Thanks, guys. Just seeing you made me feel better." Her eyes started to close.

The nurse came in. "It's the painkillers," she whispered. "She'll be out like a light. You can come back during the next visiting hours, okay?"

CHAPTER 111

Jack drove Lily home when she was released from the hospital. He tucked her up on her sofa, made a fire in the fireplace, and I brewed a pitcher of herbal tea. After making sure she was as comfortable as she could be – battered, bruised, and in a lot of pain – he left so she could get some rest. I went up to the attic so as not to disturb her.

Lily tried to rest. She pulled up a quilt around her knees and took a few sips of tea. Slowly, she started to wind down. She could feel her breathing deepen and her eyelids drooping.

Halfway asleep, she began to think that maybe the driver, whoever it was, was the killer. After all, she had been helping the cops and Phil find murderers for years. Though the cops had been careful not to divulge her name, maybe the killer found out, somehow. I have to try to visualize that driver, she thought drowsily.

If it was the killer, that could be the reason why he was after both of them, her and Phil. I need to talk to Phil, she thought, before she drifted off to sleep.

CHAPTER 112

Who Killed Who?

The blog for those with an inquisitive nose ... for murder and mayhem

CLARYVILLE, NY: Bethany Chambers, 19, of Claryville, went missing two days ago on the way home from her job at Jenkins' Candy Shop. Bethany is white, with short, blonde hair. She was wearing a blue blazer and black jeans.

If you have any information about Bethany, please call the toll-free number: 1-800-555-7362.

Miranda Grimaldi

COMMENTS:

From FredT: I know that family, the Chambers'. I'm going to check around the neighborhood and find out if anyone saw or heard anything.

From ComedyLady: Good idea. But I wouldn't go alone. In case he's still around.

From CassieB: Right. Be careful. You never know.

From TomW: I've been to that candy store. I'll check around that area, too.

From MargieY: You're all great. But please be careful.

From Miranda Grimaldi: Yes! Stay safe.

CHAPTER 113

I brought food back to Lily's from Nana's, a gourmet takeout shop in Woodstock: Raw broccoli salad with Craisins (Lily loved Craisins) and nuts; coconut carrot salad; and their delicious bread. I would not think of trying to concoct a meal for us. I contented myself with boiling water for herbal tea.

"This looks great, thanks, Phil," Lily helped herself to the salads and bread, with her aching leg up on a chair.

I forked up the salad, pulled off a chunk of bread, and poured us tea.

Lily put down her fork. "I wonder …"

"What?"

She frowned. "There seem to be more killings lately, right?"

"You're right." I sipped my tea, wondering what she was thinking.

"Look at the time frame. It was about the same time Sam started working with Jack."

I stared at her. "You think Sam is a horrible, vicious killer? I know you don't like him much and don't trust him, but Sam?"

She narrowed her eyes, a habit she had when she was determined about something. "I have a feeling. I trust my feeling, a lot more than I trust Sam. What do we know about him, anyway?

"Lily, come on, don't you think Jack checked him out before he hired him?"

She shrugged and picked up her cup.

I shook my head. "Listen, it could be any one of the people we know or don't know."

"Who do you think?"

I thought for a moment. "It could be one of my greedy relatives, or one of my dysfunctional ex-boyfriends."

"Why would any of them want to run *me* down?"

She had a point. I took another sip of tea. "Try this scenario: what if, say, one of the men we know, or knew in the past, is the killer? How would we know?"

"He's been doing more killings now because …"

"Because he's here," I said.

CHAPTER 114

Lying in bed, tucked up in her grandmother's quilt, Lily said, "I'm getting so tired." As if to prove the point, she opened her mouth in a big yawn. "All this medication is making me very sleepy."

"I could think of something that would wake you up ..." Jack gave her a fake leer. "Just kidding. I know you need your rest."

I went into the kitchen and put the kettle on for tea. "There's raisin bread in the freezer," Lily called from the bedroom. "Just put it in the oven till it's warm."

Lily's raisin bread was pronounced delicious, as always. Jack raised his eyes to heaven.

"Thanks, guys, for everything, but I'm falling asleep. I hate taking pills." She yawned again and then shook her head. "I think I'll take a little nap." Her eyes were already half-closed.

"Are you sure?" Jack asked, and she nodded. He kissed her gently on the top of her head. "I'll call you tomorrow."

As soon as he left, Lily's eyes popped open. "I need to talk to you."

I looked at her. "I thought you were half-asleep, you faker."

"Never mind that," she said. "I had to get Jack out of here first."

I sat down on the end of the bed. "Are you all right?"

"Yes, no, I don't know." She frowned. "Listen, I think it was Sam who drove me off the road."

I gaped at her. "You're kidding."

She shook her head. "There was something about the man in that car ... the shape of his head, maybe. It felt familiar." She paused, frowning again. "Doesn't Sam have a car that color, beige or tan or whatever? You know, he just seemed to appear out of nowhere to work with Jack. Another thing...."

"What?"

"When I tried asking him about his family, his hometown, he ducked my questions. Then he started asking questions about *you*." Lily gave me a pointed look.

"That was nice," I said. "Then again, maybe it wasn't. Maybe he was trying to find out about me for some nefarious purpose, like doing me in. Uh, what did he ask about me?"

"Oh, did you have a boyfriend? Did I think he should try to ask you out?"

"Hmm, this could either be very promising, or very creepy," I said. "So, what did you say? What did you tell him?"

Lily looked at me. "I think you want him to like you, and you don't know anything about him." She took a sip of herbal tea.

"Okay," I muttered, "maybe I do like him, but as you said, I don't know him. What did you tell him?"

"That I knew you went out, but not whether you had a real boyfriend. I certainly had no idea whether he should ask you out, okay?" She looked a little annoyed.

I said, "I'm sorry if I was bugging you. I was just, I can't help it, I think he's, uh, interesting."

Lily snorted. "Which part? The buns, the abs, or ..." She licked her lips and ducked as I tossed a napkin at her. "Anyway, after that, he's been careful not to get involved in a conversation with me."

"Wow, maybe you're right," I said slowly. "What're we going to do about it? Talk to Jack?" I poured us another cup of herbal tea.

Lily shook her head. "First, I want us to try to figure this out on our own."

"You are killing my diet." I snagged another slice. "This is just too good. Well, maybe you could try to visualize it."

She shuddered. "That means reliving the whole damn thing in my mind."

I chewed and swallowed a mouthful of deliciousness. "Don't, then, since it's so painful. We'll find another way."

After finishing her tea, Lily started to close her eyes. "No, nope, I have to do it. After all," she gave me a weak smile, "I've got this gift, I might as well put it to use."

I smiled back. "That would be very good use." Lily was nodding off, for real this time. I picked up the tea things and put them away in the kitchen, then tiptoed up to my bed in the attic.

CHAPTER 115

The next morning, I sipped my tea while I checked my phone for the local news.

"Whoa!" I said to Lily. "That guy, you know, Hardesty, who was renovating that old hotel down the road? When he came up last weekend and stopped at a rest area on Route 28, somebody broke into his car and bashed his head in."

Lily put down her cup and adjusted the pillow under her leg. "That's terrible. He's a nice man." She shook her head. "To think that they liked it here because they felt it was safe, after their apartment in the city was robbed. God, it's not safe around here. Is he dead?"

I nodded. "His wife's having a nervous breakdown. Wait a minute, a couple weeks ago, wasn't he in an accident on the Thruway that could've killed him then?" I poured us more tea.

"You're right, the brakes on his car failed. He was lucky he was able to pull over to the side somehow."

"Not so lucky now." I took a sip and thought for a minute. "Maybe the accident wasn't an accident. Maybe it was a rehearsal."

"You think?"

"We're talking about two life-and-death experiences, and this one, just death. Not a coincidence, I think," I said grimly.

CHAPTER 116

Norman was dead. At least Andy had taken care of that, but Gretchen was worried after Andy reluctantly gave her the details. It took a while, but she finally got it out of him. Now she was ready to scream, or kill him, or both.

They were in a bed in a motel room that she reserved under a false name. Of course, all Andy wanted to do was to have sex right away.

"Not till you tell me exactly what happened, lover boy," Gretchen said, trying for patience. No use getting him upset, because then he would sulk and not talk.

Andy looked away from her. This was not a good sign, she thought. "Please, tell me. I need to know where we are."

He turned back to her, scratching his chin. This was something he did when he made a mistake, like after he caused Norman's first car accident. When that did not do the job, it had made her so nervous.

"Jeez, doll, it wasn't my fault." He looked at her with puppy-dog eyes, begging her not to be angry.

She bit at a fingernail. "What wasn't your fault, baby?"

He grabbed her breast, and she gently pushed his hand away, saying, "Later, I promise," managing to eke out a smile.

"Uh, this car, it just appeared. I swear it wasn't there before." His eyes were beseeching her.

It was impossible for her to remain calm or nice. She could feel herself hyperventilating.

"Are you okay, doll? You look kind of upset," he said.

"Of course I'm upset. What do you think?" She was panting. "Did they see you? Did they see what happened?"

Andy turned away again. "I, I dunno, maybe. It was dark, you know."

"Of course I know!" Her voice climbed an octave, and she tried not to scream. She wanted to break every bone in his over-muscled body and underdeveloped brain. "Damn it to hell! Can't you do anything right?"

He cowered on the bed, as if he were trying to fend off an assault. "I'm sorry," he whispered into a pillow. "At least I got the job done for you. It wasn't easy. He put up quite a fight, for an old guy."

Gretchen was still panting, trying to slow down her breathing. Making herself crazy was not going to help. Think, Gretchen, maybe it was not so terrible. After all, there was nothing to implicate me in all this, is there? It was all on Bumble Brain. This could turn out to solve the problem of how to get rid of Andy: just let the cops do their job. Just think up a good story as to why Andy would off Norman. In the meantime, placate him, so he does not get suspicious. Lots of sex should do the trick. Well, that will not be too painful.

She reached over to Andy. "I forgive you, baby. I know you did the best you could."

He looked as if he were about to cry. "Doll, you know I'd do anything in the world for you," he said, as he started nuzzling her breast.

CHAPTER 117

Who Killed Who?

The blog for those with an inquisitive nose ... for murder and mayhem

KINGSTON, NY: Norman Hardesty, 53, of Phoenicia, CEO of Spotswood National Grocery Company, was a victim in what police believe to be a robbery/homicide. His body was discovered last night in his car in a wooded area on Route 28 in Kingston by a couple in another car. Police say that $500,000 is missing from the Hardestys' safe. Mr. Hardesty's wife, Gretchen, 35, was not injured.

A neighbor of the Hardestys said that Ms. Hardesty had been seen on several occasions in close conversations with a tall, fit-looking young man.

Miranda Grimaldi

COMMENTS:

From TracyL: Hey, the guy was rich. The wife wasn't hurt. And it sure looks like she had a lover. So ...

From LionelM: Yeah, it does smell funny. And the wife was a lot younger than the guy.

From MartyY: Ok, the wife or the boyfriend? Whodunit?

From PattyS: Could be both, right?

CHAPTER 118

After Phil left for a meeting in New York, Lily hobbled to the living room sofa. She picked up Phil's laptop, reading and re-reading the blog post about Norman Hardesty's murder. Finally, she put down the laptop and lay back on the sofa, pulling the quilt over her. Soon her eyes were closing, and her breathing became deeper.

She shuddered as she visualized Norman Hardesty's head crushed, hanging out the window of his car. Someone was hovering over the body. Holding something, but what? Who was it? Could she make out the face? Was it a man or a woman?

Lily's doorbell rang, jarring her out of the scene. "Damn," she muttered to herself.

CHAPTER 119

The people in the car had seen the murder and told the cops. Andy was frantic, but not as frantic as Gretchen, not by a long shot. That dumb schmuck, she thought. Of course he will blab, and they will get me too.

What do I do, what do I do? Think, girl, think, and calm down. Okay, first of all, it was dark, so they probably did not get a good description. Unless Andy does something else stupid, he – we – should be safe, at least for now.

After that, hopefully, no problem with the life insurance policy. Oh, wait, not so fast, not unless you want to look guilty, girl.

Andy will not want to wait for the money, for sure. She bit a bright red fingernail so hard it broke. "Damn," she said aloud, "I paid a fortune for that manicure."

Never mind that, there are more important things to think about. If I wait before I collect, stupid Andy could screw everything up. If I do not wait for a decent interval (whatever the hell that is), it could be more of a motive for murder, killing Norman for the life insurance.

Oh, God. Hey, girl, did you think this was going to be a piece of cake? Whoa, just slow down. You can do it. You always do, right? She grinned.

Think about dumb-ass Andy, Andy, the fly in the ointment. Well, flies can be swatted, and I think I have just the fly swatter.

He could have an unfortunate accident, a terrible accident. She grinned again.

CHAPTER 120

Gretchen picked up the ringing phone. "Doll, thank God you're there!"

Andy sounded hysterical. Gretchen felt her stomach lurch. She tried to calm down before she dealt with him. "Andy, what's wrong, baby?"

"You gotta get me a lawyer! I'm in jail! What'm I gonna do?"

Jeez, think, Gretchen. Calm him down. "Andy, hon, it'll be all right. They won't keep you there."

His voice rose an octave. "Doll, they got witnesses, the two from that other car! They got the license plate with their phone!"

Oh, God, I have to calm him down. "Don't worry, hon, I'll take care of everything. Where are you?"

"Ulster County Jail, in Kingston. Forgodsakes, get me a lawyer."

God, I better get there and show support, or he could start blabbing, the moron. "I'm leaving now. I'll be there as soon as I can. Just hold tight, okay? Don't tell them anything, nothing, understand?"

He was still moaning but managed to mumble, "Nothin', right."

When she got to the jail, she was horrified. Andy was a total wreck. His eyes were wild, and he was pacing back and forth in the visitor's room. When he saw her, he tried to grab her, until the guard interfered. "Doll, you gotta get me a lawyer, a good one, right away! They're talkin' life sentence!"

Jesus, he was a total mess, a gibbering, slobbering mess. What the hell did I ever see in him? Gretchen told him to sit down at a table. She sat across from him and took his hands. "Don't worry, sweetie. I'll take care of everything. Just leave it to me, okay?" She looked into his eyes. "You've got to get hold of yourself, otherwise…." She shook her head.

"I can't spend the rest of my life in prison!" He was banging his fists on the table.

"No, no, of course not, don't say that," she soothed. "Don't bang your fists like that, you'll hurt yourself," she said. "Try to calm down, please, for me. Try to relax, hon."

He started banging his fists harder and moaning. "What'm I gonna do? They're gonna lock me up for the rest of my life!"

"I'll be back tomorrow," Gretchen promised. "Hopefully, with a lawyer, okay? Just try to take it easy. Please, hon, I'm here for you. You know that, don't you?" She threw him a kiss and began to leave.

The moan became a wail.

Oh, God, she thought, what am *I* going to do?

CHAPTER 121

They sent a police car to take her to the station. This was so embarrassing, Gretchen thought, and in broad daylight, in full view of the nosy neighbors. They were always cool to her, probably thinking she did not belong in their precious neighborhood, not good enough to live there, not good enough to be Mrs. Norman Hardesty.

She wanted to stick her tongue out at them as she got into the back seat, but thought better of it. It was better to be restrained, calm and cool, as if you have nothing in the world to worry about. You can do it, you know you can.

They stuck her in what they called an interview room. Gretchen looked around her in disgust. Ugh, there was dust everywhere, on everything, even on the chairs. She fished in her handbag for a tissue and wiped down one of the chairs before she sat on it. What slobs, she thought, composing her expression into one of disdain. She remembered to get another tissue from her handbag to clutch in her hand – have to have the props.

The door opened and Detective Sergeant Baez and Sergeant Lang came in. Lang set a recorder on the table in front of Gretchen. Then she smiled (so phony, Gretchen thought). At least Baez was kinda cute.

"Good afternoon, Ms. Hardesty. How are you holding up?" Lang asked.

Gretchen cleared her throat and squeezed the tissue into a ball. "I, I'm, doing as well as expected, I guess."

"That's good. We will be recording this conversation, Ms. Hardesty." Lang flipped on the machine, saying, "Sergeant Amy Lang and Detective Sergeant Enrico Baez. Interview with Ms. Gretchen Hardesty."

Baez pulled out his iPhone, scrolled through it, and looked up. "Ms. Hardesty, we've been checking with the staff at the Get Fit Gym, in particular, Mr. Andrew Warner. He admitted that you two were having an affair." Baez's eyes bored into Gretchen's.

She looked down at her lap, acting ashamed and embarrassed. "Um, no, it was, um, just a brief thing that I got caught up in. It was a mistake, a stupid, stupid mistake." She clutched the tissue and blew her nose. "You have to understand that Andy is a real gigolo. He preys on vulnerable women." She sighed and looked up at Baez, wide-eyed. Thank God I bought that sexy new mascara, she thought. "Maybe it's part of his job, I mean, coming on to the women clients. It's good for business, I guess. I know I wasn't the only one there who was duped by him."

Baez looked at his notes again. "We also spoke to some of the women clients. Ms. Rachel Newman was very clear that you and Mr. Warner were an item, for quite a while, in fact." His eyes bored into Gretchen. "She said that you seemed to be bored with your husband."

Think, girl, think. Her mouth twisted in anger, effing bitch, she thought. "Poor Rachel, it's so sad. She's had a real tough life. I feel so sorry for her. Well, she always was a little jealous of me, I think. You know, I had a husband who was a good provider and all. She's a single mother, divorced from a real deadbeat. I definitely never said I was bored by my husband. Unfortunately, the more I tried to be her friend, the more jealous of me she became." She shook her head; glad she had her hair done the day before. The blonde streaks looked smashing, she thought. "She was especially jealous about Andy's attentions to me. I mean, here she was, working at a crummy job, struggling financially, and divorced and available."

Baez's hand was poised above his iPhone. "So you think Ms. Newman was, what, not telling the truth, about you and Mr. Warner?"

"Well, of course she wasn't." Gretchen did her best to look injured. "I mean, she knew that I thought it was a big mistake, that I never wanted to hurt my husband." She sniffed. "She knew I'd broken it off as soon as I could get out from under Andy's clutches."

Baez was on alert, like a pointer dog, she thought. "Andy's clutches?"

"Um, he was, actually, very abusive. I mean, just look at him. He's very strong, and he can be scary. It got to where I was afraid of him, afraid to break it off." She lifted her chin. "Finally, I managed to do it."

Lang said, "Did he get physically violent?"

Gretchen lowered her head, speaking softly. "I was so ... ashamed ... to tell anybody, and I thought Norman would find out. I never talked about it."

Baez closed his iPhone and signaled to Lang. She turned off the recorder. "Ms. Hardesty, that's all for now. Thank you for coming in."

Did I have a choice, being dragged here in front of everybody? Gretchen thought bitterly. Do not give them the satisfaction of seeing you upset by them. "Oh, let me know whatever I can do to help. I hope you can find out who did this terrible thing."

Baez's mouth was set in a grim line. "Oh, don't worry, Ms. Hardesty. We will."

CHAPTER 122

"Guess what?" Lily plopped down on the sofa and put her leg up. "One of the women from the gym called. She told me the cops arrested the personal trainer, Andy, for Norman Hardesty's murder!"

"You're kidding!" I shut my laptop.

"She said they frog-marched him right out of the gym, in front of everybody."

I got up and put on the kettle for tea. "How did they catch him? I thought the witnesses in the other car couldn't see what he looked like. Did somebody else see him do it?" I got out the teacups and spoons and reached for the containers holding fresh herbs from her garden.

"I don't know how they caught him. I tried, but I couldn't get his face." She put the tea in the pot on the table. The smell of fresh mint made me think of spring, of growing things. "Come to think of it, there was something familiar about him – his body, I mean." She smacked her lips. "What a body, delicious."

"Hey, don't let Jack hear you say that." I teased her, knowing she would never cheat on Jack. "He's very possibly a stone-cold murderer."

Lily blushed. "I was just making an observation, an objective observation." She poured the tea. "Besides that, what happened to innocent until proven guilty?"

The tea tasted as good as its promise. I put down my cup. "D'you think he – the trainer – planned the whole thing?"

"Maybe he had help, someone who had a motive. Someone who'd benefit from the murder, with a life insurance policy, for instance. Frankly, Andy never seemed all that bright to me. I mean, sure, he was definitely strong enough, but having the wits to plan it out?" She shook her head. "I don't think so."

"Proving it isn't going to be easy," I said.

"I think Norman's wife Gretchen did the planning. Andy was her lover. She could probably talk him into anything. I'd love to get my hands on her. I wouldn't trust her as far as I could throw her."

I grinned at her. "I bet you could, too, throw her if you wanted to. I have a feeling she didn't hang out at the gym for the exercise equipment, just Andy's equipment."

Lily laughed. "Well, I guess I'm doomed to leave her to the law."

"Especially since your boyfriend is an ex-cop."

CHAPTER 123

The cops sent a car to take Gretchen down to the station again. She was so nervous, she was practically shaking.

She already bit off all her beautiful silver French nails. What the hell did the idiot tell them? she thought. He was such a hysterical idiot; he could have given up the whole thing.

I should have gotten rid of him while I had the chance. Maybe I could try to convince him to kill himself – better than life in prison, right?

Baez and Lang were waiting in an interview room, recorder on the table. They look so damn smug, Gretchen thought. Baez does not look cute anymore. He looks nasty, as if he was enjoying this, and that awful Lang was staring at me. Gretchen shuddered.

"Too cold for you, Ms. Hardesty?" Baez asked, phony concern in his voice.

Act like nothing is the matter, Gretchen told herself. "Well, maybe a little." She forced a smile. Above all, make sure you do not sweat, she told herself. Think of something cold – ice cream, a cold beer.

Lang got up from her chair. "I'll turn the AC down a little."

"Thanks." Gretchen folded her hands in her lap and tried to look calm.

When Lang came back, she flipped on the recorder. "There's something you need to hear, Ms. Hardesty," Baez said.

God help me. "What is it, detective?" Gretchen smiled prettily at Baez, even though it made her want to hurl.

Baez's voice on the recorder: "Okay, Mr. Warner, we can talk to the DA, maybe make a deal, make it 25-to-life, with the possibility of parole. You have to cooperate; you have to give us something, otherwise...."

Andy's voice was high-pitched and quavering. "I'll tell you anything you wanna know. I'll do anything. I don't wanna be locked up for life."

Baez: "Okay."

Andy: "It's all her fault. She forced me, she made me do it. I didn't wanna, but she kinda hypnotized me."

Baez: "She?"

Andy: "Gretchen Hardesty."

Baez: "Go on."

Andy: "I was kinda, like, under her spell. You know how a woman can do that to a guy, right? It was all her idea, her plan."

Baez: "What was her plan?"

Andy: "To kill her husband. She wanted the insurance money. I don't care about all that. It don't make no difference to me, if I got dough or not."

Lang shut off the recorder.

Gretchen pitched forward and vomited on the table.

CHAPTER 124

Who knew who or how many people I should be scared of? That was one of the things that was so freaking scary. The other thing was that the person who wanted me dead might even be someone I had trusted, someone I was close to. Maybe it was one of the guys I broke up with, namely Elliott or Barry. Then there was the murdering escaped convict and the depraved serial killer of young women – take your pick.

It could be someone I was related to: one of my mother's horrible, greedy relatives. The whole idea of wanting to do away with a member of your own family (niecicide?) was even more frightening to me. Even if they hated my father, I was still blood of their blood.

According to my latest conversation with Henry Bradshaw, J.D., both Uncle Lucius and Aunt Martha were on a search-and-destroy mission, using whatever legal means available to undo any claim I had on an inheritance. I wondered if it were just pure greed or that they found the idea of a "mongrel" taking what they considered theirs so abhorrent. Whatever their reason, they wanted to obliterate me from the family map, maybe even from the earth.

The most important question, of course, was whether either, or both, of them were out to do more than get rid of my claim. Was the real plan to get rid of *me*? They were both relatively old and probably not all that strong, but maybe they hired somebody to kill me.

None of these thoughts helped my frame of mind, which was growing more and more paranoid. I carried my gun with me all the time now. I looked over my shoulder, twitching whenever somebody got too close on the street or in a shop. I probably seemed like a crazy person – maybe I was, at this point. I had a damn good reason.

CHAPTER 125

Who Killed Who?

The blog for those with an inquisitive nose ... for murder and mayhem

HYDE PARK, NY: Tracy Mellows, 19, of Hyde Park, went missing three days ago on her way home from Dutchess Community College. Tracy is white, with long, blonde hair and was wearing a striped red-and-white top and blue jeans.

If you have any information about Tracy, please call the toll-free number: 1-800-555-8123.

COMMENTS:

From BillK: I live near the community college. I'll try to check it out.

From FrankG: Me, too.

From CarolynP: I don't live too far, so I'll go, too.

From Miranda Grimaldi: Please, just be careful, all of you. He could still be in the area. Don't go there alone.

CHAPTER 126

Lily tried several times, with no success, to visualize the man who ran her off the road and finally decided to talk to Jack about it the next day.

After munching on cinnamon scones Jack had brought, they sat on the sofa, her injured leg resting on a stool. She took a deep breath. "I have to tell you, ask you, about something."

Jack grinned. "Okay, which is it? Tell or ask? Whatever, the answer is yes." He patted her shoulder.

Lily sighed. "Maybe you'd better wait till I tell you what it is before you say 'yes.'"

He looked at her. "You sound serious."

"I am very serious." She took his hand. "Okay, here goes. I want you to check Sam out."

"What? Why?" He gave her a quizzical look.

Lily looked down at her lap. "I think he was the one who ran me off the road."

Jack shook his head. "You're kidding, right?"

"Listen to me. Number one, he just seemed to pop up at your office out of nowhere."

"Wait a minute ..."

"Let me finish." She twirled a lock of her hair, realizing she should leave out the part about sneaking looks at Sam. "He never talks about himself, his family, his past, or anything personal. I tried asking him, but got nowhere. I heard him cursing at someone on his cell out in the lobby, and I'm afraid he caught me listening. And I saw him going into the files."

Jack frowned. "He was probably just checking on a case I asked him about. As for him not talking about his background, maybe he's just a private person."

She ignored that. "Jack, his car. It's the same kind and color as the one that did it." She took another deep breath. "I've had a funny feeling about him all along."

Jack stared at her. "Whew, that's a lot, but a lot of what? None of that makes him guilty of anything."

Lily moved her achy leg to another position on the stool. "Maybe not, but I'd feel better if you checked him out, please." She gave him a beseeching look.

Jack waved his arms in surrender. "Okay, okay, I'm sure I'm not going to find anything. I'll do it, only out of pity for a helpless invalid." He grinned and ducked as Lily threw a pillow at him.

CHAPTER 127

I made Lily and me eggs for breakfast, nowhere near the perfection that she always achieved, but better than nothing.

She hobbled into the kitchen, sat down, and hoisted her leg up on a chair. "Mmm, that smells good, Phil."

Dishing out the eggs, I said, "Let's just hope for the best. At least I couldn't ruin the juice."

"You didn't burn the toast, either." She smiled and dug in. "Hey, this isn't bad, not bad at all."

I took a tentative forkful and brought it to my mouth. "Well, it's not too terrible, I guess."

Lily laughed. "What would I do without you?"

I grinned. "You'd have the place to yourself?"

"Don't be silly. You know I love having you here. Listen, I've got something to tell you." She put down her fork and took a sip of juice. "I asked Jack to check Sam out."

"Hmm, how did he take it?"

"Not well, but he said he'll do it."

I forked up some egg. "He'll do it because he loves you."

"We'll see. Another thing: I have this feeling that something's about to happen, something very bad." She shivered.

I shivered, too. Lily's feelings were usually spot-on.

CHAPTER 128

Lily was running through the woods, trying to get to her grandmother's cottage, away from the man who took her sister.

"I see you, Lily!" he yelled. "Do you see me?" He gave a horrible screech, reaching out for her with his long arms that ended in claws. "You can't get away from me, Lily!"

If she could only get to the cottage in time, her grandmother would save her. He was gaining on her. Unfortunately, her grandmother was long dead.

Lily woke up tangled in blankets, breathing hard, shivering as she got out of bed. She made herself a cup of herbal tea to calm herself, the way her grandmother taught her. She missed Lillian terribly, though she was glad that she left this earth the way she wanted to. She just drifted off peacefully in bed one night, in the cottage that was now Lily's.

She often wondered if her grandmother helped the journey along. The doctor told Lily that Lillian had the beginnings of Alzheimer's. "She knew it," the doctor said sadly. "You couldn't get anything past that lady."

Lily realized that her grandmother was forgetting things, like remembering when Lily was due to come home from work.

"I've been so busy with the animals," Lillian apologized, pouring out cups of tea.

Another time, when Lily noticed that the oven was on, she said, "Oh, what've you been baking for us? I can't wait."

"I'll just check on the carrot muffins," her grandmother said. "They should be about done."

When her grandmother opened the oven door, Lily saw that there was nothing in it. A few days later, after Lily woke up in the morning, she went to check on her grandmother. She found her body in bed. She knelt by the bed, stroking Lillian's white hair, sobbing.

Not your spirit, Lily promised her grandmother, that will never die. Everything you passed down from our ancestors you gave to me to use: to help those who need to be helped, and to harm those who need to be harmed.

CHAPTER 129

When Gwen opened her door, she gave me a once-over. No surprise, I was sure that I looked like hell. I definitely felt like hell. I was up several times during the night, worrying about the email from my escaped-convict nemesis, and getting hang-ups on my cell in the middle of the night. I finally resorted to shutting off the damn thing. Was it him? Did he somehow manage to get my phone number?

I related all of it to Gwen, saying, "Guess I'll have to change my number again. Fat lot of good that'll do, though. I've been unlisted for years, and still, there it is. Is there such a thing as a phone-stalker, ha ha?" I was acting like it was no biggie. Who was I trying to fool?

She shook her head. "This is serious, Phil, especially about the escaped convict. Did you call the police?"

I nodded. "They said they're 'on it,' whatever that means."

"Well, that's good. What about the phone hang-ups? Do you have any idea who's doing this, or why?"

I barked a laugh. "It always lists 'unknown caller.' You're kidding, right, about who it could be? It's probably one of the many people I've managed to piss off in my life."

She leaned forward in her chair. "Can you think of someone in particular it might be?"

I sat back. "It could be somebody I exposed in an article, or a suspect in a murder I was investigating on the blog, or..." I paused. Did I want to get

into my dealings with my dysfunctional family, or my latest destructive romantic relationships?

"What were you going to say?"

She was not going to let me off the hook. She never did. I looked down
at my lap. "The Abbotts, my mother's family, are contesting my uncle's will,
which gives me an inheritance." I looked up at her. "They weren't exactly
thrilled about my existence." I described the unfortunate encounters with
my estranged relatives, finishing with, "That's my lovely family, on my
mother's side."

Gwen shook her head. "You got through it all, didn't you? You toughed
it out."

I let out a small smile. "Did I actually have a choice? Yes, I could've
begged, done obeisance, whatever. That probably wouldn't have worked and
anyway, that wasn't me."

Gwen searched my face. "Is there someone else who might be trying to
intimidate you with the hang-ups? I have a feeling that there's more."

She already knew about my past with Barry. I gave her an update about
my relationship with Elliott. I left nothing out, and the bile rose up in my
throat. I had to excuse myself and ran to the bathroom to throw up.

When I came back, Gwen had a wet towel, pillows at the head of the
sofa, and a thick, white blanket ready for me.

I was exhausted, drained, emptied of poisons in my system. I felt as if I
slept for hours on that sofa.

CHAPTER 130

After my catharsis at therapy, I went back to Lily's in a much better mood than before. I was smiling when I walked through the door.

"Hey, wow, I'm glad you're in such a good mood. What's going on?" Lily looked up from the oven, where lovely smells were wafting out. She answered my unasked question: "Pineapple cranberry muffins."

I patted my expanding waistline, but I knew I could not resist. "By the time I get back to my house, I'll have to buy all new clothes."

Lily grinned at me. "Clothes shopping is such fun, right? Anyway, what's going on with you? You actually look happy for a change."

I sat down at the kitchen table, my nose basking in the aroma of pineapple and cranberry. My mouth was watering so much, I was practically drooling. "Are they done yet?"

Lily laughed as she lifted the pan from the oven.

I had to control myself to not leap at them. Then I remembered how the last time I did that, I burned my fingers.

Finally, when they barely cooled down, I grabbed one. It never even got a chance to hit its lovely blue-and-white plate.

"Okay, now that you got your muffin fix, what's going on with you?" Lily said, putting a fresh pot of herb tea on the table.

"A good session with my therapist. It kind of put things in perspective." I snagged another muffin and sipped my rosehip tea.

Lily smiled. "That's great. It's like the old, happy-go-lucky Phil is back."

I smiled back in between mouthfuls. "That'd be nice, if only."

It was not to be. When I opened my laptop, this was waiting for me.

To Philomena Wolff:

You think you're safe, ha ha.

I'm gonna get you good. Real good.

You will pay, oh, you will pay for what you did to me. For all the years I've been locked up like an animal, you thought you were safe from me. Not anymore, never again.

I was shaking all over, so much for the feeling he could not hurt me. I had a gun. I knew how to shoot. Did I think this was going to help against an armed and dangerous escaped convict, out for revenge? That was a joke, and not a funny one.

The only thing to do was to be extra careful, extra smart, and hope to outwit him.

CHAPTER 131

Who Killed Who?

The blog for those with an inquisitive nose ... for murder and mayhem

ARLINGTON, NY: Daphne Mitford, 19, of Arlington, went missing three days ago on her way back home from her classes at Marist College. Daphne has short, blonde hair and glasses. She was wearing a red jacket and black jeans.

If you have any information about Daphne, please call the toll-free number: 1-800-555-1480.

Miranda Grimaldi

COMMENTS:

From WinnieG: OMG! That's always been such a safe area.

From LorriY; My daughter graduated from that college and there wasn't anything like that then.

From TerryL: Times have changed, LorriY. It's not safe anywhere for young women now.

From PeteB: Not until there are more cops on the streets.

From RachelM: Right!

UPDATE: Daphne Mitford's body was found in a wooded area near the college campus.

CHAPTER 132

No doubt about it, the mysterious Sam Michaels intrigued me. Even though Lily thought he was a suspicious character, for some reason. I just could not buy into her theory about him.

Maybe he piqued my interest because he was kind of mysterious. I mean, what did we – I – know about him? Well, Jack evidently trusted him enough to hire him. So far, even Lily could not point to anything about him that was – what?

He seemed so down-to-earth, so normal, so real. He must have undergone a background check before he became a P.I., for a license or a gun permit or something. Were P.I.s bonded? Did they have to check on him just because he carried a gun? I knew he did; I saw it when he took his jacket off. Besides the gun in the holster, I got an eyeful of rippling muscles under his turtleneck – six-pack abs, and a nice tight butt. He was not a pretty boy, but he had strong, craggy features: dark, almost black hair; dark eyes; a great smile. He was ... mmm, yeah.

Forgodsakes, Phil, when are you going to learn? All your man-choices have been worse than awful, horrible, terrible – sometimes downright scary, as in both Barry and Elliott who frightened me to death. Here you are, getting regular email death threats, breathing and hang-ups on the phone. Did you forget about the assault and your apartment being trashed?

Get your head on straight, Philomena, no more panting after good-looking, sexy guys.

Jeez, I was celibate for all of how long, weeks? What are you, some kind of nympho? Get your head and your whatever down there screwed on tight. As for the mysterious, sexy Sam, fuhgedaboutit. Concentrate on your work and the blog and keeping yourself alive and well for a change. Gwen would approve.

CHAPTER 133

Since Phil was out for the day and Lily's leg was feeling a little better, she decided to climb the rickety steps to her grandmother's attic. It took her awhile and her leg ached terribly, but she finally made it.

She sat down on an old bench to rest, thinking about the times she was up there with Lillian when she was little. She was entranced by the bundles of herbs, baskets (for drying herbs), a trunk full of objects meant for healing: feathers, candles, powders, stones, and waters from springs. There were notebooks filled with Lillian's writing.

When she got older and tried to open one of the notebooks, her grandmother shook her head. "No, Lily, you're not ready for this yet. When you're old enough to use what's in the notebooks, they'll all be yours."

She could still smell the sage Lillian burned for smudging (for clearing the air of bad energies) and inhaled deeply – a good, clean smell, her grandmother had said.

Right now, though, Lily was eager to dig out the notebooks. She headed for the trunk and opened the hinges. A familiar odor of dried rose petals wafted up, for healing and for Lillian's rosehip tea. She brushed a tear from her eyes. She felt her grandmother's presence here more than ever and breathed it in.

She reached into the trunk and pulled out a dozen blue notebooks. Each one was carefully labeled with the subject matter and date. She sat down on Lillian's rocker and opened the one with the earliest date: 20 years ago.

Subject: Missing and Murdered Young Women. The writing, in black script, was faded, quite hard to read, but she was determined to decipher it.

The notebook was arranged by date, victim's name and age, and whether found, dead or still missing. The first on the list was a teenager from the area who was never found: Holly Winterbourne, age 17.

Lily read through the names on the list with a growing sense of horror, and pride in her grandmother, who was instrumental in helping to find these poor young women. Then she froze. "Oh, my God," she whispered, feeling the room spin around her.

Lillian had been the one to find Abigail's body.

CHAPTER 134

After Lily finally managed to calm herself down, she grabbed her grand-mother's notebooks and slowly made her way down the stairs. She put on a kettle, made chamomile tea and took a slice of fresh-baked oat bread from the breadbox on the kitchen counter. Then she sat down at the kitchen table, sipping her tea, taking bites of bread, and spread out the faded pages.

Okay, start with this one, she thought, picking up an early page dated 15 years ago. There were three names, together with the dates the victims had been found. Her grandmother Lillian had made every effort to envision the crime scenes but had only got so far, not far enough to picture the killer's face.

I saw only a shadowy figure, leaning over each body, in what seemed to be an underground chamber, lit by perfumed candles.

Lillian had written about her frustration. "Almost, almost, I almost got it this time. He started to turn. Then it, he, was gone, damn!"

CHAPTER 135

Who Killed Who?

The blog for those with an inquisitive nose ... for murder and mayhem

POUGHKEEPSIE, NY: Emma Norbert, 18, went missing three days ago on her way home from her job at the Dutchess Deli. Emma has blonde hair in a French braid and was wearing a green-and-blue sweater and blue jeans.

If you have any information about Emma, please call the toll-free number:1-800-555-9631

COMMENTS:

From LeslieG: OMG, I know Emma. I go to that deli all the time. She's a sweet, lovely young woman. I'll go check out the deli and see what I can do.

From MichaelS: I know the deli, too. Don't know Emma, but I'm so sorry. Anything I can do?

From LeslieG: Yes, thank you. If you can, please check out the neighbors near the deli. But be careful.

From RickT: Right. Just in case. Don't go alone.

UPDATE: Emma Norbert's body was found near the Dutchess Deli this morning.

CHAPTER 136

He had a new plan to find the blogging bitch. He was able to hack into her computer, easy peasy. After all, he was an expert, right? That was why they paid me the big bucks. He chuckled to himself. This should help get rid of her, once and for all. I can track her down. Wherever she is, there I will be. He chuckled again, saying to himself, you are just so clever.

CHAPTER 137

Robin and I were having lunch at Pearl Moon, a trendy, always busy restaurant in Woodstock.

"How are you and Elliott getting along?" Robin sipped her coffee.

I made a face. "We're done."

"What happened? I thought you two were a thing." She took a bite of her burger.

I sipped my soymilk cappuccino. "Uh, we were, until he got too clingy. I felt like I was being smothered. He wanted all my attention, all the time."

"Oh, no, I didn't know he was that way, believe me. I'm sorry I introduced you."

I reached over and patted her shoulder. "I know that. Well, anyway, he wasn't exactly easy to break up with. Hopefully, he'll see the light next time he meets somebody."

She sipped her coffee. "Mmm, let's hope so. You can never tell about somebody, can you? Anyway, so what're you doing these days, about guys, I mean?"

"Jeez, I just broke up with not one, but two guys." I sipped more of my drink. "Give me a break, huh?" Oh, why on earth did I tell her there were two? God only knew what she would make of my relationship with Barry. Not good, for sure.

"Who's the other guy?"

I tried to think fast. What could I say that would not be saying anything? "Let's just say it was so wrong from the beginning. I wasn't smart enough to see it, that's all."

Robin regarded me thoughtfully. "Well, you're not going to go off men totally, are you?"

I laughed. "Who knows?"

"How about trying one of the sites for singles on face book?" she asked. "You could meet lots of guys that way. You know Mandy Jordan, right?"

I nodded.

"She met her boyfriend, who's now her husband, on one of those sites," she said. "And Mandy's not the only one."

I finished off my cappuccino. "I've got enough to do with the blog and my articles. I don't need any more distractions."

"It could be a good distraction," she said. "At least you'd get to know something about the guy before you even met him." She added, "You can't just work all the time, right?"

"What is it with you married couples? You want to pair everybody up, like Noah's Ark." I grinned.

Robin grinned back. "Just call me Mrs. Noah. Seriously, though, why not try one of the singles sites? What've you got to lose?"

"Hmm, let's see – maybe my life?"

CHAPTER 138

I took a deep breath and opened my laptop to the singles site that looked the safest. Okay, SAVVY SINGLES, here I come.

Hey, what about swearing off jumping into relationships, remember that?

Well, okay, I promise not to jump, just walk. Anyway, what could it hurt? Do not think about hurt or harm. After all, I can be anonymous and I can always depend on my trusty little weapon, just in case.

I put in as much information as I was comfortable with, saying I was single and not in a relationship. Believe it or not, I got two "likes" right away.

When I clicked on their names, it was double wow. Gerard was blonde, muscular, and very good-looking, divorced, no kids, a businessman. Marc was tall and dark and absolutely dreamy, in law enforcement, never married. That was something to find out – why?

Both of them were eager to meet a woman for drinks and conversation, no pressure.

CHAPTER 139

I got ready with as much care as I could manage for my date with Gerard. I never was one for lots of makeup and I was not about to start now. Clothes and hair, I could do. I brought my new purple top from Woodstock Design to my NYC apartment, along with a nice pair of black pants (fairly form-fitting) and black ballet flats. I hoped for a pair of purple flats, but they were nowhere to be found.

Not only did I splurge on a new hairstyle, but even went so far as sitting under the dryer hood forever for (gulp) highlights. I never dared or even wanted to do that before this. With a luscious new mauve lipstick from Jean Turmo, I was done, ready. Well, as ready as I was ever going to be. Since the forecast was warm spring weather with showers, I buckled up my trench coat and grabbed an umbrella.

I chose the meeting place, a local bar and grill, not too far from, but not too close to, my apartment. I enjoyed the walk. The sidewalks were filled with tiny plots of blooming flowers and the smell was wonderful.

Arriving at our appointed time, six o'clock, I ordered a glass of white wine. Not being much of a drinker, I figured I could sit and sip while we got acquainted.

The place was dimly lit and jammed, being a Friday night Happy Hour. It was not great for conversation, but very public, therefore very safe, to my thinking. Just in case, I had my.22 in my handbag. I sipped away, hoping I was not getting sweaty from nerves, and trying not to drip wine on myself. Unfortunately, after a few sips, some idiot bumped into my table, splattering my beautiful purple top in the process.

Outraged, I tried to mop up the mess with a napkin. It did not do much, so I hotfooted it to the ladies'. After practically bathing myself in tap water, I grabbed paper towels and dried off the best I could.

With a sense of entitlement, I went to the bar for another glass of wine. The bartender handed me a fresh bottle. "Compliments from the gentleman who caused the spill," he said, waving toward the exit. I thanked him and was about to tell him I did not need a whole bottle, for goodness sakes. Then I thought, who knows, maybe my date would want it. Speaking of my date, Gerard, where was he? I checked my watch: a half-hour late.

This was ridiculous – so much for first impressions. What chutzpah, wasting my time, not to mention an expensive hairdo and new mauve lipstick on a no-show creep. Well, mister, unless you have a damn good excuse, like death or near-death, screw you.

I thought I might as well have more wine before I go. Not wanting to hang around any longer, I drank a little faster than normal. As I got up from my seat, I felt kind of dizzy, and grabbed the edge of the table. One of the wait staff passing by asked if I was okay. I nodded, put on my trench coat, and left.

When I walked outside, I did not know who to be more furious at: my supposed date or the jerk who spilled my glass. Suddenly, I felt strange all over. My legs gave way, and I fell to the sidewalk. Before I could get myself up, I was knocked down, hard. Someone was battering me with something on my head, on my back, on my legs.

This is it, I thought, in my daze. Somebody is going to kill me. I tried to open my mouth to scream, but a hand quickly covered it, then it turned into a fist.

Then there was the sound of running feet. "Hey, you, get away from her!" was the last thing I heard before I passed out.

CHAPTER 140

A kind stranger, maybe the one who stopped my attacker, stayed with me till the ambulance got there. Luckily, I passed out again, so I felt nothing until I woke up in a hospital bed.

My head hurt horribly, especially when I tried to sit up. Not only that, there was a horrible pain in my back and my legs. "Ooohhh."

A petite nurse with short brown hair whose name tag read Cathy, came bustling into my room. "Glad you're awake, hon. I've got something for the pain right here." She was carrying a glass of water and pills in a paper cup.

"Everything hurts," I moaned, pointing to my back and my legs. "My head, too."

"I know," she soothed, pulling up the covers around me. "You've taken quite a beating."

I was stunned. "Somebody beat the hell out of me. Why? Where am I?"

"You're in St. Luke's-Roosevelt Hospital. The cops are investigating. They'll probably be in to see you soon." Cathy patted my arm.

I lay back against the pillows. "Ohh." My back was on fire and so were my legs. My head hurt the most. It felt worse than a giant headache.

"I'll bring you more pillows. That should make you more comfortable," she promised.

"Thanks." I felt myself fading back into sleep. It must be the pills. As I drifted off, I thought, who the hell would do that to me and why, forgodsakes?

Two cops walked into the room just as I was waking up. "Ms. Wolff?" the taller one, a slim African American man, said.

I tried to nod, which made my head into a ball of hurt. "Yes," I got out.

"I'm Sergeant Argente, and this is Detective Walsh." The shorter man had red hair and freckles and a paunch. "We're very sorry this happened to you. We have a few questions, okay?"

I told them yes, and they pulled up chairs next to the bed. "Tell us everything you can remember before you passed out. Where were you, what were the circumstances of your being at that bar, everything from the beginning of the evening," said Walsh.

I recounted the story of my supposed date with a man I communicated with by email. "I waited and waited, nursing a glass of white wine and he never showed up."

Argente raised his eyebrows. "That's all you had, one glass of wine? Are you sure?"

I was getting annoyed. "Of course I'm sure. That is, I ordered one glass and after a few sips, some idiot knocked it off my table. The idiot paid for another glass of wine, as an apology, I guess."

They looked at each other. Then Walsh said, "So you actually had more than just one glass of wine, maybe too much?"

I was pissed. "Forgodsakes, it was just the one glass and a few sips, all right?"

"Okay, okay." In a nicer tone, Argente said, "What happened next?"

Mollified, I said, "Well, after waiting God knows how long for my no-show date, I got up."

They leaned in toward me.

"That's when I started to feel funny, dizzy, faint, I guess. I had a hard time walking out the door, and the next thing ..."

Argente nodded. "That's when you were attacked. It sounds like somebody – the idiot? – put something in your drink so you wouldn't be able to fight him off. Do you remember the way the guy looked, the idiot?" I could see he was trying not to grin.

I sighed. "It was very dark in the bar, and of course, dark outside. You think that's what happened?"

Walsh nodded. "It seems to be. Well," he got up, "we'll check at the bar, see if the bartender or anybody else saw the guy."

Argente got up. "We'll get back to you."

"Thanks." I waved goodbye. Why on earth would some guy at a bar be out to drug me and attack me? This did not make any sense. I had to think, but my poor head said no.

I nodded off again.

I woke up sometime later. It felt like hours. I had no idea what time or even what day it was, but I knew I was in terrible shape. I rang the bell for the nurse. When she came in, she had a cup of pills and water. "Bless you," I croaked. My mouth was so dry, I could hardly talk.

"Drink up, dear," she said. "Drink as much as you can. It'll help."

I drank and drank. She started to leave, then turned, "Oh, I almost forgot. There are two friends of yours waiting to see you."

"Okay," I mumbled.

"Only for a very short time, okay?"

"Okay."

A few minutes later, Wendy and Caroline were in the room, loaded down with flowers and magazines and chocolates.

CHAPTER 141

Several weeks later, Lourdes, my editor, and I were finishing lunch at a salad cafe. "First we order food, then business," she always said.

The cafe was a relatively new one on the Upper West Side, a nice little soup-and-salad place that already had an excellent reputation in the neighborhood. Lourdes reserved a table in the corner, a quiet place for us to talk.

We both ordered the Greek salad, which was delicious and came with the best light and tasty pita bread I ever ate. The wine was excellent, too. Lunch with Lourdes definitely meant time-off from my diet.

"Mmm, I could die eating this bread." I said, raising my eyes to heaven.

"Don't say that, please," Lourdes said, with a frown. "You know how nervous it makes me."

"Right, the dreaded 'D' word." I made pretend strangling noises.

"Cut it out." Lourdes took another sip of her wine. Then she put on her glasses and fished out a file from her briefcase. As she saw me wince, she said, "I'm so sorry about that horrible attack. Are you in a lot of pain?"

I nodded. "It's getting better." I was still very sore and taking painkillers, which did not help all that much. "Anyway, I'm glad you liked my piece on the baby-sellers."

"Great, as usual," she said. "The bastard so-called lawyers are awaiting their trial."

"Hooray!" I leaned back in my seat.

"Don't get too comfortable." She grinned. "I've got a new one for you, very juicy, very dicey."

I sat up. "I love it already. Tell me."

"Illegal immigrants dying in horrible conditions when coyotes smuggle them into New York. The latest deaths were three teenage girls. They were stuffed in a trailer leaking carbon monoxide fumes." She handed me a file with notes and contacts.

"Oh, God, let me at the scumbags," I said.

Lourdes paid the bill, and we left, saying goodbye before going our separate ways.

I was so intent on the notes in Lourdes' file that I almost bumped into a woman pushing a stroller. "I'm sorry, sorry," I said. After that, I decided to wait till I got back to my apartment to go through it. I was glad the sun was out and there was a slight breeze. I was just happy to be alive, not horribly dead like those poor girls.

Then I heard heavy footsteps behind me. Shivering, I started running, and ran flat out for the next three blocks until I got to my building.

After getting my breath, I inwardly cursed for not having the guts to turn around and face my stalker if that was who he or she was. How would you even know that, after not bothering to look? I fumed, disgusted with myself. Why did you forget your gun, leaving it in your apartment like an idiot?

Maybe I was just being paranoid, right? After the latest email death threat and phone hang-ups, who could blame me? – not to mention the attacker outside the bar. Then there was the one in my Woodstock cottage. I bet it was the same guy. It only makes sense. I reached around to my back. At least it was less painful now, though very sensitive to the touch. My legs were just about better, but the throbbing in my head was still there.

I got out my key and opened the front door of my building. Climbing the stairs to my apartment and unlocking my door, I reminded myself that nothing had actually happened. See, you worried for nothing, I told myself. Remember what my friend Robin always says: Worrying about things that have not happened is a bad habit. Stop driving yourself nuts.

CHAPTER 142

Okay, trailing the blogger bitch to the bar and crashing the psychic bitch's car bombed.

It was time to make another plan or two. Those bitches are not going to outwit me, that was for sure.

Mmmm, think, guy, think. You know you can do it. You are definitely smarter than any of them.

You're such a clever boy, Sonny.

Stop that, Mother. You died, I killed you, remember? Go away. I am a man, not a boy, especially not *your* boy.

Ah, I have it! Using my charms, I will soften her up, lay it on with a trowel, when we meet: flowers, poetry, the whole works. No matter that I have to – ugh – act as if I was smitten, love at first sight with the bitch. Just do whatever it takes, guy. Go slow. Get her to trust you, trust you enough to get to meet the psychic bitch, and then ....

CHAPTER 143

I was getting excited. Take it easy, I told myself, calm down. I was about to meet Marc, my other SAVVY SINGLES date. According to his photo, he was good-looking, in a very sexy way. It could turn out to be, well, who knows? Something, I hoped, a whole lot better than my last attempt at meeting a so-called date, which landed me in the hospital.

What makes you think this one would not end the same way? Why do you keep taking chances with men?

Stop that, I told myself. What are you going to do, hide in your apartment forever?

That is not living. Try to relax, go with the flow. Well, at least, try. I put on my best cotton fuchsia top and skinny leg black jeans, and a sweater in case the AC was strong. I tend to get chilly.

We were going to meet at a hotel lounge in mid-town Manhattan: public place, check; no phone numbers or addresses check; and my .22 stashed in my handbag, which should make me feel more secure. I took an Uber. Even with the traffic, I managed to get to the hotel more or less on time – not too early, not too late.

A string quartet was playing softly. Schubert, I guessed. The lights were soft and low, and there were flowers everywhere. I looked across the room and there he was, in the gorgeous flesh. He managed to grab a table in a quiet corner. He looked just like his SAVVY SINGLES photo, so damn sexy.

He stood up, handed me a single white rose, and smiled.

I tried to control my breathing. How romantic could you get? Next, he would be reciting poetry. "Where have you been all my life?" I burst out. Did I actually say that?

"Waiting for you," he said.

OMG, was this guy real, or a figment of my imagination? "I'll just ask someone to put this beautiful thing in water." The maître d' magically appeared with a water-filled floral vase, and I stuck the flower in. "It's so lovely," I murmured.

"I agree," Marc said, giving me an approving look.

Hoping not to blush, I slid into a chair opposite him. He was even more sexy up close – wavy dark hair, deep brown eyes, long lashes, generous mouth, great teeth. (Were they genetic or caps?) He was wearing a maroon linen jacket, maroon shirt, and black leather pants. Stop staring, Philomena. Take a deep breath.

He reached across the inlaid table and took my hand, giving it a squeeze. "So happy to meet you, at last."

I laughed. "We've only been connecting for a few weeks."

"Seems a lot longer." He smiled.

After we ordered, Marc poured us wine. I sat back in my chair.

"Tell me about yourself," he said.

I took a few sips of my drink and giggled. "Well, I weighed about six pounds when I was born."

He laughed. "Okay, I got that. Seriously, I'd like to get to know you."

"Okay." I figured that starting with my love of writing made sense. I told him how I was encouraged by my college English professor, worked on the school newspaper, developed a social conscience. I finished with the exposés and the crime-solving blog. "Doing the blog is very important to me and to my friend, Lily. She's a psychic who helps the police. We work together on cases."

He did not take his eyes off me during my whole spiel. "Whew! Such an exciting life, or lives, you have. I'm envious."

"Well, it's not all just exciting." I sighed. "Sometimes, it's …" I was going to tell him about the scary stuff, the near-death experiences. I stopped myself. Maybe he would think this was boring. What was I doing? Getting all hot and bothered, that was what. Mmm, he was something else, a real sexpot. Down, girl. There is plenty of time.

"It's what?"

I managed a smile. "Sometimes, it's just a grind, interviews, research, you know." I sipped my drink. "Tell me about *you*."

He finished his drink. "Well, I weighed seven pounds at birth." He grinned. Then he told me about his childhood dream of becoming a professor, as his dad was. "My dad was the finest man I ever met." His mouth twisted.

I reached for his hand. "What happened?"

He looked as if he were near tears. "He killed himself."

"How old were you when it happened?" I did not let go of his hand. Poor kid, I thought.

"Twelve, and I was the one who found him dead in the garage." He released my hand and got out a handkerchief and wiped his eyes. "My little sister was 10. I was expected to be the man in the family, to take care of my sister and my mother. My mother sorta went nuts after that, just couldn't cope, I guess. She had to be put away in a sanitarium. Eventually, she became totally out of it." He paused. "She died a few years ago, and my sister …"

I put my hand to my mouth, almost afraid to ask, but I thought I should. It was obviously something that had a bad effect on him. "What happened to her?"

He covered his face with his hands. "She died. She was killed in an accident when she was 17."

"Oh, how awful. I'm so, so sorry." I longed to throw my arms around him, but I figured I could make up for it later. I just gave him my most sympathetic look. Then, to change the mood, I said, "Did you become a professor, like your dad?"

He blew out his breath. "Well, sort of. First, I joined the police force in a rural section of Nebraska. Later, I decided to try academia, so I've been teaching classes in criminal justice as an adjunct." He smiled. "I've also been working with a government agency, which I can't talk about, of course. It's very frustrating, sometimes, especially not being able to talk about it with anyone. In fact, you're one of the few who even has any idea what I do for a living." He sighed. "It makes me feel kind of lonely."

"Mmm," I said, "but there must be some reward, some satisfaction, right?"

Marc sipped his wine and gave the maître d' a thumbs-up. "Very good." Then he sighed. "I needed this to relax, and I'm thinking about what you said, some reward. I guess it's that my schedule is more or less my own, no nine-to-five." He made a face. "I'd hate that, having to be somewhere at a certain place and time, or else."

"I can understand that. That's why I love freelancing, no boss hanging over my desk every day, clocking my time for lunch, checking my schedule." I sipped my wine.

He turned to me. He had the most beautiful brown eyes, ringed with thick, sooty lashes. "In my free time, I've been delving into English literature, especially poetry."

I was already in love, well, maybe in lust. "I think we're kindred spirits." Then I decided to plunge right in with what I was dying to ask him. "How come you've never, uh, been married?" That's how to drive a man away, idiot, I thought. "I didn't mean to pry. Uh, that's what it said on your profile." I could feel my face burning. Now you did it.

"That's okay, I don't mind. Truth is, I've never met anyone I'd want to spend my life with. I believe that relationships are for keeps." He gave me a meaningful look.

I let out my breath. "I do, too."

He grinned. "I knew we felt the same way about things, from the first time we chatted." Then he said, "Tell me about your crime blog. That sounds like it could be, well, kind of dangerous. Is it worth it?"

I put my glass down. "Well, as a matter of fact, I was attacked pretty violently not long ago. I don't know yet if it had anything to do with the blog."

He looked aghast. "That's terrible! Were you badly hurt?"

I picked up my glass again and twirled it around. "Yeah." I nodded. "I'm taking precautions now."

"Good." He sounded relieved. "I'm glad to hear it. I don't want to think of you being at risk for whatever could happen." Then he said, "Maybe you should stop doing this dangerous work, that blog. Is it because you need the money?"

I laughed at that. "There's no money in it. You're not going to like this, but what I do get paid for can also be, uh, kind of scary."

Marc fixed his lovely eyes on me. "What is it, forgodsakes? Are you a freelance hitman, er, hitwoman, an undercover cop?"

I giggled. "Just your average investigative reporter."

He was all ears. "What kind of investigations?"

I told him about a couple of the exposés that had already been published: The corrupt big-city mayor; the crumbling tenements where children got lead poisoning; the Internet scammers who fleeced old people out of their savings; the baby-sellers. "This does give me a lot of satisfaction, especially when it has good results."

"Wow! I'm impressed!" He took my hand. "You know, you're making me think."

I grinned. "Hopefully, about good things?"

He nodded. "Maybe I can remember that I'm trying my best to do something important, something that's worth the occasional frustration and feeling isolated."

"Of course you can." I patted his shoulder. "You're already doing something important to me."

He looked puzzled. "What?"

I gave him my best lascivious look. Then I handed him the key to the room I booked, just in case.

CHAPTER 144

The rest of the evening turned out to be a disaster. It was not totally bad, because he was sweet and loving, but the actual intimacy, the sex, was a dud. Never mind, I told him. I liked being with him, cuddling and kissing. Of course, that did not work.

Marc buried his face in his hands. "Oh, I'm so sorry. I, I don't know what happened. I disappointed you. Please try not to despise me," he moaned.

I hugged him hard. "Of course I don't, you silly boy."

His face turned red and angry. "I'm not a little boy, you know."

"No, no, I didn't mean that at all. I just..." Maybe you should just shut your mouth now, Phil. Zip it. I gave him another hug instead.

He seemed to relax somewhat. I pulled him close and rested my head on his chest. Eventually, we both drifted off to sleep.

When I woke in the morning, he was gone. I found a note on his pillow: "Sorry, I couldn't stay. Call you soon, Marc."

CHAPTER 145

Who Killed Who?

The blog for those with an inquisitive nose ... for murder and mayhem

SLINGERLANDS, NY: Jocelyn Wells, 19, of Slingerlands, went missing three days ago. Jocelyn is white and has curly blonde hair and was wearing a blue striped sweater, black jeans and blue sneakers. She was last seen on the way home from her job at Lloyd's Stationery.

If you have any information about what happened to Jocelyn, please call the toll-free number: 1-800-555-4545.

Miranda Grimaldi

COMMENTS:

From JeffB: I say kill the bastard. Very slowly and painfully. And get all the goddamn perverts off the streets! Speaking of the streets, has anybody checked out who was hanging around that neighborhood that didn't belong there when that poor young woman was taken?

From TheresaM: No more soccer practice for my daughter. And I'm buying a gun and taking shooting lessons. My husband doesn't like the idea, but it has to be done.

From JimmyP: It's your job to protect your kids. I have a permit and I'm an excellent shot. Ex-Marine. Semper fi.

CHAPTER 146

Who Killed Who?

The blog for those with an inquisitive nose ... for murder and mayhem

My dear Philomena,

I had to laugh out loud at the idea of that ex-marine coming to get me. What a pathetic joke. I can outrun him, out gun him, outsmart him any day of the week, and then some. Ha ha. What a loser.

I have three words for Mr. Semper Fi:

Bring. It. On.

Sincerely, Philomena Wolff

CHAPTER 147

"So, what d'you think?"

Lily and I were sitting in her kitchen, drinking herbal tea and munching on cranberry muffins. Between sips and bites, I told my friend about my evening with Marc – *all* about the evening.

Lily put down her cup and looked thoughtful. After a few moments, she said, "Well, it could be one of a couple of things, or more than one."

"What kind of things?"

"He could be gay."

I shook my head. "I don't think so, but who knows?"

"Maybe he has ED," she suggested.

"Isn't he kind of young for that? But hey, there's always Viagra."

She took a few sips of her tea. "Mmm, let's see. He could be, well, trau-matized, maybe from something when he was growing up."

I gazed at her. "You're so smart! You know, he did have a troubled child-hood." I told her about Marc finding his father's body, his sister's death and his mother ending up in a sanitarium.

Lily stared hard at me. "Wow! That's some history! Jeez, no wonder he's got problems." She drummed her fingers on the table. "What do you know about him, besides the family tragedies, I mean? Did you ever find out what he does for a living?"

I felt a bit defensive. "What d'you mean? I told you, he's a sweet, thoughtful, considerate guy. It's about time I met someone like that, right?

He's a sensitive soul. He loves literature, especially poetry, and classical music. He seems to be a kind of free spirit."

"What does he do for a living?"

I hesitated. Then I thought, I can trust her. "Promise you won't tell, because it's sort of a secret, okay?"

She nodded. "Okay, but what's all the hush-hush? Is he in the Mafia or something?"

I laughed. "It's the furthest thing from it. He's in clandestine law enforcement."

"What's that?"

I shrugged. "That's all he can tell me."

She looked at me. "That's it?"

I shot her a dirty look.

"Well, I guess it could be the FBI, CIA, or some other alphabet. Hey, before you take a hissy fit, I wasn't questioning your judgment," Lily said, in a soothing voice. "It's just ..." She looked away for a moment. Turning back to me, she said, "He sounds as if he's been through a lot and that might've done something to him."

I was getting pissed. "C'mon, I've just been telling you how heavenly it is to finally meet somebody who treats me beautifully, is kind and loving. What more do I need?"

Lily raised her arms. "I surrender. Please, Phil, don't be mad." She got up from the table and came around to give me a hug. "I just worry about you because I care. You know that."

I felt mollified, then I grinned. "Of course, my previous relationships have all been so damn functional, right?"

She grinned back at me. "Well, you said it. Now let's have another cuppa and finish these muffins. Otherwise, I'll have to feed them to the squirrels."

CHAPTER 148

So far, so good, he told himself. All you have to do is look trustworthy and legitimate to her and the cops. Okay, you passed the believability test.

He did catch a shadow of a doubt in her eyes. No worries, because soon, very soon, there will not be doubts or anything else in her eyes. He laughed.

The critical questions: When, where, and how do you make it happen? Answers: A. as soon as practically possible. B. Upstate, downstate, in my lady's chamber. C. Does it matter if you make it look like an accident – probably not.

Now to go for a twofer and put an end to them. He chuckled. He could do them both at the same time, a challenge, but he always loved a challenge. It got his juices flowing. Meeting a challenge proved his superior intellect. He thought for a moment. Fire, that could do it. After all, I had good practice with that. He chuckled again, remembering. His mother had burned to nothing but her rings, and he was the big hero. Whenever he thought of it, he laughed himself sick. What would that silly old fag Clarence think of that if he only knew? That made him laugh even more.

Okay, we have to get both bitches in the same place at the same time. I need to suggest something to the blogging bitch that could do the trick. I can check for whatever is coming up in the area and send her a text about getting together with the friend she talked about, the psychic bitch.

You are so clever, you can fool anybody, anytime, he thought. Sometimes, the stray thought crossed his mind about what he could have been and done if he chose a different path in life. Then he shrugged. It was what it was. So far, it had all worked out well for him. His lifestyle always kept him on his toes, and, he had to admit, it could be exciting. Even the few narrow escapes he had made it even more exciting. It was as if he were holding his breath before diving into deep water. Then surfacing, realizing that he did it, he conquered his fears, met the challenge, and won – again and again.

CHAPTER 149

Marc sent me a text, saying how much he enjoyed the evening with me. He asked if we could get together soon, maybe with the friend I was talking about. He never met a psychic, he said, and would love to hear all about how it worked. He asked if there was some place or event in the area we could meet.

I was so happy to hear from him, glad that I had not driven him away by my sexual aggressiveness. We could try again, taking it slow. I know, I know, he got my juices going, but if I wanted a relationship with this sweet, lovely, hot guy – hey, girl, slow down.

Then I asked if he would like to get together at the Woodstock fireworks show that was coming up soon.

Of course, Woodstock had to be different: no Fourth of July fireworks for our town. We had them in August.

CHAPTER 150

Who Killed Who?

The blog for those with an inquisitive nose ... for murder and mayhem

SAUGERTIES, NY: Morgan Hennessy, 18, of Saugerties, was reported missing three days ago. Morgan is white, with ash-blonde hair and bangs. She was last seen on her way home from softball practice, wearing a blue sweater and leggings and blue-and-white sneakers.

If you have any information about what happened to Morgan, please call the toll-free number: 1-800-555-8888.

Miranda Grimaldi

COMMENTS:

From Ilovemovies: Protest tomorrow, DA's office, Kingston.

From LydiaP: I'm there.

From Girlygirl: Ditto.

From JosephC: Count me in.

From MeganM: I'll be there.

From Winesnob: Tell your friends.

From HenryY: Tell your neighbors. Put signs up.

From LucyN: Tell everyone. Call the radio stations.

From Ludditenomore: Put it on the web. And on Face Book.

CHAPTER 151

"I love county fairs. I haven't been to one in years." Sam said, after finding us a table.

We were having coffee at Bread Alone in Woodstock, before he headed off for the office and I got to work on the new article I was doing for Lourdes, on human trafficking. It was not a date. We both happened to land in front of the coffee shop at the same time. I noticed a poster in the window advertising the Ulster County Fair. It was a long time since I had been there, and I was looking forward to it.

"I do, too," I said, between sips of cappuccino – no pastry, of course. Sam, on the other hand, was gobbling, okay, eating, a piece of delicious-looking carrot cake. Life was so unfair sometimes, especially to short women who gained weight after even looking at pastry. "I love fairs, parades, all that stuff, such fun. I don't care if it sounds hokey or touristy."

He put down his fork and smiled. "Well, how would you like to take me to a fair or a parade?"

Coffee on the way to work was one thing, especially since it was just an accidental meeting. Going out on a date was another, even though it would be daylight in a public place. Hey, Phil, what could happen – uh, anything, right?

Getting involved with yet another guy was what could happen, another guy whom I was not sure I could trust.

"Sure, whenever there's a fair around here." What did I just do? Hopefully, he did not notice the poster in the window. "I don't think there are any parades in the near future."

Sam dug into his pocket and pulled out a flyer. "As a matter of fact, the Ulster County Fair is coming up next weekend." He grinned.

"Sure of yourself, aren't you?" I had the urge to stick my tongue out at him. Of all the …

The grin widened. "Well, I was sure such a nice young woman wouldn't turn down someone who was being so …"

I had to laugh. "Who was being so brash?"

He laughed, too. "So, is it a date? Pick a day or time on the weekend."

I sipped my drink. At least, make him wait a couple of minutes, right? The grin was getting to me, not to mention the rest of him. "Uh, what about Saturday afternoon?"

He got up to leave. "Great, I have to get to work now. I'll call you." Then he said, "I don't have your number."

I gave it to him. Why did you do that? I asked myself. That's just asking for trouble.

As soon as he left, I bit my lip till it started to bleed. I should have bitten my tongue before I said yes. I was not thinking with the right part of my body.

Well, the fair was at a very public place, with lots of people and farm animals – and I have a gun. Unfortunately, he must be a way better shot.

I could always jump on a tractor and scream bloody murder.

Why did I have to think of that?

CHAPTER 152

"Oh, look, Sam. They're shearing a sheep over there." I pointed a little way away on the boardwalk. "I love sheep. They're so ..."

He grinned. "Sheepish? Okay, let's go."

It was a lovely summer day, and we were having a good time. Surprise, surprise. Sam had a great sense of humor, seemed to be pretty laid-back and easygoing (Translation: willing to do whatever I wanted.) and, let us not forget, was a real hunk. Stop it, Phil. Remember, you do not know much about him or trust him. Down, girl, oo-kay.

After the sheep shearing, Sam got himself a lamburger, done rare, all bloody. "Ewww, how can you eat that, after just looking at your food?" I made vomiting sounds.

He took a big bite of the thing, swallowed, and said, "That was charming vocalizing. Do you do that on all your dates?"

"Only when someone does something that makes me nauseated." I said, trying not to look at what he was relishing. For my part, I got a chicken salad sandwich.

"Where do you suppose your chicken sandwich originated from, a plant?" He grinned at me, wiping off lamb juice running down his chin.

I defiantly chomped on my sandwich, but inside, I actually felt queasy, fervently wishing it were tofu. "Chickens aren't as cute as fuzzy little lambs," I said, sticking my chin out.

After we finished eating, we stopped at the pig races, which seemed to fascinate Sam. Then we wandered around the midway, looking at the exhibits. When we got to one of those shooting galleries, he said, "Wait. I'm going to try to get you one of those big blue teddy bears." He put his arm around me, which gave me a tingle. "I'm an excellent shot. Best in my class at the Academy." It turned out he was an ex-cop, too, before Jack recruited him to his firm. He hated the bureaucracy and liked the independence of being a P.I.

He hit every one of the moving duck targets and proudly handed me the big blue bear.

I looked at the huge, googly eyed stuffed animal. I had to admit; it was cute, and so was Sam.

CHAPTER 153

"Okay, we went out, and nothing."

Lily poured us cups of peppermint tea and sliced a heavenly smelling apple and walnut bread. "What d'you mean, nothing?"

I took a bite of the bread. "I could die happy eating this."

"Bite your tongue." Lily wagged her finger at me.

"Sam was a perfect gentleman." I grimaced. "He treated me as if I were made of glass and could break if he did anything."

"This is a bad thing?" She looked at me.

"At the end of the day, all he did was give me a hug and pat me on the head, as if I were a pet." I made a disgusted face.

"What did you do?" Lily said.

"I said, 'Arf, arf.'"

She shook her head. "Oh, you. What did he say?"

"He just laughed and said he'd see me around. Could you believe it?" I sipped my tea and took another delicious bite. "What's wrong with me? Am I giving off some crazy vibes that say, 'Don't touch me' or what? Some strange kind of pheromones or whatever? Something that says, 'Go slow. Go so slow that you don't go anywhere?'"

Lily sipped her tea. "Maybe Sam's screwed up from a dysfunctional family, or maybe these guys are just not that into you. I'm kidding."

I threw a napkin at her. "That's not nice, girlfriend."

"Okay, then why was Sam doing all that sneaking around, trying to find out about you, huh?"

I sighed. "God, I don't know. Maybe I should just give up on men, take a vow of celibacy."

Lily hooted at that one. "For all of five minutes, maybe?"

I gave her a dirty look. "Anyway, I was thinking about Marc. He texted me, saying he'd like to get together. Not only that, he wants to meet you and find out how a psychic works. Hopefully, that'll be a new start for us."

"That sounds good." Lily got up from the table to put away the very little remains of the apple-walnut bread. "Do you think he's commitment-phobic?"

"C'mon, you know how guys are about performing. I feel bad for him. Such a nice guy, thoughtful, sensitive, seems to be able to listen, you know?"

Lily shrugged. "What d'you want to do about him?"

I finished my tea. "The town fireworks are coming up."

"Ooh, yeah, they're so great! You know, Jack and Sam will be helping out the fire department with traffic and security."

Well, why am I worried about Sam, with me being a free agent, a very free agent? "Marc asked if the three of us could get together there."

Lily smiled. "That's a good idea. I'll get a chance to check him out."

I nodded. "My plan is to try to encourage him, gently, not pushy, you know?"

She snorted. "You, being gentle? You're kidding, right?"

"Hey, that's not fair. You know I try. It's just hard for me to be subtle. Maybe someday I'll learn how to do it." I looked down at the table.

She laughed. "Phil, please, stay the way you are and don't try to be someone you're not. You're smart, funny, exuberant, flamboyant. You're a rare bird."

"First, I'm a dog, then I'm a bird. Tweet, tweet." I flapped my arms. "Hey, we can pack a picnic."

CHAPTER 154

Marc texted that he would love to go to the fireworks. He planned to meet Lily and me at the community center at Andy Lee Field on Rock City Road, off the Village Green. The fireworks, which were always sensational and very crowded, were put on by the fire department at the cemetery next to the field.

The fact that Jack and Sam would be there, helping out with traffic and security, made me a little nervous, I told Lily.

"I'm making up my mind that I'm not going to let anything spoil my time with Marc. I hope us being together will make him less skittish."

"You think he might be more ready for a relationship now?" Lily sounded doubtful. "What about Sam? I thought you liked him."

"I know you don't trust him and maybe I don't either. Anyway," I said, "the next move is up to Sam. Somehow, I don't think anybody that brash needs a boost of self-confidence. I still can't figure out why he didn't even try to kiss me after the fair or make another date with me."

It was time to go. Lily and I left for the community center when it was still light out; easier to deal with the country roads in Phoenicia. I drove and Lily navigated. We packed a picnic basket full of deli sandwiches and chips and wine and beer, along with a blanket and flashlights. I remembered to shove my gun in my handbag, just in case the killer was lurking out there.

CHAPTER 155

By the time we got to Woodstock, it was just about dark and the summer heat was cooling down. We parked at the main parking lot off the Village Green and carried the picnic and blanket up the road to the community center. I waved to Jack and Sam in the street, who were busy directing traffic. A folk band was playing, the precursor to the main event. The field was packed, as usual. This was one of Woodstock's special family-style events, like the Memorial Day Parade and the Halloween costume parade and the town's Christmas Eve celebration. That came complete with Dickens'-style carolers in top hats from the 200-year-old Reformed Church on the Green, while everybody waited for Santa to arrive.

Marc was already there, looking smashing in a black leather jacket and jeans. I forgot how sexy he was.

I introduced Marc and Lily. He took her hand, saying he was happy to meet her, and he gave me a hug. "It's so good to see you again," he said, sounding as if he meant it.

He took the basket and blanket and we went down the field to find a good spot, where we could spread out the blanket without stepping over anybody. Lily led the way with the flashlight. I waved to Robin and Mike, who brought their children, and Jean and Rebecca Turmo.

Lily found us a good spot, not quite so crowded. She kept the flashlight on while she and I unpacked the picnic.

"Mmm, this sandwich smells great," Marc said, biting into one. "It tastes great, too."

"Have a beer." Lily turned the light on, while Marc bent his head to fish out a beer can.

"Oh," she said, putting a hand over her mouth.

Marc took a swig of beer. "Great!" Then he said very quietly, "What's wrong, Lily?"

"No-nothing," she said, turning off the light.

The fireworks were starting. I turned to Marc, "Aren't they something?"

He was focused on something shiny in his hand and moving toward Lily.

CHAPTER 156

"He's the killer, Phil!" Lily screamed, as Marc grabbed her arm.

Everything was happening as if in slow motion. Somehow, I must have moved fast, picking up my handbag and bashing him over the head. I guess the gun inside it helped. Then I jumped up and yelled as loud as I could, hoping that someone could hear, even with the booming fireworks.

Marc seemed to be stunned by the blow, but I was not taking chances. I got out my gun and trained it on him. Lily ran to find Jack and Sam. By this time, we attracted a crowd, asking what happened.

"He's a killer!" I tried to shout over the noise of the fireworks.

People were shouting, "Oh, my God!" "Thank God you've got him!"

Half a dozen firefighters zoomed in on us, surrounding Marc. He still seemed to be groggy, but alert enough to yell obscenities at me.

"Shut your filthy mouth!" Sam had his arm around me, holding me close. "You and Lily could've been killed! Thank God you're okay," he said in my ear.

The firefighters turned Marc over to the police as the fireworks were winding down. I was still having trouble taking it all in: Marc was the killer. He turned out to be Kenneth Abbott, my own cousin – and I was the one who got him.

CHAPTER 157

Sam and I were sitting in Aunt Oly's living room. After making a big fuss over me, Aunt Oly could not help scolding me.

"Why do you take such chances with your life?" She shook her head.

Sam grinned. "That's who she is, unfortunately."

"What did you say?" I was indignant.

"Well, at least now I don't have to worry so much about you. You've got Sam to take care of you." She beamed at Sam.

"I can take care of myself, Aunt Oly," I said, sticking my chin out.

It turned out that Aunt Oly and Sam's mother, who recently moved to my aunt's neighborhood, were good friends from the old country. That was why, Sam explained, he was so careful around me in the past. He also told me that his real first name was Zander.

I liked that name. It went well with Philomena.

"Your aunt knew I had police training, and that I was working in the area. She asked me to look out for you. She didn't want me to let on because she thought you'd be upset."

I did not know whether to be furious at both of them, or glad it was why Sam and I got together in the first place.

I compromised by kissing Sam and hugging my aunt.

CHAPTER 158

Sometimes, things do end well.

Kenneth Abbott was convicted of the attempted murder of Lily and the murder of his mother – life, with no parole. Authorities were also trying to tie him to the murdered young women.

The infamous escaped convict, Doug Dorgan, was captured and returned to prison with an extra sentence and no possibility of parole.

Poor Claire Anderson was glad to be released from jail, but was shell-shocked about her husband, who was convicted of first-degree murder. There never was a diamond mine.

It turned out that Jerome had been a suspect in the death of another wealthy old woman for her money.

The lawyer was right about Aunt Martha and Uncle Lucius not having a case about the will. My inheritance was being processed, as was Claire Anderson's mother's money.

Gretchen Hardesty and Andrew Warner were convicted of first-degree murder and conspiracy.

Lourdes loved my article on the human traffickers. There were no death threats – yet.

At my last therapy session with Gwen, I told her how grateful I was to her. I thanked her for all the good work we did on my self-esteem issues, which were the root cause of my self-destructive behavior.

I was not too worried about Barry or Elliott with Sam around. The fact is that he says I was getting to be almost as good a shot as he was. I must have a knack for it. Who knew? With my talent for murder investigations, he said, maybe I should think of joining their firm.

Nah. .... I plan to stick with reporting and blogging. Still, being a good shot is a handy skill to have, especially with all the bad guys around to investigate....

CHAPTER 159

Who Killed Who?

The blog for those with an inquisitive nose ... for murder and mayhem

MID-HUDSON VALLEY: According to police reports, a carjacker has been terrorizing women at the local shopping malls in Ulster and Dutchess counties. He grabbed the women while their attention was occupied by putting away packages and forced them into their car. Later, he dropped them off somewhere and took off with the car.

If you have any information or ideas about the carjacker, please call the Ulster County Sheriff: 1-800-555-7222; or the Dutchess County Sheriff; 1-800-555-3333.

Philomena Wolff

UPDATE: After the killer of young women – who also was trying to kill me – was caught, I moved back home. I was living elsewhere, to be safer. I was also using the name "Miranda Grimaldi" to keep doing this important work with you on the blog. Sorry for the deception, but it was necessary.

ACKNOWLEDGEMENTS

Thank you to everyone who read, reviewed, and critiqued *The Murder Blog*, I truly appreciate all the help: Jerilynn Babroff, Susan Baker, Brooke French, Carolyn Geduld, Claudia Hirsch, Robin Kramer, Judith Lechner, Linda Miller-Gregorius, Bill Schweitzer, Cam Torres, and June Trop.

ABOUT THE AUTHOR

Sandra Gardner is the author of six traditionally published books: three novels and three nonfiction books. Novels include: *Dead Shrinks Don't Talk, Black Opal Books*; *Grave Expectations, Black Opal Books*, mysteries; and *Halley and Me, Evening Street Press,* a coming-of-age novel. *Halley and Me* won the Grassic Short Novel Prize from Evening Street Press. Nonfiction books include: *Teenage Suicide, Simon & Shuster*; *Street Gangs, Franklin Watts*; and *Street Gangs in America, Franklin Watts. Street Gangs in America* received a book award from the National Federation of Press Women. Gardner is a former contributing writer for The New York Times.

NOTE FROM SANDRA GARDNER

Word-of-mouth is crucial for any author to succeed. If you enjoyed *The Murder Blog*, please leave a review online—anywhere you are able. Even if it's just a sentence or two. It would make all the difference and would be very much appreciated.

Thanks!
Sandra Gardner

We hope you enjoyed reading this title from:

www.blackrosewriting.com

Subscribe to our mailing list – *The Rosevine* – and receive **FREE** books, daily
deals, and stay current with news about upcoming
releases and our hottest authors.
Scan the QR code below to sign up.

Already a subscriber? Please accept a sincere thank you for being a fan of
Black Rose Writing authors.

View other Black Rose Writing titles at
www.blackrosewriting.com/books and use promo code
PRINT to receive a **20% discount** when purchasing.